THE AUDIENT AND THE PHANTOM NIGHT

SADIE HEWITT

Paperback ISBN: 979-8-9876432-3-5
Ebook ISBN: 979-8-9876432-2-8

The Audient and The Phantom Night is a pirate fantasy romance set in a world where all things wicked, dark, and dangerous collide.

This story contains elements of battle on a pirate ship, hand-to-hand combat, alcohol use, blood, brief thoughts of suicide, graphic violence, death/murder, profanity, on-page consensual sex, and mention of non-consensual sex.

Readers who may be sensitive to these, please continue with caution.

*For all of us who preferred the friendship of fictional worlds as children,
your knowledge and wit are as sharp as any blade.*

Chapter One

Devlin

"We're caught between the devil himself and the deep blue, captain!" The man shouted over the lashing rain, eyes squinted against the winds. He paused, bracing his shoulders against the helm to help his fellow sailor fight against the sudden twist of the wheel. Still, they struggled to keep it steady. "The storm is blowing us off course! Where is the Sailmaster?"

The ocean churned beneath them, waves blasting against the quarterdeck with a force that threatened to knock the men into the sea. The captain surveyed the scrambling crew, watching as their shouts were swallowed by the storm and their hands scraped against the thick ropes that held the billowing sails in place. The bo'sun had thrown himself in with the men, the silver whistle he used to keep order lay forgotten against his chest.

It didn't matter, they wouldn't have heard the shrill of it over the roaring gales anyway.

The ship rocked to the right as it dipped and a powerful wave crested over the taffrail, slamming into the mainmast. The wood creaked dangerously under the strain. Lightning forked, illuminating the black clouds racing across the sky.

The storm had come from nowhere, it seemed. Clear, blue skies had greeted them when they entered the Aeglecian Sea. But now...

"Captain?" The helmsman called out again, his voice gruff and gritty from the briny air.

But the captain's mouth had gone dry, heart beating rapidly in his chest. Something else had flashed on the horizon, a gloomy silhouette that was barely seen against the deep gray clouds. It was there for a moment before vanishing entirely. A boom of thunder reverberated over the deck and the captain felt the wood rattle under his feet. It stole him away from his thoughts in time for another wave to crash below.

"Bare poles!" The captain finally shouted, heaving himself down the stairs of the stern deck. His boots landed firmly against the slippery wood of the quarterdeck and he managed to catch himself on the railing as the ship rocked once again. "Take in the sails!"

The bo'sun hustled across the deck, shouting the captain's orders to the able seamen still battling the ropes. The sails blew back against the mast, sending a splintering crack resounding against the ear-splitting wind.

"Sails taken aback!" the bo'sun cried out. "Demasting!"

The mainmast cleaved near the middle, falling backward into the mizzenmast. Screams of pain coursed over the deck. Once the debris had settled, the captain spotted blood flowing like minuscule rivers from the injured who had gotten tangled in the snapped ropes. One man was being dragged, intelligible screams ripping from him, toward a hinged door that was held aloft by the ship's surgeon. Soaking hair matted with sea water and blood was plastered against the side of his head.

The man had finally gone limp and quiet, no doubt from the crushed leg left in ribbons where a large piece of the mast had pierced it. The bleeding had begun to slow and, from the way the surgeon locked eyes with the captain, they both knew that his death was inevitable.

From the torrential downpour and the splintered wood scattered across the quarterdeck, the captain suspected they would all follow the sailor into the afterlife soon enough.

Lightning flashed again, drawing the captain's eyes away from the sail's damaged rigging and his heart started once more. There was a man on the ship, casually leaning against the foremast at the bow. He stood there with unsettling ease, as though the rocking of the ship and the cresting of the waves were no bother to him. The captain was good with names, as well as faces, and he knew with certainty that he had never seen this man before.

And, from the ghost ship illuminated against the horizon with the next flash of lightning, he had a sinking feeling that he knew who the man was.

There were rumors, of course. Tales of a captain with so much venom in his heart that the sea herself refused to allow him rest in her depths. Stories of a ship crewed by those who were damned and dead, yet seemed to walk amongst the living as though they were still alive themselves. Demons the lot of them, their souls long sold to the gods in exchange for what, exactly, he didn't truly know.

The captain staggered across the quarterdeck, pushing past the men still working to regain control of the ship. The storm seemed to quiet as the captain approached the newcomer, the rushing wind dying to a dull roar. The man pushed off the mast, straightening to a stand.

"Your ship is going down with the storm," the man said in a bored tone, his gaze flicking over the destruction that lay on the quarterdeck. "You have a handful of minutes left, I would wager."

The captain's swallow was thick as he shifted on his feet, the waterlogged boots heavy and weighing. "You're the Specter," the captain said, his voice weaker than he wished it to be. The ship rolled to the side again and he stumbled with the motion. The man to his front stayed perfectly still, his stance wide and controlled.

"I am," the man said simply. He lifted a hand, displaying a pair of dice in his palm. They were worn and well used, the edges curved and smooth. "Captain of *The Phantom Night*."

The captain's gaze shot up and he felt his insides ice over as he took in the Specter's seafoam green eyes, an unnaturally devilish color that reminded him of stinging cold and fog-covered cliffsides.

"I thought you were a legend," the captain managed to say. Behind him, there were spouting cries of surprise as a wave crested over once again. Another rope snapped and two men were washed into the roiling sea. "Passed down through generations of sailors."

The smirk that passed over the Specter's lips was cruel. "I do wonder how the legends are born." He idly rolled the dice in his palm, the clinking of the bone on bone barely heard over the storm. "There are two options for you, James Murray." The captain didn't want to know how the Specter knew his true name. "You can go down with your ship, sink into the deep and allow the sea to sweep you into death." He tossed the dice into the air, catching them deftly with his other hand. "Or, you can wager for your crew to join with mine, barter what time would have remained. Wander the Aeglecian Seas under my sails until your hourglass runs dry."

The captain scoffed, a sound that made the Specter's brows rise. "Your crew is an abomination and your ship is a gods' damned curse."

The Specter's lips pursed in thought. "Your ship will be at the bottom of the trenches in three minutes. And mine certainly won't." There was another resounding crack as the ship's wheel split away from the stern deck. "You would sentence all of your men to death?"

"I would gladly give my men to the old gods before I allowed you to take them."

The Specter's eyes darkened, much like the turbulent sea beneath them. "The old gods have forgotten you. Your soul will spend the rest of eternity trapped in the depths below your very feet."

"Then so be it."

The Specter said nothing more as he disappeared from the quarterdeck in a hazy shadow. The captain's chest heaved as he turned to assess the damage behind him and his stomach clenched when he surveyed the splitting ship. His bladder ran dry, the warmth of his urine coating his inner thigh. He spotted the rogue wave just as it began to fold, moving swiftly on the surface of the water. The wave slammed into the broadside of the ship, capsizing it before the captain could take one more rasping breath.

"That was painful to watch, even for you, captain," the quartermaster, Booker Colby, mused. "Specter or not, we haven't gained a single crew member in months."

The Specter, Devlin Cato, didn't bother to hide his snort of irritation, though he said nothing else as the ship he had just visited plunged into the sea. The mast bobbed on the surface for a few moments more before finally succumbing, dipping beneath the waves without another appearance.

Sails and rope and wooden barrels came to float, tossed like sacks of flour by the storm. He would eventually order the crew to sweep them onto their ship, stealing away the most valuable into storage and tossing the rest back to Liddros. He let the dice roll between his thumb and forefinger, a habit he had picked up in the last sixty years or so.

"He isn't going to be happy with the progress," Booker went on, leaning his arms against the taffrail. "You know that he's been harping on us for—" He trailed off suddenly at the sharp look Devlin threw at him.

"Prepare the sails, Booker," Devlin snapped, pinning his quartermaster with a critical stare. He assessed the man's thick blonde hair and hooked nose, crooked from multiple tavern fights in his younger days. Despite Booker easily clearing one hundred and fifty years old, he still appeared as though he were a mere thirty-two. Damned curse, indeed. "I want to be in the Bay of Gildare by first light."

"The Bay of—" Booker started, tromping after Devlin with heavy footfalls. They navigated through the crew manning the quarterdeck, many returning to their posts after watching the warship's demise. The ship flared to life under the scrutinizing stare of her leader, and the two men barreled toward the captain's private quarters nestled under the stern deck. "Captain, that's impossible. We can't make that distance in such a—"

"I would suggest," Devlin interrupted through clenched teeth, his hand on the knob of his cabin door, "that you have the crew work a bit faster then." Wind tunneled through the narrow hallway. It filled the sails and sent them carving through the water. With that, Devlin let the door swing shut, burying his quartermaster's face behind it.

Devlin blew out a breath, turning to sweep his gaze along the wooden bookcases showcasing the leather bound journals, stacks of ink bottles, and bundles of quills. Polished, golden compasses and various brass instruments of all sizes were scattered along the shelves. The brine of the sea filled the space, melding with the scent of parchment and dusty, waxed pine.

He was once a brother...a son...a lover. But now he was the last thing sailors saw before their untimely demise. Some knew him as The Specter— that was mostly by the ships that passed through the Aeglecian Sea. To others, he was better known as a pirate captain. One of three, in fact, who was cursed to wander the waters around the continent. Cursed to provide souls for his master, the one who had granted him extended life.

Devlin tossed the two bone dice onto his desk, where they bounced and rolled before coming to a thudding halt against a rolled map perched near the edge. Booker was right, though Devlin would never admit it out loud. They needed men and Liddros, God of the Sea, needed their souls.

Chapter Two

Fenna

Fenna had always known her mother named her after the cove that sat a short walking distance from their two-bedroom cottage. After all, the coastal inlet was the very place her mother and father had found her wailing on the beach as the retreating waves hissed against the grainy sand. And Fenna Cove wasn't even a *pretty* cove. The rocks were too sharp, the water too brown, and the beach too protected from the cliffs above to get any meaningful sunlight.

The other children in Fenna's town made fun of her for it. Relentlessly and mercilessly reminding her that Fenna Cove wasn't the pretty cove. Just like her. Because her hair was too auburn, her nose was too long, and the way she seemed to answer unasked questions was too strange. It was merely fuel to their fire that she was named after the ugliest cove on the continent.

The only thought that kept Fenna sane was that, thanks to her mother, she was not alone. For instance, her mother named her older brother Dasos...which her mother swore meant forest in an old language she couldn't remember the name of.

It fit him, though.

Thrilling, adventurous, and spirited Dasos. Rooted like the trunks of the ancient forest trees and growing wild in every direction. Incredibly in tune with life and, yet, still aware that one slip of the tongue would send it all crashing down.

Despite all of this, the cove was still Fenna's favorite place to be. She would settle into a nook in the craggy rocks, book in hand, and watch the tide slowly creep up the shore. When the clouds darkened on the horizon, she would scale the cliffs until she could perch amongst the long grass, content to set her chin on her knees and stare at the incoming storms. And when the rains were over, she would run barefoot through the rich mud, reveling in the feeling of it between her toes.

Fenna loved the cove, the place she had been found, but sometimes...sometimes she looked where the sky met the sea and imagined the possibilities of what lay beyond. Then, she would shake her head and scoff at herself, knowing that it was her brother who was the adventurous one and she was destined to stay in the town where she was raised.

Tucked away. Safe and quiet.

"I believe it's cause for celebration!" Dasos said, the wide grin splitting his face. His cheeks were tinged pink, the flush of excitement spotting them. "Dasos Terrigan, newest seafarer and future lieutenant of *The Polperro*."

"Dasos Terrigan," Fenna retorted with a mocking smile, "newest ordinary seaman and current scrubber of the poop deck."

Dasos leaned over the table to ruffle Fenna's hair, a barking laugh crackling through the small tavern. "What am I gonna do without your terrible jokes?"

"Think of your own, I hope," Fenna said, batting his hand away.

Gods, she's awful. So lanky.

What is she wearing? I thought she would dress better after her mother died.

And her freckles...

Fenna's swallow was thick as she regarded the wood grain of the table. Dasos must have sensed her shift, because he reached out a warm hand and clasped it tightly around her forearm.

"What are they saying?" He asked softly, leaning forward to tilt her chin upward with a single finger. The motion forced her to peer up at him.

"The usual." Fenna lifted her hand to self-consciously smooth her hair, making sure the freckles of her ears were covered. "Nothing unexpected."

Dasos sat back in a huff, crossing his arms over his chest as he surveyed the tavern. The three women in question, each around her own age of twenty-five, were pinning Dasos with interested stares. He dutifully ignored them, always the good brother.

"Remember what mama always said—"

"Yes, I know." Fenna paused to sigh. "Don't reply out loud to the thoughts in my head."

"And."

Another sigh. "And ignore them. They wouldn't think on it if they knew I was listening." It still wasn't a comforting thought.

Her *gift*, as her mother called it, was a heavily guarded secret in the Terrigan family. The first time Fenna had responded to a thought of her father's, he had nearly leapt out of his skin. The second time, he made sure that she understood the gravity of her gift.

More importantly, how outward shows of magic were strictly forbidden in the continent and would surely end with her dangling from a rope. That didn't stop her ability from blooming, though, and by the age of eight she knew exactly what the other children thought of her.

Dasos said that he didn't know what he would do without her. But the truth was, Fenna always knew Dasos would do something dangerous and exciting. He was too big for their town. He had just been waiting for the right opportunity to present itself.

A body fell into the seat next to Fenna, jolting her from her thoughts. A sudden deluge of wild mint and warm vanilla flooded her nose, and Fenna glanced over to see her best friend, Imogen, setting her stein on the table. Wild haired, bright eyed, and creative Imogen. She was her brother in female form and the only one who gave her a chance in their days in the learning house.

"Dasos Terrigan, the newest member of the continent's navy!" Imogen started, brushing a lock of dark hair from her brow. Her perceptive stare darted between brother's flared nostrils and sister's slumped shoulders. She locked onto Fenna's sullen face. "Who was it this time?" She spun in her seat, eyes narrowing on the three giggling women, all whom buried their grins behind the rims of their steins.

"It's no matter." Fenna tugged a grin onto her lips. She knew it looked more reminiscent of a grimace, and struggled to right it. "We're here to celebrate the newest sailor. In the King's name!"

"In the King's name!" Imogen repeated, twisting to grab her stein, but not before sending a rude gesture toward the three women with her right hand. They blanched, mouths slackening as they turned away.

They each took a sip and Fenna coughed when the amber-hued fion hit the back of her throat, burning a path of smoky fire on the way down. Dasos and Imogen exchanged knowing smirks.

"Please promise me that you'll teach her to enjoy *fion*," Dasos said, placing the stein back on the table with a dull thud. He raised his voice as a fiddle began to play. Chair legs scraped against the wooden floor as people rose to dance. "I'm begging you. I need to be able to have a drink with my sister when I'm on leave."

"I've been trying since we were teenagers," Imogen replied, taking another sip and smacking her lips to savor the taste. "No such luck."

Who can't drink fion *at her age?*

What a child. She dribbled on her stays.

I wonder if there were any new books at the shop this week.

"Yes, there's a great one about a princess and an old castle. I think you would like it," Fenna answered Imogen, who started with enough force that some of her drink sloshed over the rim of the stein and onto the wooden table. Fenna bit her lip, a flush rising in her cheeks when she realized what she had done.

Dasos sent her a long look before leaning forward, bracing his forearms on the edge of the table. "We just talked about this, Fenna."

"I know, I'm sorry," Fenna said quietly, shame brushing her tone. Imogen swiped the *fion* up with her cloth napkin, setting it in a wet and rumpled bundle at the corner.

"Do I need to stay home? Are you not ready to—"

"No." Fenna's head shot upward, gaze connecting fiercely with her brother's. "No, I— I'll be fine. It was just a mistake. It won't happen again." She softened her voice at the bright, pleading stare Dasos was giving her. "You deserve to go; you've waited for too long now. Please."

Imogen took another sip of her *fion*. "I'll be here to watch over her, Dasos. She's right. You should go." She leaned back in her seat, sending a sultry wink his way. "We've already said goodbye to you. Don't make us regret it."

Fenna flicked her gaze between her best friend and her brother, an uncomfortable squirm worming its way through her lower belly. She had always known that her brother was one of the most eligible bachelors of their town— had equally known that dark-haired, charming Imogen was chased around by every man aged twenty-two to forty. But from the glances passing between the two...Fenna cleared her throat.

"See?" Fenna finally said, taking a second tentative sip of the *fion*. "I'll be fine." She swallowed back the cough tickling the back of her throat.

"You don't need to finish that," Imogen said with a tight-lipped smile, reaching forward to place her palm on the opening of the stein and pushing it away from Fenna's mouth. "We all know you don't like it."

Fenna merely sent her a sheepish grin.

The used bookshop was Fenna's second favorite place in town. It was nestled near the end of an alley, which meant they didn't get nearly as many patrons as the bookshops on the main thoroughfare. And it was almost always dark, even on the sunniest days. The books were well-read and dog-eared at the corners, which were both things that Fenna found endearing. It meant they had been loved.

The shop smelled of old carpet fibers and the acrid scent of burning oil from the lamp that lit up the counter. Shadows danced on the ceiling, bobbing and dipping with each flicker of the small flame that swayed within the glass flaretop. The bustle of the mid-afternoon crowd could be heard down the narrow cobblestone path, murmured conversations pinging off the brick buildings. It was small and it was cozy, but it felt like home.

Fenna took in a deep breath as she turned the page of the book spread in front of her, feeling the dry parchment beneath the tips of her fingers. This one wasn't new to the shop, but it was a story that she had read a handful of times already. It was a love story, first and foremost, with echoes of an unexpected journey, men who fought in heroic battles, and animals who talked. Delving into it was a comfort for her, one that she came back to every so often.

A ding of the bell above the door drew Fenna from the book and she glanced upward with a furrowed brow.

"Quite the day for your brother to embark on the warship," a voice called from the other side of the shoulder-height bookcases. "Rainy and overcast. Certainly not the day I would choose to set sail."

Fenna's answering smile was wide and knowing. "I actually think he prefers it this way. Dasos never liked for things to be easy."

The owner of the voice came from around the corner. Algie was a squat man, shorter than Fenna's average frame, with broad shoulders and a round belly. What was left of his wispy hair was white, as were the whiskers that pebbled his cheeks, and his walk was more of a waddle. But his eyes were kind and he was the only bookshop owner who would hire Fenna, choosing to ignore the gossip that littered the town.

"*Woman of the Solstice* again?" His gaze dropped to the counter, where the book was still opened flat against the surface. "I know what that means. What's on your mind, my girl?"

Of course he knew. Algie always knew. It was his own gift, the ability to read her mood based on whatever book was propped in front of her at the time. Fenna surmised it was due to the seemingly endless amounts of time they spent together.

"Worried about Dasos, that's all." It wasn't a lie. Leaving him at the docks as he readied to board the giant warship was one of the hardest things she ever had to do. Almost as hard as when they had to bury their mother just the year before. And both made equally hard by the pitiful stares and the sour smell of rotten fish that pierced the busy barges.

Everyone in the town knew she was alone. Now it was just official.

Algie's eyes drifted over her features, the leveling stare both warming and penetrating. He heaved a sigh, one that lifted his belly off his upper thighs. "Did you catalog the new arrivals?"

"As soon as I opened the shop."

"And exchanged the citrus tea for the cinnamon one? The wet season is here, you know. Dry season tea won't do."

"Brewed the cinnamon tea this morning. Freida from the bakery already came to pour a cup."

Algie seemed mollified enough as he sent Fenna a curt nod. "Good girl." He peered at her for a few seconds longer and Fenna felt his roving gaze search her face once more. He let out a grunt. "There is a bundle coming on the next ship from Irongrave. Keep an eye on the bay for a few days, will you? My knees have been stiff since last night. I doubt they would allow me to make the trip."

It was only two staircases and a series of roads to the docks, one that Fenna knew Algie had no issue making. She smiled and nodded, nonetheless. She was grateful for his willingness to make her feel useful.

Chapter Three

Devlin

Four months later

"This is the one, captain," Booker said, his heels bouncing excitedly against the wood of the stern deck. "I can feel it in my bones."

"Relax," Devlin replied tersely, though the knot in his chest had eased a bit since they had anchored. He let his hand drop to his side, not realizing he had been rubbing his knuckles against his sternum. "Nothing is settled."

Booker followed Devlin down the steps and onto the quarterdeck. "This is a warship. They don't come around these parts very often—" The rest of his reasoning was lost to a sudden gust of wind. A storm was approaching, though that wasn't the reason the warship at their port was sinking.

Devlin grasped a loose rope as he hauled himself onto the taffrail. Glancing over a shoulder, he spotted Booker's tanned face, his brows set in a furrow. "Prepare to board," he commanded, raising his voice to allow the other men to hear. "The ship sinks when the last of the storm breaches the horizon."

He turned to glance at the weather, where heavy clouds were stark against the otherwise blue sky. *The Phantom Night* bobbed beneath him. In the distance, Devlin could see the streaks of rain blurring the skyline against the sea. Clutching the rope with both hands, he pushed from the taffrail and swung across the gap between ships, landing with a sharp thud on the deck of the warship.

At the sound of his boots, the nearest man's head snapped up. Devlin felt a zing of pleasure when the man's eyes widened and his lips parted in terror. Devlin rested an easy hand on the pommel of his cutlass, reaching into the pocket of his frock coat.

"Care to point me in the direction of your commodore?" Devlin said as he retrieved the set of bone dice, allowing them to roll in the palm of his hand. "Unless you want to take a look."

The man's breath seemed to catch in his throat as he swept his dilated stare along the open sea. Devlin knew he wouldn't be able to see *The Phantom Night*, despite it being only feet away. The ship was invisible when Devlin willed it to be. That terrified gaze returned to Devlin and the man seemed to realize who was standing before him. "*Specter!*" he shouted, lurching forward in a fool's attempt to run toward the bow of the warship.

Devlin withdrew a dagger from the belt at his waist and threw it with a flick of his wrist, sending it sailing through the air. It embedded between the man's shoulders with deadly accuracy. He dropped to the deck with a loud crash, and he continued to slide a few feet across the wood from the force of his fall before coming to a crumpled stop against a pile of unused rigging. Heads swiveled toward the sudden sound, a comical range of emotions flitting over each damned face.

Devlin sighed.

This could go one way or another— it always did. In one version, the men would lay down their weapons and fall to their knees to helplessly beg for mercy. That never worked and, truthfully, it only managed to irritate him further. The alternative was much more his speed.

And based on the number of men currently drawing their swords, the alternative was far more likely.

Devlin couldn't help the smirk that lifted a corner of his mouth as a man emerged from the jeering crowd, a scrawny boy shouldering past the crew behind him. The silver pendant in the boy's hand glinted in the sunlight, dulled from the wisp of early gray clouds racing across the sky. He made to pin the metal back to the lapel of the commodore's coat when the man sent him sprawling to the deck with a quick crack.

The commodore placed his hand back at his side, as though he hadn't just split the servant boy's lip with the broad edge of his golden ring. "You aren't welcome here, Specter. We are already patching the keel."

Devlin clicked his tongue against the roof of his mouth at the sight of the boy prodding his fat lip, and Devlin's hand flexing against the pommel. A shot of agitation clattered through him. If one spent enough time on the Aeglecian Seas, it was inevitable that one would cross paths with Devlin. The commodore, for example, had worked his way up the chain of command over the last twenty years. It had been quite some time since Devlin had to deal with him, the last being a series of deaths due to plague when the commodore was merely a lieutenant.

"Commodore Keetes. Your warship has taken on too much water. You're destined to sink."

If the news rattled the commodore, he didn't show it. Keetes took a brazen step forward, his own hand now wrapped around the hilt of his sword. "You are mistaken. We cannot sink, *The Polperro* was designed to perfection. She's the principal ship of the king's naval fleet." He let out a chuckle and laughter rippled through the crew. "Unless there is another reason for your appearance, I would suggest allowing us to be on our way."

Murmurs of shock followed on the heels of the laughter and, by the sudden heat against Devlin's right elbow, he realized Booker had appeared at his side.

"He doesn't seem to know about the secondary hole in the hull, captain," Booker said, running his forefinger over the sharp edge of his dagger. Devlin didn't need to look at the quartermaster to imagine the violent gleam in his eye.

"No, he certainly doesn't," Devlin replied, though the commodore's cool mask of indifference markedly dipped at Booker's statement. "Ah, now he does." His smirk grew as the commodore slowly drew his sword from the sheath at his hip. "That isn't necessary, Commodore Keetes. Your ship will be at the bottom of the trench by nightfall. You've sailed your crew into the graveyard and ripped open your hull in the process." He rattled the dice in his hand. "I've already offered one of your men the chance to join my crew. What say you?"

The sword lifted from the sheath with a sharp zing as Keetes leveled the end at Devlin's heart. Devlin sighed again. This time, it was wistful. Storing the dice back into his pocket, he walked forward until the point of Keetes's sword dug into his chest, caving the skin beneath it. Keetes's eyes widened as the sword passed through Devlin's flesh and slipped between two ribs, a sickening sound of metal against bone squelching out. He would fix it later.

"You forget your place, Keetes," Devlin hissed out as the commodore released the hilt of the sword, staggering backward. Keetes knocked into three of his men, each of their dirty, sun-bronzed faces twisting with disbelief and horror. Devlin wrapped his hand around the hilt and pulled, the sword sliding out with relative ease. Red coated the blade and steadily stained his tunic. "Death has come for you and now you must heed her call."

In a flash, Devlin's hand lashed forward and slit the commodore's throat. Keetes swayed on his feet, grappling at the sudden opening at his neck. There was a choked death rattle of wet breath and blood bubbling from the wound as Keetes fell to his knees. He landed in a sprawled heap against the deck, eyes unseeing and feathered hat askew on his head.

Devlin lifted his gaze toward the nearest crewman as he tossed the dead commodore's sword to the side. It clattered loudly in the span of silence emanating from the deck. "Now, who is the commodore's second?" The men shifted uncomfortably on their feet, sweeping glances at one another. "No one? Not a soul?" Devlin heaved a dramatic sigh, letting the breath whistle through his nose. Now that the protective barrier that was Keetes was dead, the crew didn't seem as prepared to banter with Devlin.

Or, perhaps, it was fifty of the pirate captain's men that had appeared, flanking him equally on both sides.

"We go down with our ship."

Devlin's eyes darted to the right, spotting a man with his arms crossed over his chest. By the way his fingers were trembling, Devlin recognized the stance for what it was– a poorly executed show of force. He glanced down to the front of the man's tunic, where a white badge was pinned against his broad chest. A Chief Petty Officer. The ranks of officers had fallen back, allowing this one to assume leadership. He couldn't help but think it was a shame.

"What's your name, sailor?"

The man shifted on his feet, discomfort apparent on his weather-beaten face, though he straightened his back as though Devlin had shoved a metal rod down his spine. "Litton, sir. Litton Vaughn."

Devlin ran a finger along his lower lip. "Well, Mr. Vaughn. Water will breach the quarterdeck when the first crack of thunder reaches you and the waves will pull you all down with her—"

"We go down with our ship," Litton repeated in a rasp, though his throat bobbed with the force of his swallow.

Booker cursed under his breath as Devlin's smirk turned glacial. "Very well. May Samael, God of Death, have mercy on you or may you choke on Liddros's briny waters when he does not. Men, raid the stores. Bring anything of value to me. Put all of the food and clean water in our underdecks." Devlin tipped his head toward the crew of nearly two hundred men, all huddled together as they awaited their inevitable demise, and turned to board *The Phantom Night*.

"Wait! Wait."

Booker and Devlin exchanged looks of surprise before Devlin turned to glance over a shoulder. A man had pushed to the front of the crew, his chest heaving and his dark hair disheveled.

"I want to join. I want to roll the dice."

Devlin slowly spun on the balls of his feet, dragging an assessing stare from the man's widow's peak to the tips of his worn, black boots. He was tall, yet lankier than Devlin preferred his crew to be. Thin ropes of muscle had barely begun to build on his shoulders and chest, and their appearance was laughable in contrast to his age. The tips of his ears were flushed pink and his cheek pulsed on the left side with every clench of his jaw.

"Back away, boy," the officer growled amidst rising snarls and hisses. "We go down with our ship. It's the way of the naval command."

The man ignored him, dark eyes boring into Devlin's.

"How old are you, sailor?" Devlin asked, placing his hand back on the pommel of his cutlass. The move was not lost on the man, who tracked Devlin's hand with wide eyes.

"Twenty-eight."

"Old for a deckhand," Devlin grunted. No officer's pins adorned his tunic, no feathered hat sat upon his matted head. The man was ordinary, undeniably so, and Devlin was rapidly losing interest. "That's child's work."

"I joined only four months ago. I needed to wait until my mother died," the man pressed on, taking a tentative and hopeful step forward. "My sister, she—"

"I don't give the king's right sagging sack about your sister." Devlin watched the man fidget under his piercing stare and the jeering laughs of the crew behind him, knowing full well that he was going to allow the man to roll the dice. He didn't have the choice to be picky. "What's your name?"

"Dasos Terrigan, sir."

Devlin plunged his free hand into the pocket of his coat, retrieving the dice once more. "Pick your mark and state your rules, Dasos."

Dasos's face fell. "I don't— I've never—"

"Choose two numbers, both between one and six," Booker shot over Devlin's shoulder, his irritability puncturing the air like a sharpened claw. Devlin knew his quartermaster was clambering for dinner. "You roll a pair of numbers over what the captain claims and you win a spot on the crew, but be warned. What you choose is how long you are fixed to the crew."

"And if I don't?" Dasos asked, voice shaking and weak. "Win, I mean."

"We'll get to that later," Devlin replied with a biting smile. "Pick your mark, boy, before I lose my temper."

"A pair of fives."

Devlin smirked. "A pair of ones." He threw down the dice before Dasos could realize what he had done. A rumble of chuckles resounded from his crew as the dice tumbled to the deck.

Dasos's eyes cleared with realization as they fixed on the two dice, one sporting a three and the other a six. "You cheated."

Devlin cocked a brow as a sharp ping of energy crested over his soul. A payment to Liddros. "You failed to state your rules, that isn't cheating. And you'd be well to remember that next time." He took a step forward, staring down at the terrified face of his newest crew member. "Welcome to *The Phantom Night*, Dasos. A pair of fives was your mark, and twenty-five years is your debt."

"He's going to be a weak link in our chain," Booker muttered, sidling up to Devlin and resting his forearms on the railing overlooking the quarterdeck. "He doesn't have enough experience to work the sails."

"He'll learn," Devlin replied, watching the newest member of his crew struggle to haul the thick ropes back to the mainmast. A whip cracked in the air followed by a shrill cry of pain. The bo'sun had laid the thin leather straps across Dasos's back, splitting his shirt in two. "Or he won't."

"Captain!"

Devlin's eyes slid from Dasos and came to rest on the man standing at the foot of the steps leading to the stern deck. Whit Risley had been a member of his crew for nearly eighteen years. He was a formidable sailor and an excellent swordhand. Whit swept the unruly strands of blonde hair from his cheeks, a wicked smile on his lips.

"I want a challenge."

The crew manning the deck stilled, save for Dasos, who was still attempting to tie the rope off. Devlin could see the trails of blood across the fibers where Dasos's hands had opened. The skin still needed to thicken.

Devlin pushed off the railing, taking deliberately slow steps to the stop of the staircase. The tendrils of his long, dark hair brushed against his brow. Even the wind in the sails seemed to die down, the sound of flapping cloth suddenly disappearing. "A challenge, you say."

"Aye, captain." Whit folded his hands at his front. "My years are up tomorrow. I want a challenge."

Devlin began to descend the stairs, letting the splinters of the wooden railing bite against the palm of his hand. The sun was already halfway hidden against the horizon, the clear skies casting a golden glow on the deck. The crew shuffled away from their posts, surrounding Whit and Devlin in a half-circle.

Challenges, though uncommon, weren't rare. Devlin would have wagered that nearly a quarter of the men who entered his service would go on to challenge him. The risk was worth the reward. Whit would die when his debt was repaid. Or, he could win a roll of the dice and live out the rest of his days in peace. But if he lost...

"Pick your mark and state your rules."

Whit crossed his arms over his broad chest. "No siren's eyes." He sent a knowing grin toward Dasos, who only flushed in response. The crew laughed loudly at Dasos's expense.

"And no sixes for you, then," Cato said in turn. Whit replied with a curt nod. "Your mark?"

"A four and a two."

Cato dipped a hand into his pocket, rolling the dice between his thumb and forefinger. "A three and a five." His hand flew out as he tossed the dice down. They bounced against the wood of the deck, one of them coming to rest by Whit's boot and the other wedging into a narrow crevice in the flooring.

A deckhand, nicknamed Tabs for the amount of time he spent labeling each item they acquired in their raids, leaned over the dice to read the marks. Whit kept his eyes trained on Devlin.

"A two and a four, captain."

Whit loosed a breath, nearly imperceptible, if not for the fluttering of the locks close to his mouth.

"Again."

Tabs scraped the dice from the deck, depositing them into Devlin's outstretched palm. No die could match and they would roll until they didn't. Devlin threw them down again.

"A five and a three, captain," Tabs called again.

Tricky little bastards. "Again."

A third roll was much the same: a five and a three. But the fourth roll...

Cato's heart sank to his feet when Tabs called, "a one and a two, captain." His voice was notably quieter than before. Tabs peered toward Whit, his lips pursed and his brow lowered in a sorrowful expression.

Whit was nodding his head slowly, gaze fixed on the dice still perched on the deck. Finally, he lifted it and the corner of his mouth quirked, though the action didn't quite meet his eyes. "Only a few minutes left, then." His stare darted to the horizon. "It's been an honor, as you well know, captain."

Devlin's gaze followed, seeing the final rays of the sun dyeing the sky a deep orange. "You were one of the best, Whit. Send our regards to Liddros."

Whit's face was cast in shadows as the sun sank below the sea, darkening the water to inky black. The quarterdeck was quiet, save for the waves lapping at the hull and the men working to shift the new items acquired in the raid to the storage compartments below. Whit's breathing was fast and ragged, as though he couldn't draw it into his lungs deep enough. Then...

A choked gurgle skittered along the wood as Whit fell to his knees, one hand on his throat and the other on his chest. His eyes widened to saucers. The men had removed their hats and head covers in respect, but a single cry of terror broke over them. Devlin didn't need to find the source to know it was Dasos. He had never seen a drying before.

Whit's body began to shrivel, starting in the tips of his fingers and quickly moving to his wrists, forearms, and shoulders. It was as though he were having the water sucked out of him, second by second, inch by inch. The skin on his face shrunk against his skull, giving him a skeletal appearance that hollowed out the spaces of his eyes. His mouth contorted into a silent scream, the breath whooshing out of him as the flesh of his body whittled down until there was nothing remaining. Whit's remains collapsed to the deck in a heap of skin and bone, still covered in the tunic, breeches, and leather boots.

Devlin had never seen a body that had been dead for months, but he always imagined this is what they looked like. Something behind his navel tugged, and grief curled like a cat in the spot where his heart should have been.

Whit had always been one of his favorites.

The men took no time to wrap his body in a shroud and pitch it over the side of the ship, where it entered the deep of the sea with a weak splash. In the same moment, Dasos had flung his upper body over the gunnel and emptied his stomach.

CHAPTER FOUR

FENNA

The days were too short and the nights were too long in the week since Fenna had been given the news. *The Polperro* had been downed in the waters to the north off the continent's coast, presumably pierced by one of the many sunken masts hidden just below the surface. It had been commonly known as the graveyard, though many weren't quite sure why the commodore had sailed them through it.

None had survived.

Imogen had taken to staying with her, sleeping in the bed that had once belonged to Dasos. Fenna could hear Imogen crying at night. It didn't take much for her to imagine her friend curled against Dasos's old pillow, soaking up the last of his scent. Once it would have sent her stomach into a roil of discomfort, but now...now she took solace in knowing that Dasos was truly loved by more than just her.

The rainy season had shifted into the bitter season, where the cold winds of the inner continent clashed violently with the warmth of the sea. Fenna knew it wasn't nearly as cold as it would be hours inland, but it was cold enough to warrant a fur-lined cloak when she left the confines of the cottage.

Which she tried to do as little as possible.

The stares of the city folk were filled with pity— not much better than the weary stares that blanketed their features before. Now she was just the weird woman with the dead brother and their thoughts reflected as such. They had taken to peering through the windows of the bookshop, hoping to catch a glimpse of her. They would never come inside, though. That would have been too crude.

Fenna took the pathway that led to the cove, pausing at the first border of sharp rocks that separated the forest from the sea. She stared at the horizon, a silent plea thrumming through her for her brother's return. She wished for the warship to appear against the clouded sky, masts high and sails full. The longer she looked, the darker the clouds became.

Fat droplets of rain fell against her cheek. Fenna lifted her hand to wipe them away, unaware that her cheeks had gone numb from the wind. She focused on the crash of the waves against the grainy shore, followed by the sharp hiss of their retreat. The smell of brine and fresh seaweed had always been a reprieve for her, but now it was mocking.

She couldn't help but think of the last moments of Dasos's life. Surrounded by the cold, salty air before the currents pulled him below. She had once loved the sea and it had betrayed her.

Fenna turned her back to it, trudging toward home. Her boots sank into the thick mud of the trail as she crested the hill leading to the cottage. She saw the smoke from the chimney curling above the tree line before she saw the flicker of candlelight against the window panes.

Imogen made the one-sided decision to stay with her and Fenna could almost taste the spicy warmth of the beef stew Imogen planned on making, though she wondered if it would turn flat against her tongue like everything else she had tried to eat. Her swallow was thick as the lump in the back of her throat grew.

Even with Imogen taking up residence in the cottage, Fenna knew it wouldn't last. It was only a matter of time before she was alone once again. And it was going to be a long and lonely existence...for however many years the gods deemed her worthy of.

Sharp *thwacks* on the door woke Fenna from her restless sleep. Her eyes cracked open in confusion before clearing with rapid blinks. The gaslamp next to her bed had burnt out, recently it seemed. The embers on the tip of the wick still glowed against the dark backdrop of her bedroom.

Rain pattered against the window, streaming down the glass in thinly formed trails. Fenna wiped the sleep from the corners of her eyes. The pounding must have been her dream. She couldn't remember exactly what that dream was, just that it wasn't a good one. She had nearly begun to nestle back into the mattress when another series of sharp *thwacks* cracked against the front door.

Heart drumming a ferocious beat in her chest, Fenna tossed the covers off before swinging her legs toward the floor. She shivered as her bare feet hit the cool wooden planks, but she ignored it. Instead, she reached between the mattress and the bedframe to pull out the small knife she had hidden there.

When Dasos had been home, she didn't bother with it. As a single female living in a cottage on the outskirts of the city, she had quickly changed her mind.

Clutching it tightly in her fist, Fenna crept toward the living space, the scent of the beef stew from dinner still lingering in the air. She peered over her shoulder when she heard the door to Dasos's old bedroom creak open.

"You heard it then?" Imogen whispered as she wrapped her arms across her chest.

Fenna nodded and opened her mouth to respond when a third series of *thwacks* had her leaping back, her fingers fanning over her sternum. Her breath was shaky as she took a hesitant step forward. Reaching for the door, she shifted the curtain away from the small window framed in the wood and dropped the knife from her hand in disbelief.

"Dasos!"

The sharp cry of shock from the back of Imogen's throat was nearly drowned out by the sound of the iron lock sliding against the wooden door. Fenna yanked the handle toward her and, in the next moment, flung her arms around Dasos's neck. She didn't care that the rain rolling off the roof was soaking through her nightgown or that the air was so cold her breath came out in a misty fog.

Dasos was here. He was alive.

Hands encircled her waist and pushed her across the threshold. Fenna withdrew from Dasos, looking up at him for the first time. In the firelight flickering from the hearth, she took in his pallid cheeks and trembling chin, both covered in patches of brown hair. His terrified glance darted around the room before turning over a shoulder to sweep across the front garden.

"Dasos—"

He said nothing as he forcefully shut the door, rattling it in the frame. With minor difficulty and jerking movements, he managed to slide the iron lock back into place. He continued to stay silent as he whirled around and Fenna watched as his eyes landed on the poker leaning against the stone surrounding the hearth. He made a beeline for it, tripping over his feet as he grasped it. His footsteps thudded against the floor as he raced toward the door, shoving the poker through the handle and embedding the sharp end in the frame.

Dasos's throat bobbed as he took a step back, sucking in gulping breaths. His eyes remained fixed on the small window as he backed into the living space, coming to a stop when his shoulders connected with the wall directly across the room. He slid to the ground, tunic snagging against the exposed brick, and buried his head in his arms.

Imogen and Fenna exchanged worried glances. A silent conversation danced between them for a long moment, unanswered questions written on pale, ghostly faces.

"What is—" Imogen finally started, bending down to place a gentle hand on Dasos's forearm. She quickly retracted it when his body flinched against her touch, knuckles fading into white when he tightened his fingers into a fist.

"He's going to find me," he whispered to no one. The stiffening of his shoulders eased, though an uncontrolled shaking had taken its spot. "He's going to find me."

Fenna sank to her knees in front of her brother. She made to reach out for him but thought better of it, and allowed her hand to fall back into her lap. "How are you here? Who is going to find you?"

Dasos's whimpering ceased at the sound of her voice. His head lifted long enough for him to swipe a shaking hand across his brow. Fenna hadn't even realized it was covered in a sheen layer of cold sweat.

"Fenna—"

Fenna's eyes landed on Imogen, drawn from her brother with the urgency in her best friend's voice. She stood at Imogen's frantic hand motions and wound her way to Dasos's side. Fenna's rasping inhale hitched in her chest at the sight Imogen was motioning toward.

As though he had been whipped, the back of Dasos's shirt was stained with blood and split in criss-crossing patterns. Fenna reached forward to lift the shredded cloth from his back, sucking in a whistling breath through her nose. The skin was ribboned, healing in thick patches of scar tissue that clumped along his back. Angry, pink strips marred his flesh while deeper, open lacerations still leaked red-tinged fluid onto his tunic.

"What is this, Dasos?" Fenna demanded, placing the back of her hand against her lips to keep the sick from creeping up her throat. "Who did this?"

When he remained silent, rocking on his tailbone as though trying to soothe himself, Fenna imagined sending tentative tendrils into the air between them. The golden bands of light snaked to his temple and pushed into his mind. She hated using her power on her brother, had, in fact, been banned from doing so at a young age...but she had to know. This was Dasos. Strong and infallible Dasos.

Who could have possibly done this to him?

She began to sift through his thoughts, words crackling before her like the final passages in a burning book. *Pirate. Specter. Dice. Death.* Dasos whipped his head up to glare at her, anger clearly etched into the furrows of his brows and the downturn of his mouth.

"Do not," he snarled, his hand shooting upward to clasp around Fenna's wrist. "Do not read me, Fenna. You cannot know. You cannot—" His face crumpled into feared despair once again and his hand slid from her wrist, landing against his knee.

It was Imogen who kneeled next to him this time, her fingers reaching forward to brush the locks from his temples. "Dasos. Tell us how you got home."

His next breath was ragged and tears pricked at his red-rimmed eyes. For a long minute, Fenna didn't think he was going to say anything. He took in one more harsh breath as he turned his ashen face toward Fenna. "I've seen things. Terrifying, unnatural things."

Imogen ran her fingers through his hair in gentle, soothing strokes. "What things?"

"*The Polperro* went down, the underside torn open from a hidden mast," Dasos began as he dragged his blank stare toward the hearth. "We spent hours trying to fix the keel, but didn't realize there was a second hole in the hull. There was a ship that— that...I made a mistake. I found passage on it through a debt I can never repay." He sniffed, wiping the end of his nose with the back of his hand. "There are legends of specter ships that haunt the seas. Ghost ships that collect souls of those damned to the bottom of the deep. That's the ship I owe my life to." His gaze lifted to meet Fenna's and he went quiet once more.

Fenna's brow knitted together as she studied her brother's pleading expression. An unwelcome feeling prickled the back of her neck. "A ghost ship? Dasos, I—"

"I know how it sounds," Dasos interjected with a curt shake of his head. "I wouldn't have believed it myself. But I've— I watched a man die as though his very self was sucked from his body. I watched as the crew worked for days without food, without water. I—" He paused to take in another breath. "I found myself without the need of sleep, without hunger. I jumped ashore at the first sight of land, into the town of Pinehollow to the north. I've been boarding ship to ship for days now to get home."

"You just need some rest," Fenna pressed on as she wrapped a hand under Dasos's arm and tried to tug him away from the wall. "Come, let's get you to bed. It's been a harrowing journey home, not to mention the sinking—."

"You don't understand. He's hunting me. I need to hide. I need you to hide me."

His insistence made Fenna hesitate. Her grasp on his elbow slackened.

"Hide you from who?" Imogen asked, her worried gaze roving Dasos's face.

"The captain. Devlin Cato. He'll be coming for me."

Something about Dasos's words sparked fear within Fenna. Her hands trembled, though she couldn't pinpoint why. For the few minutes that followed, the only sounds that emanated through the cottage were the crack of the logs splitting in the hearth and the rain pattering mindlessly against the roof.

Dasos was just exhausted. He was imagining things, his mind working overtime to make sense of the trauma he had been through. Fenna was sure that was it. There was no other explanation...wasn't there?

The first *boom* was quiet. So quiet that she almost missed the echo of it flooding the forest. It cleaved apart the peaceful veil of night, shredding the usual moonlit calm, and drawing her attention away from her brother.

"Is that..." Imogen started as Fenna straightened to a stand, her stare pinned to the door as though she could see through the wood if she squinted hard enough.

"He's here," Dasos sputtered out, a fresh sheen of sweat breaking across his hairline. His hands shook as he buried his face in the crook of his arms. "The captain. He's here."

A second *boom* ricocheted against the trees and, this time, screams from the citizens of the town followed on the heels of it. The massive bells above the church in the square began to gong, ringing an alarm that signaled an attack on the bay.

Fenna felt each toll in her chest, her pulse setting a devastating pace as she squared herself to Dasos. "What did you trade for?" she asked quickly, crouching down to meet her brother's eyes at level. "What did you give the captain that he might be looking for?"

A third *boom* followed, this one closer. Fenna could hear the snapping of bricks as the cannonballs collided with the buildings at the port.

Dasos's pained gaze searched her own. "My soul. I gave him my soul."

Chapter Five

Fenna

Fenna usually took her time dressing: the layers of her shift, stays, and petticoats were notably harder to work with after the death of her mother, who always helped her dress. At the sound of the cannons still firing in the bay, though, she pulled everything on in record time.

"I'm going into town," she said between rapid breaths, tugging on her boots and lacing them just as quickly.

"Fenna, this is madness," Imogen hissed. She left Dasos's side, who had curled himself in an armchair with a steaming cup of tea in his hand, and managed to catch Fenna at the forearm as she pinned her cloak around her shoulders. "It's too dangerous out there. You should stay here—"

"The bookshop is blocks away from the port," Fenna responded with reason. "I'll be safe from the attack. I want to open it for the people who may be seeking shelter."

Imogen's grasp only tightened. "Unobstructed cannon fire can go a long, long way."

Fenna snaked her arm from Imogen's hand and delicately squeezed her best friend's fingers. "Then let's hope the cannons have not taken down every building between the shop and the port." She swooped down to plant a kiss on the top of Dasos's head, his hair still cool and damp from the rain. "Put the poker back in place when I leave and hide him in the root cellar out back. It may buy you a few minutes if they come looking here."

"Stay here with us," Imogen pleaded one final time. She wrung her hands, twisting her fingers into knots. "The people of the city were never kind to you. They don't deserve your help."

Fenna felt her chest constrict at the words and she fought back the panic that boiled hot in her stomach. "My help isn't offered as a reward for their kindness. They need a safe place to stay and I'll give it to them." She yanked the poker from its place within the door handle and let it rest with a *thud* against the brick wall. "I'll see you both soon."

Then, she took off into the darkness.

Water droplets, remnants of the rain that had since stopped, leaked from the forest trees above her. The cool light of the moon was barely visible behind the thick clouds that raced across the black sky. Fenna felt the air saw against her throat, a cold humidity that sank deep into her chest. The bitter season had made its mark, the wind biting at her arms and collarbones despite the cloak pinned around her.

Her boots suctioned into the mud of the pathway and she felt the splashes of it against her ankles as she drew her petticoats up. The hems were already dirty and wet, but Fenna pressed forward. The booms of the cannons had yet to cease, only growing louder with every passing minute.

She raced into the city, nearly sliding into a fall as the mud transitioned into slick cobblestones under her feet. The *gongs* of the bells above the church were ear-splitting, nearly covering the hysteric screams of the people scurrying as far from the port as they could get. Fenna surged deeper toward the city square, navigating the crowds with difficulty as they grew thicker and thicker.

Fenna shouldered past a woman, her young son tucked safely under her arm and blood dripping down the bridge of her nose. The woman's shift, soaked and nearly see-through despite the layer of dusted plastering, clung tightly to her body. She shivered uncontrollably, as did her son, and didn't give Fenna a passing glance as they ran toward the cover of the forest.

Taking in a deep breath, Fenna scented smoke in the air, a congested and heavy contrast to the fresh salt that blew off the sea. Scanning the tops of the buildings, her heart stuttered when she leveled her gaze on the bright orange glow that licked against the port. Something was on fire. She dipped to her left, taking a narrow passage that she knew dumped into an alley near the bookshop.

It was dark and confining, not one Fenna preferred to take when the sun had set, but it was the quickest route from where she stood.

A younger man, his coat singed and his cheeks smeared with ash, pushed past her. Her shoulder bit painfully against the wood exterior of the building. She slapped a hand over the spot, knowing it would more than likely bruise, and bit her inner cheek to keep from crying out. The shoulder let out an aching throb in time with her heartbeats.

A cannon blasted again and, this time, Fenna heard the iron ball burst through a building only a block or two from her. The wood of the building's exterior splintering mixed with the new shouts echoing from the square, creating a disastrous song that echoed through the alleyway.

Fenna rounded the corner, stumbling over her own feet, and locked her wide eyes on the destruction before her. Where there had once been a bustling square lined with vendor carts crammed with fruits, clothing, and pottery, now lay smashed framing and littered debris. Meat still on the skewers and spilled bags of nuts rolled in the gutters. Sun-faded fabrics that had been strung above the wooden stalls hung limp and torn. Soldiers were running, broadswords in hand, toward the port.

No one paid her any mind.

"Come to Algie's bookshop down the alley," Fenna stated, wrapping her hand around the arm of a woman running across the square. She flew past, kicking loose fruit with the toe of her house slippers. "I know of a safe space, please," Fenna tried again, this time to a teenage boy who merely sent her a disgusted sneer and continued on.

Fenna swallowed back the sting of hurt and Imogen's words rang through her mind. She didn't want to dwell on them, not now when there was so much pain and anguish. Those thoughts were shoved back a moment later as an icy grip seized her chest. Shouts reverberated down the main road that led to the port, loud and boisterously out of place in the calamity surrounding her.

"Find him!" The male voice ordered. The harshness of his tone was evident, even above the near constant cannon fire.

Fenna took another tentative step forward, but tripped over something in the darkened square. Her lips parted in shock, hands flying to her mouth to cover the scream threatening to claw its way out of her, when she saw a body at her front. The back of the man's head was split in two, likened to an overripe melon, and blood still slowly seeped from the wound. It looked as though someone had wrenched their weapon from his head; the edges of his exposed skull crudely fractured.

At the sound of pounding footsteps against the cobblestone, Fenna lifted her head. She froze in place, open and exposed, as dozens of men in tricorn hats and stained tunics flooded into the square. Most had cutlasses gripped in their hands, each one dripping with blood and flecked with mud. The men fanned out from the mouth of the road, twisting into the alleys and kicking open the doors of the shops.

But, they weren't what kept Fenna stilled in place. No, it was *him*.

He emerged from the middle of the pack, cutlass also in hand, an air of arrogance enveloping him. His dark hair brushed against his shoulders and it hung loose under the red kerchief he had tied tightly around his head. His jawline was square and cutting, tense in a way that made Fenna shiver in her boots.

He was the most beautiful man she had ever seen. Maddeningly beautiful— dangerous and unforgiving.

His dark eyes swept across the square, pinning her in place just as she had the nerve to attempt a move into the shadows. The flickering fires set by the men cast his face in sharp relief. He walked toward her, at ease and seemingly unaware that she was whirling around to sprint back up the alleyway.

Fenna lifted her skirts to keep from tripping on them and sank into the refuge of the narrow passage that led to the bookshop. Her hand fumbled in the pockets she had tied around her waist, her rapid heartbeat thumping against her ribcage. She felt her throat constrict painfully with realization as she felt nothing but cotton fabric...the key to the shop had fallen from her pocket.

She glanced toward the entrance of the alley, her stomach dropping to her feet when she saw the silhouette of the man standing idly with his hands crossed at his front in a casual display of power. He casually leaned his cutlass against the wall, as though knowing that no one would dare take it. Smoke billowed from a shop window behind him.

Fenna turned back to the bookshop and wrapped her hand in her skirts, protecting her knuckles as she reeled back and punched the glass insert of the door. She didn't know why she thought it would work, perhaps because she saw one of the invaders doing it, but her fist bounced painfully off the window. She swore under her breath as a chuckle tickled the back of her neck, prickling her skin.

A hand wrapped around her upper arm and twisted her around to face its owner. Fenna inhaled deeply at the sudden movement, her senses deluged with the smells of a morning breeze off the sea and old, cured leather. She trained her eyes on the vee of his tunic, staring at the tendrils of dark hair that poked above the seam.

"I don't like to chase," the man rumbled, "at least in this sense. I prefer other reasons to do it."

Fenna let out a huff of disbelief. Men didn't make jokes like that to women, but especially to her. And it felt distinctly out of place in the midst of a raid. Something tight coiled in her belly and she tempered down the shudder that began in the base of her spine. When she said nothing, the man went on.

"I'm looking for someone, love." His voice was a purr against her skin, deep and husky. He took a step closer, pressing her to the wall. His breath fluttered onto her cheek and her skin pebbled traitorously beneath the sensation. "A man named Dasos."

Fenna lifted her gaze to meet the man's, though it wasn't out of bravery, but pure self-preservation. Her heart stuttered when she saw that the man's eyes weren't dark at all, but a shockingly light green. "I don't know a man by that name."

The man's full lips quirked to a grin and he raised a hand to brush a finger along the shell of her ear. "Your liar's blush says otherwise." She heard every word, despite his voice dropping to a murmur. "And you're going to tell me where I can find him."

Fenna swallowed loudly as she fastened her back as far into the brick wall as she could. That only made the man step closer, his hips holding tightly against her own. A large bulge rested on her upper thigh, hard and wanting despite the layers of her skirts. Her eyes closed as he leaned forward to bracket his hands on each side of her head.

"Come on," he cooed, running his nose from the corner of her jaw to the crook of her neck, "the sooner you tell me, the sooner we leave. I didn't want to spend my one day on land searching for him, but I do what needs to be done to keep my property in line."

A cold raindrop fell onto the back of Fenna's neck, sliding between her shoulder blades. It broke the spell of his touch and she let out an angry *whoosh* of breath. "What do you want with him?"

"You do know him."

Fenna opened her eyes, once again allowing her gaze to connect with his. She was thrown to see how close his lips were to her own. She wagered it wouldn't take more than a lift of her chin to taste them. "I didn't say that."

"It was implied in your question." His grin widened, flashing a white set of teeth. He paused, assessing her with a strict scrutiny that had her squirming. "What's your name, love?"

"It isn't love," she snapped back, only causing his grin to widen even further. "Fenna."

"Fenna." He said her name like a caress, rolling it on his tongue as though he were savoring it. "Where is Dasos, Fenna?"

She immediately regretted telling him. "What's your name?" She asked, hoping to distract him long enough to buy Dasos and Imogen time to lock themselves in the root cellar. If they hadn't already, any-ways.

His head tilted as his eyes narrowed down at her. Glass broke in the distance as another cannonball ruptured from the ship in the bay. For a long moment, she didn't think he would answer. "Devlin."

Fenna suspected who he was by the aura surrounding him, but hearing confirmation of the captain's first name made her stomach clench.

"You've heard of me, then?" His eyes danced gleefully as a shrill scream pierced the square. A raucous course of laughs followed and Fenna wasn't sure she wanted to know what had happened. "From Dasos, perhaps?"

"What do you want with him?" Fenna asked again.

Devlin pushed off the wall, taking a series of steps away from her. She sucked in a deep breath, unaware that she had been holding it at bay in his stead. "Dasos owes me a debt. And I always collect my debts."

"What's the debt?"

"Aren't you just the nosy one?" The question was a stark warning in whiplash opposition to the casual way he leaned against the far wall and hooked his right ankle over his left. His arms crossed over his chest. "Nothing you can afford, I promise you that."

Fenna leveled him with an assessing stare. "Entertain me then."

Devlin's eyes darkened mischievously, a slyness spreading across his grin. "Gladly."

"The debt, Devlin."

He bristled with the use of his name and a shot of pleasure rocketed up Fenna's back. She was getting to him, wearing him down like she did to her brother and Imogen. "You can call me Captain Cato. But the debt is twenty-five years of servitude on my ship. Won fair and square."

Fenna considered him for a minute, studied the way his mouth set in an unhappy grimace and his eyes crinkled at the corners. "You need to leave the city and never return," she finally said.

Devlin let out a barking laugh. "I don't need to do anything. I know he's here. It's only a matter of time before I find him."

"Alive?" Fenna inquired, sweeping her eyes to the mouth of the alley. Flames crackled merrily from the broken windows, licking at the billows of black smoke that followed. "You're sure that you would find him alive?"

"My men know better than to kill him. I assure you, they have better restraint than that."

"I assure *you* that Dasos would rather kill himself than return to your ship. And where would your debt be then?" She thought back to Dasos's ashen face and sweating brow, knowing in her heart that she was right.

Devlin stilled, leering down at her. "Your assertion seems personal."

"Dasos is my brother." Fenna shifted on her feet. She never knew she had the strength to do what she was about to do, the words that were just on the tip of her tongue. But the thought of Dasos, beaten and broken, had the statement tumbling out of her. "I will pay his debt."

Devlin cocked a brow, his lips downturning in a frown. "His debt is twenty-five years of servitude aboard my ship."

"I understand."

"With no reprieve."

"I gathered that."

"And no way out. If you escape, as your brother did, I will tear the continent apart to find you. Starting with Dasos."

"I do understand how debt works."

He scratched at the stubble on his jawline before running a hand down his cheeks. "You would do that? Trade your soul for his?"

Fenna raised her chin. "I would do it to save my brother, yes."

Devlin's step toward her was graceful and full of swaggering confidence. He threaded his fingers through her braided hair, holding the back of her head steady as he traced a finger into the hollow of her collarbone. "Say it again."

Fenna couldn't contain the shiver this time. "I trade my life for Dasos."

Devlin closed the gap between them, sealing his lips against her own. She gasped into his mouth at the suddenness of it, allowing him enough of an opening to run his tongue along hers. On instinct, Fenna's lips moved against his, matching his ferocity with a level she didn't know she possessed. He was warm despite the cold rain, his taste a sensual mix of peppermint and *fion*. A jolt of pleasure rang through her and he softly bit her bottom lip as he drew back. The kiss was over before she realized what had happened.

But when she did, Fenna placed her hands on his chest and shoved him away. Anger tore through her. Anger that he kissed her, anger that he was here and threatening her brother, anger that she reacted to the kiss like a lust-filled teenager, and anger that she liked it. He didn't move, merely chuckling at the attempt.

Devlin's fingers left her collarbone to trace along the spot of her lip where he had bitten her. "Welcome to *The Phantom Night*, Fenna." She swore his voice had lowered, the huskiness deepening as he spoke. "Twenty-five years is your debt."

Chapter Six

Fenna

"We have to go back," Fenna said, her attempts to yank her arm from his hand were negligible against the steadiness at which he held her. "I—I need clothes and supplies—"

"You'll be on my ship for twenty-five years," Devlin grunted. "There will be plenty of time to find you a new ruby necklace and gold-trimmed boots."

He was leading her toward the port, deftly navigating the debris that scattered the main road. The wreckage was even worse than she could have imagined— buildings torn in half, bloody body parts strewn like a macabre painting across the smeared red cobblestone, and smoky ash falling from the sky as the fires finally began to temper. The screams had ceased, blanketing the city in an eerie silence that only magnified the moans of those still left alive.

Not for long, it seemed, as Devlin's men making up their rear were happy enough to finish off any survivors that stood between them and their ship.

Beyond the tattered brick walls and the unlucky merchant vessels that happened to be docked at the time of the attack, Fenna spotted *The Phantom Night* bobbing in the deep waters of the bay. There was a thick rope cast over the side, anchoring the ship in place. The sails were tied down, leaving the three large masts bare against the dark sky. And a siren figurehead, bare-breasted and staring longingly at the sea before her, was carved at the bow.

Fenna's heartbeat quickened when her eyes fell on it and, even though she felt Devlin's glare heating her cheek, she kept her gaze forward.

"It's not about jewels and shoes," Fenna snarled at him, beginning her tugging once again. "You won't even allow me to say goodbye to my brother?"

"Your brother is a coward who would prefer a woman go in his place," Devlin replied.

"He doesn't even know—"

Devlin rounded on her, one hand still clamped to her upper arm and the other rising to pinch tightly around her chin. Fenna jerked her head in response, her mind unwittingly drifting toward the kiss they had shared.

No, Fenna chided herself, *the kiss he had* forced *on her*.

She had been kissed before. Once. She was still in her learning days— newly fifteen-years-old. The boy's name was Artemis. Fenna had feelings for Artemis, ebbing and flowing over her youth, but never leaving entirely. His hair was a darker shade of blonde and she often daydreamed running her hands through it. Freckles dotted his cheeks and he almost always smelled like the fisherman's boat his father owned.

Artemis had found her in the garden of the learning house one afternoon and planted a kiss on her lips. It was wet and close-mouthed, but Fenna leaned into it, nonetheless. She had been over the moon thinking that someone had chosen her for once.

The realization came crashing down when two of her learning mates, Mabel and Alice, darted out from around the corner to laugh at her. A second boy, Henry, had placed a gold coin in Artemis's upturned palm.

Fenna ran home crying that day and didn't appear back at the learning house for nearly a week. The only reason she did return was due to the learning master threatening to remove her from the class roster.

But the kiss Fenna had shared...*no, didn't share*...with Devlin was different. Scorching and passionate. She could still feel the tingle of him on her lips. Her belly curled traitorously at the thought of doing it again.

It was the knowing curve of his mouth, where her eyes had inadvertently planted, that made her snap her gaze upwards. By the darkening of his expression and the gleam in his eye, she knew that he could tell exactly where her thoughts had strayed to. He leaned down, close enough that his breath ghosted the tip of her nose.

"He still would have allowed you to go. I know men like him. He would have you take on his debt, so he can stay in his shitty town and have his bed warmed by the most average cunt he can find. He'll give her children and thrill her with tales of his non-existent sailing days while sliding his cock into every other average woman within four leagues of his home port." Devlin inhaled sharply. "And I'm not going to give you the chance to be disappointed by him."

A flush had crept up Fenna's neck at the crudeness of his words and she reeled her head back, though his fingers remained on her chin. "This is for me, then? You shuffling me away in the middle of the night is merely altruism?"

Devlin's brows rose as his scrutinizing gaze swept over her face. He studied her for a long moment, as though he had never heard someone of her social standing use a word like altruism. Or, perhaps no one had dared argue with him since he became a captain. The thought had Fenna briefly wondering when that could have been.

He snorted, though the sound was not out of amusement. "This is for me, so I don't have to hear you blubbering about my ship for the next twenty-five years." He released her chin and turned to continue their trek down to the port.

Fenna was nearly in a jog to keep up with his wide footsteps. "You don't know Dasos. He fought tooth and nail to get back home to me—"

"Is that what he told you?"

"He's brave and selfless and honorable, traits that you could never even imagine finding within yourself."

Devlin's boots halted at the edge of the port, where the wooden docks met the bay. The water to Fenna's right was lapping against the posts anchoring the docks in place and the sulfurous smell of the waves was enough to make her eyes glaze over. The bay was the one place in the city where the citizens disposed of their garbage and waste. It remained murky, sludgy, and smelly for most of the year and Fenna hated having to come on Algie's behalf.

"That very well may be, love," Devlin said. His head danced back and forth, as though he were considering something important. "But honor only extends so far when you're the only man on your warship who takes a deal from the devil himself."

Fenna opened her mouth to scathingly reply, but Devlin had already nudged her from the dock. And she went careening into the dirty water below.

Fenna had enough sense to seal her lips together before she crashed into the waves. Still, nothing could have prepared her for the shock of her sudden immersion into the cold waters of the bay. She sucked in an involuntary gasp when her skin tightened into a burn and her lungs seized inside of her. She was sure needles were piercing her, hammering into every exposed inch. She was also vaguely aware that she was sinking— the faint orange glow from the fires above becoming weaker and weaker as she fought to thrash against the sodden weight of her petticoats.

There was a dull splash and a trail of bubbles, followed by a figure carving a path through the water. A hand reached out, grasping onto her forearm and tugging her upward. Fenna's head broke through the surface a moment later and she let out sputtering coughs that still didn't clear the heaviness from her chest.

Devlin's hands were clutching at her waist, the wet locks of his hair plastered to the sides of his neck. The knot from the kerchief tied around his head floated on the waves.

"Do you not know how to swim?" he asked, shaking the water from his eyes.

Fenna didn't want to know what she was covered in. The water smelled something awful and there was a mysterious slimy object bumping against her ankle. It didn't feel like a fish.

"Of course I don't know how to swim," she shot back angrily. "I work in a *bookshop*. I've never even been on a ship—"

Devlin gaped at her, lips parting in disbelief. "You traded your life to the sea knowing *full well* that you didn't know how to swim?"

Fenna bristled. "I didn't think you would toss me into the bay at your first given chance." She sent a splashing wave of the disgusting water at him, where she was pleased to watch it splatter into his open mouth.

He spit the water back out, sending her a glowering stare. "How did you expect to get back to my ship, then?"

"A rowboat!" Fenna shrieked, lifting her hands to wipe her eyes of the salty brine stuck to her lashes. Her teeth began to clack together, forcing Devlin to drop his attention to, what she knew was, the bluish tinge of her lips. "Normal sailors take a rowboat."

Devlin's eyes narrowed on her and she could feel the current created by his treading legs billowing her petticoats. "You didn't take to the debt correctly."

"What are you talking about? You kissed me, didn't that seal it?"

His grin was back, wolfish and shrewd. "That kiss didn't make one lick of difference in your debt, love."

It was Fenna's turn to gape. She raised her knees under the water and pressed her boots against his chest, flinging a kick powerful enough to tear her from his grasp. She slowly turned toward the ship, paddling her arms in a poor effort to remain upright. She began to sink just the same.

Devlin sluiced through the water with easy strokes, barely making a ripple on the surface. He reached her just as her nose dunked beneath the waves and he grasped her waist once again to hoist her up. "Slow and steady movements," he said, running his hands toward her forearms and working her limbs to imitate the motions he was doing. "Embrace the water, caress it like a lover."

Fenna was gloriously upset, but she understood the importance of learning how to keep herself afloat. And she hated that she didn't mind the feel of his surprisingly gentle hands around her wrists. Her petticoats were heavy, though the slow kicking he taught her kept her head above the waves.

"The kiss had nothing to do with the debt?" she asked, her lips pursed into a thin line. She didn't know why the thought had her core thrumming, though anger still seeped through every pore of her body.

"I kissed you, because I wanted to. Because you looked ruthless while the city burned to the ground behind you. And I really like ruthless things."

Fenna hadn't felt ruthless while she was in the square. Truth be told, she was on the edge of wetting herself with fear when she saw Devlin and his men spill from the main road. She certainly wasn't going to tell him that. Instead, she lifted her chin to look down her nose at him. His brows rose in response.

"You're a pig," she said, shoving him away once more, "and I want out of the bay."

Devlin didn't reply, though he pressed his lips together to keep from smiling. Fenna just scowled.

Fenna hadn't given a second thought to how the other crew members reached the ship, as none of them had made the cold crossing with her. At least, until she saw figures bursting from the surface of the waves and scaling the side of the ship like crawling insects. Her heart pattered in her chest, a drumbeat of a rhythm that she felt in the tips of her fingers.

"You didn't take to the debt," Devlin repeated.

Fenna realized that he had been watching her reaction. He didn't give her time to respond as he thrust her forward and pushed her onto the rope ladder that led to the starboard bulwark. Her body trembled as she climbed, the whipping breeze coming off of the open sea beyond the bay biting her wet skin. Shivers wracked her body, sending her teeth to noisily click together. She wished she were seated in front of the hearth, the warm bath of firelight drying her skirts and stays.

Instead, she imagined she was scrambling up the cliffs that stood high over the cove, climbing higher and higher until she reached the grassy peak at the plateau. The moonlight was the rays of the sun behind the misty fog that rolled over the bay. And the flapping of the newly released sails were her skirts in the wind.

As soon as Fenna reached the final rung on the ladder, fingers wrapped under her arms and tugged her over the side of the ship. She spilled to the deck, a wet and heaving mess. Her shoulders and legs were sore from the swim, the muscles aching from the weight of the sodden clothing. Water pooled beneath her, only adding to the bone-deep chill that had set into her chest.

Devlin heaved himself over the bulwark, palm planted on the gunnel, as though he had done it a thousand times before. He remained upright as the cold water streamed from his breeches and down the black leather boots. "This is Fenna," he announced to the crew. "She'll be joining us for the foreseeable future."

"Where is Dasos?" a voice called above the crowd.

Fenna didn't look up, still struggling to calm her erratic breath.

"This is Dasos," Devlin said cheerfully. Fenna could feel the eyes of the crew turn toward her. "At least, she took on his debt. I trust you'll treat her as one of our own." He paused and Fenna glanced up to see him surveying each and every member present on the deck. "And nothing more."

He twisted away from her, boots *thunking* against the quarterdeck as he stalked toward his cabin door. Fenna kept her stare trained on his back, even as a pair of hands helped to lift her to her feet.

Devlin never looked behind him.

CHAPTER SEVEN

FENNA

Only two members of the nearly two hundred person crew had taken enough pity on Fenna's relentless shivering to tuck her underneath their proverbial wings.

Loma Netley was a stout woman, one of six female crew members, with a shorn head and an eye for map reading. The helmsman weighed heavily on her expertise and, while Fenna didn't know much of anything regarding course navigation, she was impressed that Loma did. Fenna ate her supper of dried meat and old bread quietly as she watched the woman pour over various charts and maps that made no sense to Fenna.

The second was a man called Waller Rudges, though he was more commonly known as The Drunk, and Fenna learned within the first hour on *The Phantom Night* that he was aptly nicknamed. He staggered everywhere he went, bouncing from the walls of the berth and tangling in the hammocks hung from the ceiling, a bottle of *fion* clutched tightly in his hand the entire time. At first glance, Fenna was convinced that he was truly no more than that...a drunk.

But when Loma and Waller gave her a tour of the ship, after providing her a dry set of skirts and stays, Fenna learned that Waller knew everything there was to know about cannons and ammunition. He could recite the names and widths of each cannon, how much gunpowder they required, and where they were located on the ship. He knew how far each cannon blast would carry, the weight of each iron ball, and the damage that could be inflicted on every type of material.

The two together were an unlikely pair, rooted only in friendship, as both preferred the company of females. And they treated Fenna as one of their own, even helping her set up the hammock that would be her bed for the next twenty-five years.

Fenna lay awake that night, staring at the ceiling of the berth. She swayed with the ship, rocking back and forth, and listened to the heavy snoring of the men. When the pleasure-filled moans started beneath her, from Loma and another woman named Esta, Fenna squeezed her eyes shut and pretended she was somewhere else...anywhere else.

She imagined being on a quest, submerged within the pages of her favorite book and surrounded by her favorite characters. If she were the heroine of the story, she would have a cutlass stashed underneath her skirts and she would be hustling the men playing cards in the corner of the berth.

But, Fenna wasn't the heroine. She was just...Fenna. Quiet and often overlooked, one to happily slip into the background. Smart, she supposed. At the very least, she had excelled at the learning house.

At that moment, the first time since she had boarded the ship, Fenna desperately wished Dasos or Imogen were with her. They were better equipped for this situation. More outgoing, more social. They would know what to do and what to say. She quietly brushed away the tear that slid down her cheek. She wouldn't cry, not here.

As Fenna turned over in her hammock, careful not to up-end herself onto Loma and Esta, she wondered if she could be one of those heroines. And how it would feel if she were.

The sun was bright against the cloudless sky when Fenna emerged from the berth the next morning. Two men were positioned at the helm, Loma behind them with an intricately decorated spyglass clenched tightly to her right eye. She swept it across the horizon, seemingly looking for something one of the helmsmen had called her to find.

On Fenna's other side, the deck sprawled before her. Hundreds of feet of billowing sails, ropes pulled taut and tied against the three masts, and men scrambling to complete their morning assignments.

Her auburn hair, swept behind her with the wind, was already beginning to knot. It would need to be braided before long, she was sure of it. She hopped out of the way as a man carrying a full bucket of soapy water shouldered past her, slopping some over the edge and onto her boots.

Fenna awkwardly stared after him, uncertainty curling in her belly. She spent much of her time back home doubting her interactions with others, but now...

She took a tentative and wobbly step toward the side of the ship, then another, and another until she wrapped her hands around the wooden railing and looked out into the endless vast of blue. She could have never imagined the expanse of the sea, how it surrounded her, the feeling of the waves crashing against the keel, or the smell of the salty air that continued to tangle her locks. The breeze back home was freshest in the cove, where the tall cliffs kept the wafting scents from the city at bay, but this…this was clean and rejuvenating. This was how Fenna would have described the way a sunrise smelled, when the light arched over the horizon and painted the sky with streaks of orange and gold. It promised new opportunities and adventures.

Fenna planted her elbows on the taffrail and leaned far over the railing, eager to watch the ship carve through the water. Here, embraced on all sides by various shades of blue, she thought she could reach out and brush her fingers against the sky. She even tried, stretching her hand outward to let her palm feel the pressure of the wind as they moved at impossible speeds.

"What do you think you're doing?"

Fenna pulled her hand to her side, whirling around to face Devlin, who was standing behind her with his arms crossed tightly over his chest. She tucked her forearms behind her back, steadying herself against the sway of the ship.

"Do you have a death wish?" Devlin went on, his lips pressed in a tight, white line. "One rogue wave and you'll be pitched over the side, lost to Liddros before any of the crew would even know you were gone."

Fenna opened and closed her mouth, unsure how to respond.

"I see you found a change of clothes." He took a step forward, unraveling his arms to reveal an apple held in his left hand. He lifted it to take a bite, the crunch of it between his teeth audible despite the noises of the ship.

A pang of annoyance rang through her chest. "No thanks to you, Devlin. You left me on the deck to die from the cold." It was a surprise how effortless it was for him to pull these reactions out of her. She was normally even-tempered and easily agreeable, sometimes to a fault, but there was something about the captain that prodded her into anger.

Devlin's brows rose as he took a second bite of the apple. "It's captain to you," he reminded her smoothly. He shifted his gaze over her shoulder to survey the sea behind her. "And you certainly wouldn't have died. Your clothes would have dried eventually."

Fenna took a moment to peer up at him, gliding her eyes over his dark locks pulled into a ponytail, the fit of his tunic against his shoulders, and how his breeches clung to his waist. His appearance was relaxed without the cutlass strapped to his side or the kerchief tied around his head. He looked less fierce, though she knew that he was just as dangerous.

"Like what you see?"

Her gaze darted upward and connected with his. She recognized the glimmer of amusement dancing within his eyes as the one he held before he ducked down to kiss her. It felt like a lifetime had spanned since then.

Fenna scowled. "You have a stain on your tunic."

Devlin smirked. In the light, she noticed a dimple grooving into his cheek that she hadn't seen before. He stepped closer, his boot heavy against the wood under their feet. Fenna sucked in a soft breath as he stooped forward, the wind catching the underside of his shirt and pulling it away from his chest like a sail on the mainmast. She swallowed as she spotted the muscle underneath cording his shoulders and chest– a body built by a lifetime of working on the water.

For a moment, Fenna thought he was going to kiss her again. Press his lips against hers and sweep his tongue to taste her own. Her heart skipped at the thought. Instead, he stepped to the side to place his forearms on the railing, and looked back out at the sea.

"What were you looking at, anyways? There isn't anything to see."

Fenna carefully twisted on her toes and placed her hands gently on the gunnel, keeping in mind to not lean over the railing. "Nothing to see?" she repeated, disbelief threading her tone. "It's breathtaking. Look how the sun reflects against the waves. Feel how the warmth of it sinks into your skin. Listen to the cry of the gulls or the crash of the waves against the ship." When Devlin remained silent, she changed course. "I read in a book that there are nearly a thousand different kinds of fish that live in the sea. Is that true?"

Devlin shrugged a shoulder and took a final bite. "It won't take until the end of your twenty-five years before you're tired of this." He gestured vaguely in front of them before letting the core of his apple drop from his hand, where it was lost to the water in Fenna's next breath. "I'm willing to bet it'll be within the next few months."

Fenna rolled her eyes, though she couldn't help the grin that tugged at the corners of her lips. "That very well may be, but this is the only time that I'll ever see this view for the first time. I'm going to remember this moment when the cold seeps in and my skirts are soaked through." She turned to glance at him, expecting her eyes to land on his cheek, and was taken aback when she caught Devlin staring at her. Her grin faltered. "What is it?" She suppressed the urge to swipe a hand down her face, briefly wondering if a piece of her breakfast was visible to him.

"You're nothing like your brother."

The words made Fenna's heart sink to her stomach. She tore her gaze from Devlin's and dropped her eyes to study the grains patterned into the wood of the gunnel. She didn't need the reminder of her weakness in comparison to Dasos's strength, especially here and now.

"You should be angry with me, not conversing about the fish that live in the sea."

Fenna heaved a sigh, allowing her eyes to harden before turning back to look at Devlin. Delighted curiosity marred his features and he let out a chuckle that nestled deep into her bones. "I'm here to settle a debt," she replied after a long minute. "There's no reason to be angry when I'm here of my own volition."

"Right you are," Devlin stated, straightening himself to a stand. "And you'll take over his duties, as well." Planting his hands on the tops of her shoulders, he spun her around until she faced the crew still bustling around the masts. "Royden Alby cleans the stern deck. You'll be assisting him and his men today." He must have guessed the look on her face, because he leaned down to whisper in her ear, "Did you think you would get out of work for being a woman? I treat everyone on my ship as equals. And that means starting at the bottom of the ship's ledgers."

With that, Devlin lightly shoved her forward.

"Yes, *Devlin*," Fenna sneered over her shoulder. She didn't bother glancing back to see his reaction of her refusal to address him as captain, but she imagined him bristling based on the way his fingers curled into the laces of her stays.

She said nothing else as she stomped away to find Royden Alby and his group of stern deck-cleaning men. Just as the night before, she allowed her thoughts to sink into her favorite book. When Royden placed a whiskered brush into her hand and directed her to begin at the back of the helm, she daydreamed the soap were an antidote to a poison coursing through the prince and it was up to her— and her scrubbing— to clear it all away.

CHAPTER EIGHT

DEVLIN

"A woman is no more than a raised skirt and a gripping cunt."

At least, that's what Devlin's father had beaten into him. From an early age, women were meant to be seen and not heard. To be taken with pleasure. To suck, be fucked, and finally discarded at the soonest possible port.

And those were words Devlin lived by...until *her*. But he didn't like to think about *her*. And he definitely didn't like to think about Fenna.

In fact, Devlin was regretting ever agreeing to allow Fenna on his ship. He should have turned down her offer and dragged Dasos back to *The Phantom Night* by the skin of his teeth. Because, more often than he wasn't, Devlin found himself watching Fenna.

That wasn't a new feeling, of course. He had entered that damn square, sweeping his gaze along the wreckage, to see her staring at him. And he had been temporarily struck stupid by Fenna. She was stunning— her curvy body strong beneath her skirts and stays with freckles dotting her nose and upper cheeks. Her hazel eyes, despite the fear, were filled with a shocking fierceness that had him following her, as though she grabbed him by the cock and dragged him into that alley.

Devlin felt like an animal. Not because she had run or because he had been forced to chase her, but because his desperate need to know her name outweighed any need to track down her brother. He would never forget the look of her auburn hair, braided behind her back, or how she seemed to glow under the cool light of the moon. The feeling of her lips against his, the softness of her skin, and the way she tipped her chin fearlessly toward him had him wanting more.

And that was the primary problem. Devlin didn't *want* to want more. He loathed it. He wanted to shed it as though it were an outer layer and toss it into the crashing waves below him.

With all of that coursing through him, he desperately needed Fenna off his ship.

Devlin stood on the quarterdeck, his hip leaned heavily against the taffrail. The sun was high in the sky and the heat from the rays sent beaded sweat running between his shoulder blades. The wind had died down since the morning and *The Phantom Night* crawled at a snail's pace, patiently slicing through the calm waters of the sea.

The Drunk stumbled by, a bottle of *fion* in one hand and a cannonball tucked underneath the other. Devlin didn't want to know why the man had a cannonball or what his plan was for it. It was a common occurrence that Waller did experiments with the ammunition, especially when their stocks overflowed from a recent raid. And the raid from the port town had been plentiful.

Instead, Devlin swiped the bottle from The Drunk's hand and took a sharp swig. The liquid had barely coated the back of his throat when Waller whirled around, steadying himself against the bobbing ship by throwing a hand out into the ether. Devlin cocked a brow as Waller looked up at him, struggling to focus his bleary gaze.

"Isssyou, cap'n," he managed to slur out, stumbling backward a series of steps before catching himself once more. "You can haaaave it, I p-promise I won't demand it from you."

Devlin sighed, the sound whistling through his nose. "What are you doing with a cannonball, Waller?" The curiosity had gotten better of him.

"She wants it."

"Who wants it?" Though the sinking feeling had already begun to dig a hole under Devlin's heart.

"Fennnner...Fennis...Fenren...Fenru..."

"Fenna?"

Waller snapped his fingers. "Yes, cap'n, that's the one. Fenna." The cannonball dipped in his arms and he scrambled to catch it before it hit his boot-covered foot.

Devlin took another swig of the *fion*, grinding two fingers into his throbbing temple. "And why, pray tell, does she need a *cannonball*?" He chanced a peek at the stern deck above him, seeing six of his men gathered around an animated Fenna. He didn't know what she was saying to them, the flaps of the sails and the groans of the men working the deck behind him were far too loud.

Waller's shrug was casual, though the cannonball nearly slipped from his hands once again. "She'ssss telling the scrubbers a story to pass the time. The crew working the sails stopped their shanties, sir, when the winds died." He hiccuped. "She didn't know the words anyways."

Devlin plucked the cannonball from The Drunk's hands, who stumbled forward with the sudden shift in weight. He planted the bottle of *fion* into the crook of Watters's elbow, much to the chagrin of his crew member.

The last thing Devlin needed was his men distracted by a woman in a skirt. He generally liked women in skirts, especially when said garment was hiked up around their waist and he was buried deep beneath them. But he also understood the limitations of his men, who rarely interacted with women in skirts. And he knew nothing would get done as long as they were busy gawking.

The deck needed cleaning and Devlin wanted it done. Now.

His boots thumped against the wood as he climbed the stairs to the stern deck, cannonball pinned between his torso and his forearm. The men spotted him as he rounded the helm, their eyes darting to the half-filled buckets of soapy water at their fronts.

Fenna, who was kneeling with her back to him, hadn't quite gotten the message. Her hands arced into the air, the droplets from the bristled brush spraying Devlin's tunic with suds, as she continued her story. The men had begun furiously scrubbing once again, averting their eyes from where Devlin stood, still as a mast.

"And the prince drew his sword from his scabbard, readying to plunge it straight into the heart of the wyvern—" Fenna thrust her brush out in front of her, still wildly unaware of the shift between the crew members. "—and swung the blade back until his shoulders strained under the weight." She arched her hand back, once again soaking Devlin's tunic with suds.

One of the men, Parsons Nottley, a black-haired man with large ears and an unhealthy obsession with fermented fish, was biting his lip to keep from laughing. The sight made anger surge, hot and quick, in Devlin's chest.

Devlin crouched behind Fenna, slamming the cannonball against the deck. The wood groaned, threatening to splinter, as the grin slid from Parsons's face.

"Do you find it funny to keep my men from their work?"

Devlin watched as Fenna's shoulder stiffened. She seemed to suck in a slow breath before daring to glance over her shoulder, her eyes lifting to where he was hunched overtop of her.

"I—I was just..."

"Having Waller do your bidding around the ship? Retrieving ammunition for stories that have surely distracted my crew?"

The six men were frantically scrubbing now, their heads dipped so low that their chins were tucked to their chest. The tips of Parsons's ears were stained red with a flush that was slowly making its way down the back of his neck. His eyes still peered up through his thick lashes, running a gaze over Fenna that had Devlin's stomach twisting with discomfort.

"Devlin, I—"

Only one woman had ever addressed him as such and she had died over one hundred and fifty years ago. Another shot of anger rose up his spine. Never again.

Devlin wrapped his hand around Fenna's upper arm and stood, dragging her up with him. She knocked over a bucket of water with her knee, soaking the front of her skirts. His hand came to her throat and he felt her thick swallow beneath his palm.

"You will address me as Captain," Devlin stated, his tone dangerously close to a growl, "or I will have you thrown off this ship with bricks of gold tied to your ankles. Am I understood?"

Fenna's nod was curt, though her eyes were wide with terror. A knot clenched behind his navel and he was suddenly aware that the six scrubbers, two helmsman, and Loma were watching them with bated breath. He released Fenna and she stumbled back, tripping against the overturned bucket and falling into the puddle of soapy water.

"Back to work," Devlin said as he turned away, drowning the conflicted regret until it no longer resembled anything aside from bitter irritation.

Devlin leaned back in his seat, the wood of the chair groaning. The map Loma had stretched flat on his desk was still pinned down in front of him, coordinates etched in black ink covering the margins. There was a chance of a storm near the east end of the sea, one that he suspected merely by the smell of the wind and the angle at which it hit the sails. He had asked Loma to pull a series of maps from her stores, something she was more than happy to oblige.

Leaning forward to plant his forearms on the edge of the desk, Devlin brushed a thumb along the back of the brass compass held tightly in his hand. He turned it over to study it, watching the needle bounce back and forth with each rock of the ship. He flipped it once more, running his thumb along the engraved words.

Property of Symon Cato

The compass had belonged to his father— an admiral in the king's navy. He had assisted in helping Devlin reach the title of lieutenant before his demise and Devlin often wondered if his father ever came across someone like him. Whether a pirate captain appeared on a specter ship and demanded his soul in exchange for more time at sea. He wondered whether his father had taken it or if he went, laughing, into his watery grave like most of the others.

He also couldn't help but wonder whether his father would have been proud of the exchange he made. Devlin snorted at the thought.

No, his father would have been appalled, absolutely disgusted at the act.

Devlin did it for love...or so he thought. His father would have also found that unacceptable. He barely held fleeting lust for Devlin's mother and only returned to their port home long enough to ensure the continuation of the family line. Which he intended on maintaining whether Devlin's mother wanted to or not.

It was due to the pleas of mercy he heard as a child— the midnight begging that came hard and fast out of his mother— that Devlin knew he could never take a woman in that way. Or allow any of his men to do the same.

Shortly after becoming The Specter, it finally happened. Devlin locked the man in the brig long enough to attract a few sharp-toothed predators that lurked in the deep with buckets of old fish parts. Then, he ran the man through with his cutlass and tossed him overboard, where his screams were still heard echoing through the night as they sailed away.

Devlin supposed he was different from the other pirate captains in that way, but he didn't mind. He just—

His thoughts were interrupted by a sharp rap on the door.

"Aye," Devlin rasped before clearing his throat. He shifted in his seat once again, tossing the old compass into the open desk drawer to his left.

The door cracked open. Booker balanced at the threshold of the office, leaning a shoulder against the door frame and crossing his arms over his chest. "You've been hiding, captain."

Devlin clenched his jaw so tightly his molars began to ache. "I've been thinking."

"About *her*?"

Devlin shot his quartermaster a glare of warning. "About our voyage."

Booker clicked his tongue against his teeth. "Aye, the voyage." His tone conveyed cool indifference, but Devlin knew Booker meant otherwise by the way he cocked a brow. "A rumor circulates that you laid hands on our newcomer. That you grabbed her breasts, shoved her to the ground, and threatened to return her to Liddros if she didn't agree to be yours."

"A portion of that is the truth, yes."

"Which portion?"

"I did threaten to return her to Liddros. Accompanied by two bricks of gold at her ankles if she distracted my men again." Devlin paused to take a deep breath, nostrils gently flaring. "As for laying hands on her...I regretfully grabbed her arm and nothing more." His eyes narrowed on Booker. "With whom does the rumor begin?"

It was Booker's turn to shoot him a look. "You know with whom the rumor began, captain. And additional word is that, with your blessing, he plans to claim the woman as his own tonight."

Devlin knew exactly who it was. Parsons fucking Nottley. He was newer on the ship, within the last two years, and frequently engaged in bending the truth in order to bolster his social standing with the other men.

"Some of the crew are concerned that your allegiance to women has begun to shift. That your...fondness of the new one is exacerbated by your inability to take a courtesan while on land. Others know that Parsons is nothing, save a blustering speech. But..." Booker's hesitation made Devlin's gaze darken. "There are two others who have joined Parsons's plan. I fear it's only a matter of time before she is approached."

While it had been true that Devlin preferred the company of a courtesan or two during his day on land, many on the ship were not privy to the fact that he had frequent dalliances with Esta, the most recent occurring the day Dasos slipped from his ship. Even if he hadn't the privilege, Devlin knew better than to take what wasn't his.

His own mother had taught him better. It seemed a few newer members of his crew needed to be taught that same lesson.

And he certainly wasn't going to allow a scrubber of the stern deck the chance to touch Fenna, whether she wanted him to or not. The thought of Parsons's hands gripping her hips, reaching between her thighs, seeing the look of ecstasy on her face as he worked her to pleasure.

Fenna was *his*. Not Parsons. Not anyone else's. *His*.

The unwanted thought clattered within him and he managed to kick it back, as unwilling as it was to go.

Devlin stood from the seat, the wooden legs scraping against the floor of the office. "Ready the irons and my tarred tails. Bring Nottley and the others to the quarterdeck." He briefly glanced down at the map, sweeping his gaze over the marked parchment. A glint of metal caught the corner of his eye when the ship bobbed against the waves. Devlin's decision was sealed when he pulled the pistol from the glass case behind his desk. "And have Waller draw up gunpowder as well as two shots from the magazine."

Chapter Nine

Fenna

There was a dark whisper on the ship that night. Fenna couldn't make out the cause, but it settled uncomfortably deep, pulling at her navel.

She had spent the rest of the day hiding from Devlin...*Captain Cato*. She scrubbed the deck in silence, ignoring the leering of Parsons Nottley whenever she bent over to dip the bristled brush into the nearest bucket of water. She ate the fish stew supper in her small corner of the berth, tucking herself into the swinging hammock earlier than she would have normally. She waited to untangle her braid and comb her fingers through the knotted locks until Parsons had turned his attention toward a card game.

But Fenna still felt his hungry gaze on her, one that wasn't appreciated nor welcomed, and she sank below the upper edge of the hammock to stay out of sight. Boots clomped, heavy and loud against the floor of the berth, as the whispered voices snuffed into silence. Fenna's heart hammered in her chest as the footsteps ceased and she didn't dare lift her head above the hem to see who had approached her.

Fenna had never been touched by a man before, but she instinctively knew what the owner of the boots wanted. She ran through the options in her head. She could chance running– overturn the hammock and stumble onto the deck in hopes of finding someone that would help her. She could put up a fight, though she knew it wouldn't last long. Perhaps she could struggle long enough to draw attention to herself.

A bell deafeningly clanged from above and the sound reverberated into Fenna's chest.

"All souls to the deck!" Fenna heard the familiar voice of the quartermaster yelling from above them. "All souls report to the mainmast!"

A huff of irritation sounded from Parsons and Fenna felt a surge of relief lighten the coiled tension within her. The lamp, dimmed from Parsons's silhouette, brightened once more as he navigated the crowd headed to the staircase. Fenna took deep, soothing breaths before creeping out of the hammock, afraid that any sudden movement would have the men descending on her.

The night air was cool, all humidity from the early afternoon burned away by the final rays of the setting sun. Stars spackled the sky above and the half-moon gave off a silver glow that cast the ship in shadow, but still illuminated the small patch of sand to the right.

She wouldn't have described it as an island, it was far too small for that. It ran half the length of the ship and nearly its width. Only washed up seaweed, dried from the time in the sun, littered the beach.

Fenna's skin pebbled as the breeze tickled her exposed arms and danced along the hems of her petticoats. It took her a moment to realize the ship had stopped moving and that one of the two heavy anchors at the bow of the ship had been lowered. She could hear the empty wooden cask tapping against the hull as it floated, signaling to the deckhands the location of the dropped anchor.

She didn't know what was happening and the wall of nearly two hundred men blocked the base of the mainmast from view, but her determination outweighed the underlying unease that skittered along her bones. Fenna pushed through the crowd, making her way toward the taffrail nearest the sandy isle. Grasping onto one of the taut ropes that held the sail in place, she hiked up her skirt and hauled herself onto the railing. The smooth wood was slippery under her boots, but it was no different than the rain-slickened cliffs that she scrambled at the cove.

Fenna's gaze glided over the heads of the men, coming to rest in a clearing at the base of the mast. Her heart skipped a beat, thumping unnaturally in her chest, when her eyes landed on Devlin...*Captain Cato*.

The sleeves of his tunic were rolled to his elbows, revealing inky black tattoos that decorated his muscled forearms. His hair was pulled back in his short ponytail. Even with the distance, Fenna could see his jaw ticking with every clench of his teeth. He held a whip in one hand, each of the nine leather tips dipped in thick tar, and a single pistol was strapped to his waist.

His eyes were sweeping along the crowd and Fenna considered that he was looking for someone in particular. It was when they darted upward, landing on her for the first time, that he seemed to relax his shoulders enough that the whip dropped a fraction of an inch toward the deck. Booker stood behind him, three iron clamps clutching tightly in his fists.

Fear rippled through the crowd of men, restlessness settling like a thick blanket over top them all. Devlin took a single step forward and the first row of the crew struggled to take the same step back, their spines straightening as though pitched with a rod as they hit the chests of the men behind them.

"Mr. Nottley! Mr. Quint! Mr. Whitewall! To me!"

Fenna's skin prickled once more, though this time, it was due to the command sent forth from Devlin. The crowd folded and contorted as the crew shuffled to part for the three men who had been called to the clearing. Shoulders hunched and ragged breaths tearing from their lungs, Fenna could see two of the men wiping their palms on the legs of their breeches. Her breath caught in her throat when Booker clapped the irons around the wrists of each man before forcing them to kneel before the captain.

"You've each been caught conspiring to force a woman aboard my ship," Devlin started, his voice a deep growl. Anger flared in his seafoam green eyes as he fixed his gaze on each of the men on their knees before him. The words sank into Fenna, hard and fast. She struggled to deepen her breath and she began to panic from the choking feeling of it getting caught by a lump in her throat.

"Captain, please—" The man on the far left began, his tone wavering and tight.

Booker stepped beyond Devlin to punch the man clean across the jaw. "Enough out of you, Quint."

Quint whimpered as he lifted his shackled hands to his face and, from the way he dabbed delicately at the spot where he had been struck, Fenna knew that Booker had drawn blood.

"Thirty-nine lashes and a maroon is your punishment," Devlin went on. Another shudder rippled through the on-lookers.

Fenna tightened her grip on the rope, both afraid to watch and afraid to turn away. Fascination kept her attention rapt on the three men before Devlin, rage boiling within her veins at the thought of them going through with their plan. And, oddly enough, a worm of sympathy wriggled its way into her mind at the sound of Quint's shuddering cries. She had read about sailors' punishments for breaking the maritime laws and she had known from the rumors at the port that many captains ruled their crews with iron fists.

But Devlin wasn't just a captain and this wasn't just a crew.

Fenna dared a glance to the sandy isle where they had anchored and she wondered for the briefest of moments whether their punishment fit the crime. From the way the other men winced at even the smallest movements from Devlin, she had a strong suspicion that it had been a very long time since they had become witnesses to his wrath.

Devlin nodded to Booker, who reached forward and hauled the man named Whitewall to his feet. Fenna watched as the captain waited patiently for Booker to grasp the collar of Whitewall's tunic, tearing it in half. The moonlight glowed against his bare skin, illuminating it like porcelain under a dying lamp. Whitewall was led to the mast and bent forward, his chained hands clamping around a knob of wood used to tie off the sails.

Fenna wasn't sure what she expected to happen. She had seen men hanged before, though it wasn't a common occurrence in her town. It was a brutal way to die and she had nightmares of purple-faced prisoners for months following each one. But this...

Devlin laid down the whip against Whitewall with a fury that left Fenna gaping in shock. The first crack of the tar-tipped cables against the bare of the man's back echoed across the otherwise silent sea. The skin split on impact, revealing puckered pink tissue and rivers of blood that ran into the waistband of his breeches. Whitewall's knees threatened to buckle, but his hands tightened around the wooden knob at the mast, whitening his knuckles.

"One," Whitewall seethed through pursed lips.

Devlin reeled back and slammed the whip down again. And again. And again. Blood coated the cords, tissue flicking back onto the crowd of on-lookers with every cast of Devlin's elbow. When thirty-nine lashes had been counted and dealt, Booker dashed forward to release the irons from Whitewall's wrists.

"Into the sea," Devlin ordered two of the closest crew members. "His passage on my ship is revoked. He must submit to the mercy of Liddros now."

Fenna recognized one of the men as Haig Atterton, the scrubber who had asked her to tell them a story when the shanties had died down. Haig and his partner hauled Whitewall up from beneath his arms, dragging him toward the side of the ship. Fenna's lips parted in wide-eyed shock as Whitewall's unconscious frame was tossed over the side. She didn't expect...didn't think...surely they wouldn't let him drown after receiving thirty-nine lashes.

But, Fenna watched as Devlin seemingly waited, his head cocked toward the sandy isle. And her eyes were trained on the bubbling column that followed Whitewall's sinking body. Ten seconds passed by, then twenty. Suddenly, as though he had been raised from the dead, Whitewall surged upward and broke the surface of the waves with resounding screams of pain that nearly knocked Fenna from the taffrail.

The salty water, infiltrating each and every open gash on his back, was burning him to his very core.

Whitewall struggled to swim against the loose tunic, his arms flailing as he clawed his way onto the beach before collapsing against the dried seaweed in a heap of shuddering sobs.

Devlin turned back toward the two men still in his charge, once again nodding to Booker, who seized the front of Quint's tunics and placed him square in the pool of Whitewall's blood. Quint was far more vocal than Whitewall had been, with squeals of pain bleating out of him with each stroke of the whip. He collapsed to his knees with ten lashes remaining and went unconscious soon after.

Nonetheless, Haig and his partner threw Quint over the side of the ship. Fenna watched him sink past the keel and saw the plume of unsettled sand as his body plummeted to the sea floor. He did not resurface.

Booker had already placed Nottley at the mast when Devlin turned away from the isle, sweeping his gaze along the crowd before connecting his stare with Fenna's. A shiver ricocheted up her spine at the darkness that shadowed his green eyes.

The thirty-nine lashes took just as long as the first two, though Nottley held in any noise with tightly pressed lips. When Devlin threw down the tarred tail, though, Nottley glanced up at him from over a bloodied shoulder.

"I would have taken her the moment she was alone," Nottley said, pinning Fenna from across the deck with a dangerous smirk. "I would have had her knees around her ears and—"

Fenna never heard what else Nottley had planned for her. Before Booker could reach forward to unlatch the iron clasps around Nottley's wrists, Devlin had hoisted the man to his feet, marched him to the side of the ship, and tossed him over without another word. The iron clasps must have been heavy, as Fenna watched Nottley struggle to surface under their weight.

But when he did, his shout came out as an angry hiss. "You owe me a pistol with a shot, Captain Cato." His voice was taunting, a gesture of a laugh hidden within its depths. He shook the sea water from his eyes, managing to free the plastered locks from his brow with a swipe of his wrist. "Maritime law states—"

Devlin unholstered the pistol from his waist and let off a shot that rang across the deck. She leveled a stare on Nottley, expecting to see a small hole in-between his eyes. Instead, he continued to meet Devlin's gaze with a murderous one of his own.

"Your shot has been taken," Devlin replied in a hardened tone, so unlike the seductive one he had peppered Fenna with the night they met. He holstered the pistol as Fenna swung her gaze to the isle. She choked back a gasp when she spotted Whitewall lying on the sandy beach, his unseeing eyes staring at the star-speckled sky above him. "You're in the hands of Liddros now."

"Do not leave me here like this," Nottley warned as eight members of the crew moved to hoist the anchor back into place. "You will regret this night for the rest of your gods-forsaken life if you do not kill me right now."

Devlin merely placed his forearms on the edge of the gunnel. "I commend your soul to Liddros and may he not have a lick of mercy on you."

Fenna felt the ship lurch underneath her as the sails caught the night wind. Her hand clutched at the rope, wrapping it around her wrist as she stayed on the railing to keep her view.

"See this as a warning to any and all of you who have entertained the thoughts of taking one of our women by force," Devlin shouted over the grunts of working men and the flap of the sails. "It will not be tolerated on my ship."

Fenna caught the exchange between Devlin and the three women closest to him— Loma, Esta, and the third named Maud who Fenna hadn't met yet. Loma sent Devlin a small smile, nodding her thanks of approval before taking the steps to the helm two at a time.

"I didn't ask you to do that," Fenna called out as Devlin waltzed past, making a direct line for the door to his cabin.

Devlin froze as his gaze flicked up toward her, gliding his stare from the toes of her boots to the locks of her auburn hair billowing in the wind. She wondered what he made of her, standing on the gunnel with her hand wrapped around the rope. She half-expected him to demand her return to the deck, but surprise coursed through her when he grabbed hold of the rope and hauled himself onto the gunnel next to her.

Fenna's brow barely tipped his chin and she was forced to crane her neck in order to keep her hazel eyes connected with his. She took in a deep, steadying breath when his blood-soaked hand wrapped around hers, the twanging, vibrating rope stilling beneath her palm. His face was flecked with red splotches and, had his tunic not been a dark shade of blue, she imagined that she would have spotted the stains there too.

His smell was a salty freshness that had become familiar to her, though it was melded with the tang of iron that only told Fenna that she was right in thinking his shirt was covered in blood.

Devlin's eyes went molten as he stared down at her, his gaze flickering down to her lips. He lifted a hand, seemingly to sweep her locks of wild hair from her face, before thinking better of it and resting it on the butt of his pistol.

"I didn't ask you to do that," Fenna repeated, though her voice shook with nerves that she hoped he couldn't identify under the *thwaping* of wind pressure against their ears. "I don't want you to think that is my expectation of you."

His answering smirk told her that he did.

"No, you should have expected it from me," Devlin said, lifting his hand once again to tuck a lock behind her ear. As though he couldn't help but touch her. "My mother would have expected it from me. The women who have signed themselves to my charge expect it from me. And, furthermore, I expect it from me." He paused to trace a light finger down Fenna's jawline. Her skin pebbled for the third time that evening, an involuntary shiver imploding at the base of her neck. "No one will touch you, except when you want to be touched."

Fenna swallowed past the lump in her throat. "What if I never want to be touched?" What she wanted to ask was...what if no one ever wanted to touch her? But she settled for the first question instead. Self-doubt swelled like a bullfrog inside of her.

Devlin's smirk grew, deepening the dimple that sunk just below the prickled hair dusting his face. Fenna resisted the urge to reach up and stroke it, wondering what it would feel like beneath her fingertips. Wondering if his skin would pebble like hers and his breath would hitch in his chest at her touch. Then she wondered why she was wondering about it at all.

Devlin's finger left her jawline, tracing down the column of her throat. "I promise you, Fenna," he started, leaning forward until his breath brushed along the shell of her ear, "that one day you'll be ready to be touched." He traced his fingers along her collarbone. "To be explored." His fingers went to the crest of her shoulder and traced along the crook of her neck. "You'll want your breasts massaged and your nipples tweaked between roaming fingers and for a tongue to lap at your cunt until your voice is hoarse from crying out with pleasure."

Fenna's eyes fluttered closed and she nearly moaned as his fingers dipped to run along the outer swell of her breast.

"And when you're ready for that day, it will be me who does it. No one else."

Devlin palmed her waist and Fenna cracked her eyes open, confusion settling against her belly. Earlier that afternoon he had been threatening to toss her overboard and now he was set to seduce her. Fenna's heart sank when she recognized it for what it was— a game.

One that Artemis had willingly participated in a decade ago, much to her own heartbreak.

She drew away from Devlin, shifting her weight back on her heels until breathing room had been reestablished between them. She had been a fool once, but it wasn't going to happen again.

For a long minute, Devlin studied her. In the next, he suddenly swung down from the gunnel, boots planting heavily on the deck. The sound was hollow, echoing into the berth beneath his feet. "Set course for the isles, Booker," he shouted at his quartermaster as he began his path toward the cabin once again. "And get off my ship's railing, Terrigan, before you get lost to the sea." He said nothing else as he closeted himself inside his private quarters, slamming the door shut behind him.

Chapter Ten

Fenna

Ten days passed before Fenna saw land again. The ship sailed south, carving through turquoise waters so clear that she was able to spot the fish swimming under the surface. When *The Phantom Night* slowed to a crawling pace, and the crewmen working the sails had begun to lower them, Devlin ordered the anchors to drop.

Fenna was itching to leave the ship and the endless rocking of the sea. Her eyes dragged over the island before her, taking in the tall, curved trees that she had only read about in books. Their leaves, spread wide to soak in the bright sunlight from above, swayed in the warm breeze coasting off the bay. The illustrators of those books hadn't quite done their beauty justice.

Wallers was the first to approach the side of the ship, breezing past her with surprising quickness. His eyes were clear for the first time in days and his hands remained free of the bottle of *fion* he had been touting around. But it was when Fenna allowed her eyes to drift past his face that she froze, her cheeks heating in a blush.

Wallers was naked as the day he was born, his cock on proud display as he clambered onto the gunnel with impressive ease. He jumped from the ship before her thoughts could thaw. Fenna stepped forward, lips parted in horror, to scramble to the railing. Her hands clasped the worn wood as she peered over, sweeping her eyes over the ripples and bubbles obscuring his frame from view.

"He's just gone to shore," a voice behind her stated.

Fenna briefly glanced over her shoulder before whipping back to stare wide-eyed at the island. Her flush deepened as the man, name unknown to her, sidled up to the taffrail and hauled himself up with a quick tug against a thick rope. His bare leg was just within Fenna's peripheral view. Her chin tipped to her chest in a sore effort to look away, but her shifting gaze still caught on the dusky sack that hung between his muscular thighs.

Her eyes trained on the wood-grained pattern beneath her fingers as he, too, leapt from the ship and entered the water with a resounding *splash*. And now Fenna knew to not look behind her. More and more men, each just as naked and just as eager to leave the confines of the quarterdeck, climbed onto the railing and followed the two men into the sea below. Wallers, on the other hand, had waded to the sandy beach. Water ran like rivulets down his bare back.

"You should go."

Fenna chanced one more look behind her and was relieved to see Booker Colby pointedly staring at her, his brows high on his forehead. She gulped, though the motion was painful against the dryness that coated her throat. She dutifully ignored another faceless and naked man who brushed past them both.

"What are they doing?" she asked quietly, though she wasn't sure why she was whispering. Discomfort twisted her belly and the feeling that she was witnessing something she shouldn't rolled over her like a cresting wave.

"Going to bathe," Booker said, tilting his head toward the island. Fenna could hear the men scurrying to land, the water sloshing noisily against their knees. "And you should go too."

"I— I don't know—" Fenna began, managing to sputter the words out despite the brain-numbing fog that had descended on her.

"You don't smell like a bouquet of flowers yourself," Booker pressed on through her hesitation and his arms crossed in defiance over his chest. "It's for the good of the ship that we all bathe and your hair still smells like the water from the bay. That's not a compliment."

She snapped her mouth shut, teeth clicking together. "I don't think I can...I mean, I can't really—"

"She can't swim, Booker."

Devlin leaned against the doorframe of his cabin, the laces of his tunic undone and open to reveal the chiseled top of his chest. Fenna was equal parts unhappy and filled with sharp desire to see that his eyes roved over her. Longing and greed pulsed through them, shadowing the light green that haunted Fenna every moment she was alone. She tore her gaze from his, planting it back on Booker's face with misplaced satisfaction.

She *knew* that she needed to bathe and the curl of Booker's upper lip confirmed it.

"Captain, she—"

"She can bathe in my cabin," Devlin cut in, a wicked smirk dancing on his full lips. "Have the men bring extra fresh water to me."

Fenna reeled back, regret for the action coursing just as suddenly though her with the new batch of naked men sauntering up from the berth. She pressed her hand against the side of her face, blocking the men from view. "No, I don't...I just..."

Devlin's smirk turned devilish as he pushed off the door frame and stepped forward. "The way I see it, you have three choices, love." Fenna let out an irritated sigh that only strengthened the smugness of his face. "One, you can strip off your skirts and stays to join the men. I'm sure one of them would be far happier to have your breasts against their back as you clung to them on their way to shore. Two, I can have the men bring fresh water to my cabin and I can strip off your skirts and stays off myself before I scrub you down. Three, you can agree to bathe yourself of your own volition in the privacy of my cabin."

Fenna stared at him, disbelief clouding her every thought. At first, she told herself that she couldn't be certain that she heard him correctly and she fought against the urge to ask him to repeat himself. Treacherous heat wound through her core as she replayed his second option in her head.

Thump, thump, thump.

Her heartbeat pounded against her ribcage, the sound reverberating into her ears as his anticipation and her stunned silence twined. Her wide eyes narrowed to a glare.

"You wouldn't force me," Fenna blurted out, the first thing that came to mind once the haze had cleared and her disbelief morphed into spilling anger. He was toying with her...working her up... again. "You said so yourself. You would never touch me unless I said that you could."

Devlin's smirk slipped into a sneer that should have sent a shiver of dread up her spine. She knew she had caught him in a corner, though, and that thought overruled any instinct of self-preservation that was still within her. He hitched a shit-eating grin on his face, replacing the broken smile, just as Fenna felt a bare arm graze against the laces of her stays.

"Bathing is meant to keep all of us sane," Devlin retorted, thrusting his chin in a gesture over Fenna's shoulder, "and if you don't want my assistance, I will have one of the women do it. Loma!"

Fenna's breath seized in her chest, painfully squeezing her lungs. Daring a peer behind her, one that turned Devlin's grin into a feral smile that told her he now had her cornered, she spotted Loma and Esta slinking to the side of the ship. Loma's head turned at the sound of her name and Fenna felt herself blush again at the sight of her heavy breasts bouncing against the roundness of her stomach.

"Captain?" Loma asked, taking a step away from Esta, who was equally naked and eyeing Devlin with interest. Jealousy tore through Fenna with surprising intensity and she couldn't quite temper the new feeling. Sadness, anger, happiness…all of those she had extensive experience with. But jealousy? She had never been given a reason to be jealous. She didn't have a reason to be jealous now.

"It's no bother," Fenna snapped in retort, enraged at herself for the lack of her own control. She shouldered past Booker as she stomped toward the captain. "I'll bathe myself." She couldn't quite shake the image of Devlin thrusting into Esta and the envied awareness that awoke in her along with it.

"Excellent," Devlin said and Fenna heard the pompous gratification in his tone. "All the way passed the desk to my cabin, love. You'll find a wash tub at the foot of my bed."

The door clanged shut behind her and Fenna's steps comically halted at his words. In her all-consuming temper, and her desperation to rid herself of the naked crew still crossing the deck, she had marched directly into Devlin's personal cabin. And he had shut the door behind them.

Fenna took a moment to sneak in a slow, deep breath.

The cabin was larger than she expected, with an imposing wood-framed bed layered with dark-colored quilts and furs centered on the left wall. Much like the neatness of the rest of the room, the coverings were methodically piled at the foot of the mattress. Four windows, each spanning ceiling to rug-strewn floor, were built into the far wall and overlooked the bobbing waters below. She knew that, had the ship been moving, the windows would provide a clear view of its wake. A small, circular table was placed in front of the window wall. A single plate, fork, and pewter tankard ladened the surface, which was polished to a gleaming perfection.

Devlin strived for cleanliness. The knowledge of that felt strangely intimate.

The bathing tub had been placed in the middle of the cabin and Fenna spotted the heating rocks bundled beneath the clean water. The steam curling from the tub only accentuated the scents of old gunpowder and melted wax from the candles on the shelves near the...

Books. Fenna's heart swelled with longing when her eyes landed on them. She could almost feel the leather-backed spine and crinkled parchment beneath her fingertips. And she couldn't help but imagine Devlin seated at the table, an ankle hooked over a knee, as he studied the contents of one by the light of a dimly lit lamp.

She stiffened as he walked past her. He bent at the waist, wrapping one hand onto the rim of the tub while dipping the other into the water. The tunic stretched over the expanse of his upper back and the muscles of his shoulders shifted with every sweep of his hand into the basin.

"You'll need to undress to get in," Devlin murmured as he straightened to stand. She thought the size of the room would have made him seem smaller, but that couldn't have been further from the truth. The cabin only seemed to shrink with him inside of it, his dominating presence seeping into every inch of the space.

Fenna swallowed as his knowing gaze flicked down to land on her. Her feet shuffled, the boots scuffling against the worn run underneath. "Not with you in here." She lifted her own gaze to connect with his, tilting her chin upward in a defying confidence that she couldn't quite convince herself that she had.

With a gait that threatened to wobble, Fenna walked forward to check the water for herself and Devlin caught hold of her wrist when she attempted to glide past. The warmth of his palm against her skin temporarily cleared her mind of any thought, giving him enough time to tug her closer to him without fight.

"Are you certain? The laces of your stays seem intricate. I'm not sure you can manage on your own with them." His breath caressed her cheek and a shiver began to bloom at the base of her spine, the threads of heat worming into her belly.

"I think I can handle them alone, thank you." Her voice was quieter than she willed it to be and worry burrowed through her when she wondered whether he could hear her thundering, traitorous heart beating for him. The tension between them was suffocating, made only deeper by the thick of him that brushed against her front hip.

"As you wish, then." Devlin took a step back and released her wrist from his grip. "There are clean clothes of mine in the chests, ones you can use until you find skirts and stays in storage. I'll be just outside of your door. Just in case you...require anything of me."

Fenna's breath finally came in a whooshing exhale as the door clanged shut once more. The effect Devlin had on her was new and uncomfortable, both wanted and not. It fizzled her thoughts and sent her innards roiling like live snakes. She lifted a trembling hand to tug at the laces of her skirts and stays, allowing the linens to fall into a heaping pile on the rug. They seemed out of place, a direct contradiction to the neatness at which Devlin kept his cabin.

Desire bolted through her, sudden and unexpected, when her eyes darted to his bed. She fantasized what it would feel like to slip between the quilts and furs, entangling within the musk of his scent, the weight of him on top of her...the hardness of him between her legs. She shook her head to rid the thoughts from her mind.

The water was shockingly warm as she slid a foot into the tub and a groan slipped from her lips as she settled into the large basin. Fenna only had the rare opportunity to run a damp cloth over her body in the last few weeks, something she did only within the safety of her hammock. But it certainly wasn't the same as scrubbing.

Fenna froze when a creak of wood followed by a thump against the door sounded through the cabin and her head turned sharply toward the entrance. "Devlin?" she called out, wrapping her arms around her exposed breasts.

"It's Captain Cato," he retorted in a gruff voice, one that tightened her nipples. She bit her lip to contain her smile.

Reaching toward the cloth and bar of soap that balanced on the rim of the tub, Fenna quickly worked them together, watching as the suds began to lather against her hands. She suppressed another groan as she ran the cloth against her skin, scraping away the dirt and grime that layered every inch of her body.

"Tell me a story."

Fenna paused, her hand halting its continued swipe down her shin. She glanced toward the door, slightly surprised to see that it was still tightly shut in the frame. "What?" A boot dragged against the wooden flooring and she imagined that he pulled his knee up to rest a forearm against it, the other leg still straightened in front of him.

"A story, Terrigan. I'm out here and you're in there. I know that you read, I saw your gaze on my books. You use words like *altruism*. Tell me your favorite."

Fenna renewed the soapy lather on the cloth before sinking beneath the surface to soak her hair. "All of my favorites are of princes and princesses. I don't think you have any interest in that."

His resounding snort echoed under the seam of the door. "Try me, love."

Fenna scrubbed the cloth against her hair. "The book I read again and again while working in the shop was *The Lost Queen of the Sanguine Desert*. It's about a girl who is sold into servitude after her kidnapping and grows up to learn about her true heritage as heir to the throne." She cleared her throat. "But, I'm sure you have better things to do right now."

"Tell it to me." His voice was soft despite the commanding words.

Fenna drew in a breath and leaned against the back of the tub, the metal basin cold against her bare skin. "There was once a princess, beloved by her people, and raised in a desert palace—" She closed her eyes, conjuring the image of the book in front of her, and launched into the story.

Thieves and battles and a journey of self rang from her. Fenna voiced every detail that she could remember– from the sweat dripping down the prince's brow under the sweltering sun to the first time he spotted the lost princess, desire and longing clicking into place within him. She described how the prince stole her away in the night, how he struggled to contain his growing feelings for her, how he wanted to touch her–

Fenna stopped, the words faltering in her throat. For a long minute, she thought Devlin had left his spot against the door. Immersed in the story, she hadn't paid him any mind...until now. Until she remembered the first time the prince and princess had joined as one in explicit and unending pleasure. Her gaze drifted to the door, straining to see whether his shadow stirred beyond the threshold.

"And what did the prince do?" Devlin asked, his voice low and husky.

Fenna let out a sharp breath, twisting away from the door as though he could see straight through it. The linen cloth against her skin felt rough as she dragged it against her nipples. She discarded it with a wet *thwack* onto the wooden floor of the cabin. "He kissed her," she whispered, though she didn't know why she said it.

"Where did he kiss her?" he responded, barely audible through the thick door. A gull cawed as it sped past the windows, circling the back of the ship before landing heavily on a tree in the distance. The branch bent with its weight, the large leaf waving in the shift. "Did he taste her?"

"Yes." Fenna's very blood heated as she thought back on the words. How the prince slipped his tongue inside of the princess, how he made her come with steady, stroking licks.

Devlin's chuckle was like silky velvet. "Did he slide his fingers into her? Rub his thumb over her clit until she tightened around him?"

The question jolted her heart and she felt her inner thighs slicken. She pressed them together to relieve the pressure, water sloshing over the side of the rim. She wanted him to keep talking to her like that, in that tone that made her core mercilessly throb. "He made her come twice before he thrust his cock inside of her." She felt emboldened by the door between them and sensual pride burst forth when she heard his light groan.

"Touch yourself for me."

Fenna's mouth went dry. "Wh-what?" She had only touched herself in the dead of night, when she was alone in her bed and even the brightness of the moon through the window was like the flaming torch of a ship's guidehouse. "Why?"

"Because having you on my ship is driving me to the brink of insanity and this is as close to touching you as I can get." The admission was a shock to Fenna's system and her toes curled at the thought of it. "Tell me to stop and I will—"

"What do you want me to do?" she interjected, settling her hand on her stomach. Her skin was flushed and needy. She had never done anything like this before, even when the thoughts of the boys long grown into men entered her mind. When they begged to be her first, when they thought of how her breasts would look and how her tongue would taste. She only took those thoughts and pleased herself with them.

"Roll your nipple between two fingers, pinch it until it hardens."

Fenna lifted her hand, letting her fingers skirt between the valley of her breasts. It didn't take long for the skin to perk and tighten beneath her touch and her back arched at the thrill of it.

"Put your other hand between your thighs and circle your clit with your thumb."

She let her other hand drift below the surface of the water, coming to a halt when she cupped herself. She hesitated for a fraction of a moment before desire sliced through her once again and she dragged her thumb over the round swell at the apex of her legs. Her back arched at her own touch and she couldn't help the moan that escaped her lips as she circled her clit again and again and again.

"Slide in a finger, tell me how you feel."

Fenna did as he said, allowing a finger to glide into the slick of her. "Warm and soft," she said, still circling with her thumb. She thrust in again. "Wet and needing." The words tumbled from her before she knew what she was saying. "I'm adding in a second finger."

More water sloshed over the side of the rim as Fenna spread her legs further, allowing the second finger to dip in with the first. The brim of her palm skated against her sensitive arousal and another stifled moan fell from her lips.

A close-lipped groan, primal and hungry, echoed from the other side of the door. "Let yourself moan, Fenna. I want to hear what you sound like when you come."

The words rocked through her, fracturing the heat that had built in her lower belly. Pleasure coursed like a cannon blast, exploding from her center and cresting like a storm's wave, washing over every naked inch of her. She panted, chest heaving, as she came down and extracted her fingers from inside.

Fenna felt wonderfully full and wholly satisfied in a way that she hadn't felt before. And yet...she felt equally exposed. She knew that Devlin had been ready to play from the moment he accepted her onto his ship and she had unwittingly fallen directly into his lap. Shame and embarrassment swiftly replaced the satisfaction as she quickly lifted herself from the tub to dry off.

Gods, she had been so stupid. Of course this was what he had wanted from her. To take pleasure in any way that he could, to rip her apart just to see her squirm. Like the others had...like they all had.

Devlin was still on the other side of the door and, while what she really wanted was to dig a hole through the ship and sink into the depths of the sea, she decided to face him with her head held high. Fenna was sure he would sneer at her, much like the other men in her town had done, and she braced herself for the barrage of thoughts that were surely readying to come her way.

That is, if he wasn't willing to voice them aloud.

Fenna, dressed in Devlin's breeches that nearly reached her ankles and a shift that was three sizes too big, took in one more breath of resolution before tugging the door open. And what she found on the other side wasn't a sneering, glowering man filled with delight and disgust.

Devlin was standing now, his hands held fast against the door frame. He looked down at her, eyes filled with a darkened lust that had her core clenching tightly again. Her thighs began to tremble at his assessing gaze and she felt a betraying jolt in her chest at the intensity of it.

He must have sensed her hesitation, because he reached for her in the next breath and placed her chin gently between his forefinger and thumb. "Never feel shame for taking your own pleasure," he said softly. His swallow worked the column of his throat and Fenna watched it closely. "I'm going to stroke my cock to the sound of that moan for the next twenty-five years."

Fenna's eyes flared wide as she flicked her gaze upward, astonishment parting her lips.

"Speaking of that," Devlin went on, letting his hand drop from her chin. He inched around her and she spun on her toes until they had swapped places. His head bent forward, low enough that the tip of his nose brushed against her own. "I'm going to start now, if you'll excuse me."

Fenna stumbled backward at his statement. He let out a breathy chuckle as he reached up and yanked his tunic over his head. Fenna's mouth went dry at the sight of his naked chest, bronzed from the sun and well-sculpted. She couldn't help her roving gaze that slid from his shoulders to the vee of his hips. An aching bloom began in her sex at the thought of reaching out and grazing a finger over the hardness that tented his breeches.

"Don't you want to change the water?" She managed to ask, despite the thickness of her tongue. "I've gotten it dirty."

Devlin paused to wrap a hand around the door. "Make no mistake, I'm going to worship that water for the rest of my damned life. I'm going to bathe in it and bottle it, taking pleasure in the fact you came while submerged in it. I'm going to spread it on my palms before stroking myself at night. And I'm going to lock it in my safe and no one, except you and me, will know what I use it for."

Fenna stood in stunned silence as a wild grin quirked his lips and he said nothing else as he slid the door shut. But, a moment later, she heard the splash of water crest over the rim of the tub just the same as he made an audible show of climbing inside of it.

Chapter Eleven

Fenna

Fenna spent the next two days scrubbing every inch of the ship, including the gunnery, the storage cabins, and wherever Devlin Cato wasn't. She liked to think she wasn't avoiding him…she was just acutely aware of his location at all times and made sure she was elsewhere.

And that worked for some time, though she was never quite sure whether it was because he allowed it or not. Devlin ran his ship on a tightrope and nothing happened without his knowledge or approval.

But Fenna had a sneaking suspicion that he had begun to look for her. She watched the way he swept his gaze across the deck, studying every face as he passed. She hid behind the casks of fion or crates of root vegetables whenever she heard the clunk of his boots descending the stairs. She had learned the cadence of it, had memorized the way it sounded when his heel struck the wood flooring in the hammock-filled berth.

Her heart hammered a betraying beat that vibrated against every bone in her body. She prayed to the old gods that he wouldn't find her...and then begged them that he did.

The last place Fenna thought to hide was in the crow's nest, positioned high above the quarterdeck and with easy viewing of the cabin door Devlin usually sequestered himself behind. And that's where she first met Iris Larsa.

Iris Larsa was the fourth of the six women that had sold their souls to Devlin...*Captain Cato*. She was taller than average. Her height rivaled most of the men on the ship and freckles coated every exposed inch of her tawny skin. She was thin and lacked any curvy definition beneath the breeches and tunic she preferred to wear. She could sing the shanties louder than any of the men working the sails and one stern look from her sent the likes of even Booker scurrying away.

The woman merely sent Fenna a surprised glance and didn't bother to comment on the climb Fenna had to make to get there— one that made the hardened sailors, many who preferred keeping their boots firmly on the deck, queasy. Fenna had thought of the tall cliff sides when she scaled the mast leading to the crow's nest and, for the briefest of moments, it almost felt like home.

"You shouldn't be up here," Iris finally said, her lilting accent bordering on casual. Her eyes stayed trained on the horizon. "You should be scrubbing the deck."

"Not that it's any of your concern, but I finished scrubbing the deck," Fenna responded, though she kept her own gaze pinned on the helm below. "And the galley and the brig." She cleared her throat. "And since we're just now meeting, there isn't a reason for you to question how I do my daily chores."

Iris let out a snort that would have offended any of the highborn ladies that haunted the town streets. "He'll still find you up here, you know. There are better places to hide."

Fenna whipped around, the tendrils of her hair snaking across her face in the wind. "I'm not evading him, I—" She paused at the smile curling Iris's lips and her spine straightened with the scorn rising within it. "You speak out of turn."

"Of course." Iris leaned against the mast, allowing her gaze to trail toward Fenna for the first time. "I must have been mistaken. For the last two days, I haven't been watching you scurry the ship like a mouse running from a cat. And I haven't been watching him pretend that he doesn't know where you are."

Fenna brushed away the confirmation of his knowledge and peered over the side of the crow's nest. He was gone from the helm, and Fenna's body responded by bottoming out her belly. Her stare became desperate as she squinted against the bright rays of the sun, each one reflecting off the wake of the ship and refracting into long bars of color.

All the same, she chided herself when she realized that she had been seeking him out too.

Iris's second snort twisted into a cough at Fenna's sharp glare. "You're right, I speak out of turn."

Fenna leaned her elbows against the edge of the railing, taking deep, soothing, sea-filled breaths. "He won't look up here," she stated with a curt nod. "He wouldn't think me brave enough to make the climb." She wrung her hands as secretly as she could. Iris didn't need any more ammunition than she already had.

"I think anyone would think you brave enough the moment you made the climb." Iris reached toward the waistband of her breeches and pulled out a small glass flask wrapped in a thick leather hide. She popped the cork from the top with her thumb, expertly catching it with her other hand, and took a long swig. Fenna shook her head when Iris made to hand it to her. *Though I am surprised that a woman barely sure-footed on the deck would have risked it.*

Fenna turned to respond, but jolted to a halt when she realized Iris hadn't spoken the last words out loud. It had been the first time she had heard any thoughts since joining the crew and she had gotten used to the silence it finally provided. "I've never seen you outside of the berth," she said instead.

"I prefer to be alone." Iris sent her a stone-faced look before taking a second swig. "And I prefer the warmth of the sun on my face and the smell of it heating the wood. It reminds me of home."

Most of the crew skirted away from the topics of where they hailed from, who their families were, and any loved ones they left behind. Fenna learned, despite it being their choice to remain within Devlin's employ, the ultimate goal of even the boldest pirates was to win a challenge and return home.

"Where is that for you?"

Iris pressed the cork back into the flask and tucked it back into the waistband of her breeches. "Forrey Haven."

Fenna didn't miss the way Iris's shoulders tensed when she spoke and curiosity burned through her. She peered over to the woman, who was now busy kicking the toe of her boot against a soft slice of wood. "That's in the south, isn't it? Surely past the continent that houses the king. What brought you this far north?"

Iris's boot scraped against the grain patterns before stilling and drew her gaze down Fenna's front. "Don't you have Loma to pester?"

Fenna felt her confidence evaporate like a puddle of water on a hot summer day. "I— Loma has been— I mean to say she's—"

Iris must have felt an inkling of pity for her, because she relaxed just enough for it to be noticeable. "Loma only wants the ones who will allow her to tongue their cunts at night. She lost interest in you the moment she realized that Esta was willing to warm her bed at night."

A blush bloomed on Fenna's cheeks when her mind flitted to Esta's gentle face and the moan Fenna heard her elicit late in the night. She hadn't quite grown used to the language used by the crew aboard the ship. "Loma has just been busy as of late."

"That's one way to put it." Iris sighed and turned to sweep her gaze along the horizon once more. Her lips, chapped from the constant battering wind, pulled to the side in thought. "To answer your question, a lover brought me this far north. A man with whom I shared a deep connection."

"And you came aboard this ship how?"

"Are you always this meddling or are you finding new ways to avoid the captain?"

"I'm not *avoiding*—" Fenna's brows drew in, a sudden pang of annoyance pulling her nose into the beginnings of a sneer.

"And that, Terrigan, is where you're wrong."

Fenna's breakfast soured her stomach. Her throat bobbed with her swallow as Devlin's boots fell heavy against the wood of the crow's nest. Iris's spine straightened in a show of respect and it only took a silent command from Devlin for her to back to the other end of the lookout post.

Fenna just barely held herself from clutching onto Iris's forearm in an attempt to keep the woman in place. Even here, on nearly the highest point of *The Phantom Night*, she wasn't safe. She felt her guard rise up like hackles on a wild hound. Never again— never again would she allow him any leverage over her. She glanced over to him, willing her lungs to thaw from the iciness that had gripped them, and looked down her nose at him in a way that she hoped would convey cold indifference.

"Devlin. What brings you to the crow's nest?"

"It's Captain Cato." He leaned a shoulder against the mast, meeting her gaze with a steady stare of his own. And damn if her traitorous heart didn't zing at the sight of him before her. "I could be asking you the same question. I believe I remember assigning you to scrub the deck. If you have the time to distract Iris, certainly you have time to—"

"I scrubbed the deck," Fenna interjected with a blistering tone that quirked the corner of Devlin's lips, "and the galley."

"Don't forget the brig," Iris called from her end of the crow's nest, the threat of a smile brimming her tone.

"Yes and the brig," Fenna said with finality. She didn't like the way Devlin was studying her and she *definitely* didn't like the way she watched his forefinger trace along his lower lip.

"You need a new job," Devlin responded. The winds rippled along his tunic, where the fabric draped against the cords of muscles along his shoulders and biceps. "You need a new job that will keep you from climbing my ship like it's a tree in the jungle."

The scowl Fenna had been hitching onto her features fell away in shock. Faint scents of salt and sun-warmed linen dusted along her inhale. "Have you seen a jungle? A true jungle?" For the second time in minutes, curiosity burned through her. She had read the description of them in passages, and had only seen them hand-drawn on the parchment pages of the more expensive books that littered the shops on the main street.

Devlin's dark brows rose. "Of course. The seas have taken me all along the continent."

Excitement bubbled inside of her, along with a tangle of other emotions that she couldn't quite identify or temper. "Will we get to see a jungle?" More thoughts peppered her mind. "Or an ice floe? Oh, what about a flaming mountain? Or the coastal temple ruins of the old gods?" Fenna's voice died out. She hadn't realized that, in her enthusiasm, she reached forward and wrapped a hand around Devlin's wrist. She retracted it, embarrassment thrumming along her bones.

"In time, I'm sure you'll see it all." Was it her imagination, or did his face dip at the removal of her touch? "Until then, get out of the crow's nest, leave Iris to her work, and follow me."

Devlin's idea of a new job was one that nearly had Fenna leaping off the side of his ship. And, had he not barricaded his cabin on the way back to the helm to keep her from leaving, she was sure she would have. Cleaning his captain's office and cabin felt overreaching in a wriggling and uncomfortable way. She hadn't witnessed *anyone* enter his space without strict instruction and they were out within a minute if they had.

Yet, here Fenna stood, locked in his office with a bucket of soapy water in one hand and a stained washrag in the other. She hadn't given much thought to the office that preceded his sleeping chambers, decidedly marching straight through it to reach the bath instead, and now that she was here, it felt oddly...personal.

There was a large wooden desk centered along the far wall. Much like the table in his cabin, the desk was meticulously kept. Ink bottles and quills lined the top, while a stack of parchment was neatly tucked against the corner. Brass instruments that Fenna knew assisted with navigation lay aside a large map of the sea that spanned the middle. She recognized the markings Loma had written in the margins.

The wood of the chair didn't quite match the desk and the stain of the tall backrest was faded, either with age or from the sun. Fenna wasn't quite sure. A bright red cushion had been placed on the seat, flattened and worn from the time Devlin spent sitting on it. At the end of the armrest on the right side, she noticed a slim scratch, less than an inch in length. She imagined him running a fingernail along it, lost in thought, as he stared down at the map in front of him. A shiver ran up her spine and she quickly turned away.

A small rug, red to match the cushion on the chair, was placed at the foot of the desk. A trail of boot prints worn down the middle of the fibers. It was an intimate detail to know that he often paced in that very spot.

In the corner of the office, tall bookcases were bolted to the interior wall. More brass instruments were precisely placed along the middle shelves, while rolls of used parchment and stacks of leather-bound journals took up the rest of them. There wasn't much dust on the ship, the whipping winds took care of any that dared to settle, but the office was protected enough that a light layer coated the very edge of the shelves.

She ran her fingers along the spines of the journals, paying close attention to the ones that bore tracks through the dust. Those were the ones Devlin had looked at recently. A flame of inquisitiveness sparked in the recesses of her brain and Fenna quickly set down the bucket, looping the washrag through the handle. She plucked the book with the least amount of dust from the shelf and cracked it open.

At first, Fenna didn't quite know what she was looking at. The writing, scrawled quickly in sweeping strokes of a quill, was blotched in places, as though by the accidental swipe from the meaty side of a palm. She flicked through the journal, the subtle scent of dried ink and old parchment wafting upward with every turn of the page. With dawning realization, it occurred to her that she had taken one of Devlin's personal journals from the shelf rather than a book. She made to close it, a creeping sense of unwanted closeness tingling her fingertips, when a passage caught her eye.

Four types of Clairs, otherwise named Clear Mystics, known to the continent. All receive their magic and capabilities through unknown channels. All are highly sought after for war, pirating, and for the king's personal spies. It is unknown how many Clairs reside on the continent, but it is suspected that there are, at least, four dozen in total.

1. Voyant. Clairs who are able to see through visions and visual impressions. This may include fully-fledged conceptions or through subtle influences, such as colors, shapes, and symbols. They are also able to plant visions in the weaker minds of others.

2. Sentient. Clairs who are able to sense through shifting feelings and energy. They are able to sense non-visual and non-verbal cues of another individual's emotions. This is called "the detection." They are also able to project certain feelings into the weaker minds of others.

3. Audient. Clairs who are able to hear voices of other individuals in their minds. This may include voices of those alive or not, with weaker minds more likely to imprint their thoughts on an Audient. They are also able to shift the immediate thoughts of another.

4. Cognizant. Clairs who are able to know things without tangible evidence or facts. This is called "the knowing" and may include insight, information, and ideas. It is unknown the other powers of a Cognizant, as they are the rarest of the four, but it is highly suspected that they are able to access information in other worlds.

Fenna's thoughts turned fuzzy and her ability to think was dampened by the rush of information before her.

This...this had to be fiction, the inner works of a mind lost to the sea. There wasn't a possibility it could be true. Her parents would have told her, she would have come across it in the bookshop, someone would have surely said *something*. Rumors had flown in the town of her peculiar talent and most had chalked it up to her being a shy girl who listened too much. And the few who thought her odd made it known to her every single day.

Fear, uncertainty, and panic swirled around her like the winds of a heavy sea storm. Her heart thundered against the inside of her chest as she read the passage again and again. She hadn't realized she was biting her lip until she tasted the metallic tang of blood against the tip of her tongue.

"I sent you in here to clean, I believe, not to snoop."

Startled, Fenna's head jerked upward and she tightly gripped the sides of the journal. Her breath hitched in her throat, catching along the narrowing of her windpipe and sending squeaks erupting from her where words should have been. She had been completely absorbed in the book, however long she had been in here, and hadn't realized Devlin came to check on her progress.

His seafoam green eyes dropped to the journal in her hands and he reached forward to pick it from her grasp. It fell away with ease, her fingers unraveling with the shock still thrumming through her. He glanced down to graze the passage. "Clairs? I didn't think you would be one to believe."

"Is it true?" Fenna's voice came out barely a whisper, her chest still tight and heaving. "What you have written, I mean. Is there such a thing?"

Devlin tucked the book between his arm and his side. "You are on a specter ship surrounded by sailors who have gambled their lives. And you question the existence of Clairs?"

The raging wind containing her doubt and hesitation spun into a hot, desperate storm of rage. Fenna lunged for Devlin, stunned surprise lifting his brows and parting his lips, as he easily side-stepped her. She barreled into the corner of his desk, a shock of pain reverberating from the bony point of her hip. She whirled on him, the hair from her braid loosening with her sudden movement.

"I want you to stop playing games with me, Devlin Cato, and *tell me what you know.*"

A thoughtful, smug smirk quirked the corners of his lips as he lifted the journal into the space between them. A chuckle rumbled out of him, one that would have curled her toes if it weren't for the frenzied rashness careening through her veins. "And what, pray tell, would you give me in return?"

Fenna had enough. She rounded the desk with determined stomps and haphazardly grabbed the map spanning the desk with a quick clutch of her fist. In the next moment, she unlatched the small, square window and pushed the panes outward. "You tell me what you know and I won't pitch every map, every instrument, every quill from this desk into the deep."

Devlin's gaze darkened, though not in the way she had hoped. He slowly approached the other side of the desk and leaned forward to place his knuckles against the edge. The shift made his tunic tighten against his shoulders. "I have every map on this ship memorized better than I have my own palm memorized. I can lower anchor in three days time to allow my crew to find replacements for every instrument and quill you discard. What that doesn't answer for me, however, is why you are so utterly fascinated with this journal."

Fenna drew on instinct, accessing a piece of herself that her mother and father had been quick to dampen. As a child, she would receive severe punishments for using it. She still had the markings from the switch her father had laid across her back. And now, she used this piece of herself so infrequently that she wasn't even sure it would still work.

But when Fenna reached for him with tendrils from her soul, akin to the coils of smoke that rose from a dying hearth, she pierced through the first layer of his mind with ease. Devlin's eyes widened as those tendrils scraped against the thick door that held her back from him. She caressed it, lovingly stroking it, willing it to open for her.

Devlin was around the desk in a flash, cutlass in hand. Fenna snapped out of her trance with the sound of the journal falling against the rug and, in the next three heartbeats, found his hand wrapped tightly around her throat. He shoved her against the bookshelf, some of the brass instruments wobbling dangerously above her head, and pinned her in place with his hips and the point of his cutlass.

"What are you?" he demanded, his gaze wildly searching her own. Gone was the darkened lust, the playful gleam. In place was deep unease and misplaced betrayal. He tightened his grip on her throat, lifting her chin with the edge of his blade. "What. Are. You."

"I don't know," Fenna seethed through gritted teeth. Her thoughts were a muddled mess of their closeness, his hips against her waist, and his briny, wooded scent. The truth tumbled out of her. "I was found on the outskirts of town as a baby. My parents called it my *gift* and I was forbidden from using it. No one, not until I read that passage, had ever given my ability a name."

His chest heaved with pent up breath as he released her throat and staggered away. He swiped a hand through his hair, sliding it down his cheeks until it rested heavily on his jaw. "Which one?"

"I—"

"Which one are you?" The question wasn't gentle or soft, but demanding and forceful.

Fenna swallowed. "I— I think an Audient. I can hear the thoughts of others. I—I can access them if I try—"

Devlin's hand tightened on the hilt of his cutlass as he raised it toward her once more. "If you try that on me again...if you attempt to breach the walls of my mind...I will run this blade through you and dump you over the side of my ship. Do you understand me?"

Fenna stayed silent, tears pricking the corners of her eyes, as she flapped her head up and down. Devlin turned from her and nearly ran from the room, leaving Fenna with a heaviness to her legs and the raw sensation that every nerve in her body had been flayed open for the world to see.

Chapter Twelve

Devlin

Devlin didn't know how long he waited after extinguishing the candle. The cool light of the moon marched across the desk, illuminating every isle, bay, and coast that Loma had mapped out over the last fifteen years. He sat back in the wooden seat, stiff and shadowed, not daring to even flip through the pages of a book to keep himself occupied in fear that Fenna would hear.

And Devlin knew she would come. If not tonight, though he suspected she would, it would be tomorrow night at the latest.

Fear had rolled off of her like an impenetrable fog when he held the knife to her throat, but within the hazel of her eyes, Devlin saw threads of defiance, fury, and a promise for retribution. And it was within those threads, that quiet strength, he was lost.

He thought back to *her* and how different *she* was to Fenna. Loud and boisterous with a love of all things violent. *She* sniffed out the weak and desperate like it was an addictive drug, reveling in their misery and begging for their deaths.

And Devlin loved it...for a time. He craved the ups and the downs, soaked in the way her eyes lit up at the sobs of those at the gallows, and how passionate she was in bed when she recounted it afterwards.

That is, until he fell victim to it himself and he was cast aside the moment he was no longer necessary. He couldn't even truly call himself the victim, because he knew who and what she was the moment he decided to become a sail tangled within her storm cloud.

Looking back on that time of his life was painful. Thinking about *her* was painful. But Fenna...Fenna was a fierce light, shining goodness, and steady peace—

A click at the door pulled Devlin from his thoughts. The corners of his lips tugged into a small grin as it cracked open, squeaking in protest, before the person behind it paused. Ruffled, ragged breathing echoed through to the desk and Devlin waited in anticipation for them to continue. Through the growing gap, a fan of auburn hair haloed by the moon blocked the sight of the closest mast. The fabric of her skirts ruffled with the sea breeze and Fenna dropped a hand to stifle the noise.

She crept into the room and, quiet as a mouse, shut the door behind her. Devlin leaned deeper into the shadows, tracking her movements toward the bookcase. She halted just outside of his cabin door, seemingly listening for any creak of a bed or rustle of the sheets. Satisfied by the silence, she continued on.

By the slivers of silver light shining over his shoulder, Devlin studied the sweep of her eyes and the trail of her fingers across the spines of his journals. He took a soft inhale and the salty, soap-heavy mix of her scent powered over him. Intoxicating him. She leaned in, eyes narrowed and nose scrunched in an attempt to adjust her sight to the dark. She pulled one journal out, thumbed through it, and returned it.

She did it to a second, a third, and a fourth journal, her brow becoming increasingly more furrowed as time passed.

Devlin became impatient. As Fenna reached for a fifth journal, he pulled the one she was searching for off his lap and let it drop to the desk with a loud *thunk*.

Fenna froze. Her shoulders stiffened and her spine straightened in a comically clunky jerk as she whirled around to face the sound.

"Looking for this?" Devlin drawled. He rose from his seat, tenting the fingers of his right hand over the leather cover of the journal. He struck a match, expertly re-lighting the candle. "Somehow I knew that you would be unable to leave well enough alone."

Her jaw ticked as she clenched her teeth, but she remained silent.

"And knowing you're an Audient certainly gives me an advantage over the king," Devlin went on. Fenna's face curled into a grimace. "I could sell you. Give back your time and trade you for every chest of treasure the continent has in its stores. He would take that deal, you know, to have you in his employ...in his bed."

"You wouldn't do that," Fenna rasped. Her arms crossed in the defiant way that made Devlin's cock twitch. "You wouldn't sell me to him."

"Oh?" He knew that she was right.

"You don't have much use for jewels and fine clothing, you told me yourself. Anything of that nature you could instruct your crew to steal for you. Matter of fact, you have a decent amount in the stores of this very ship."

Devlin quirked a brow. "We have been snooping, haven't we?" He clicked his tongue against the roof of his mouth. "And I thought we had a chat about that."

Her eyes narrowed even further. "I was scrubbing. On your orders, might I add."

He tapped his forefinger against the cover, the thick leather rough and aged beneath his touch. "What are you doing here, Fenna?"

Fenna shifted on her feet. "I want to know more about the Clairs. Or is it not obvious?"

Instead of commenting on how much he wanted to bottle that sass and pleasure himself to it, he twisted the journal and pushed it toward her. "Go on, then. See what you can find."

She lurched forward before coming to a halt and her lips pressed into a tight line. "Why?"

Devlin feigned ignorance. "What do you mean why?"

Fenna's gaze lifted from where it had settled on the book. "You're making this too easy and I have a pressing feeling that isn't in your nature. So again I ask...why?"

Devlin said nothing as he reached down and opened the journal. Despite the only light being the flickering flame of the candle, he knew by her widened eyes that she saw what he wanted her to see.

"Why would you do that? Why would you rip the pages out?" Her voice rose, each word more hysterical than the next, and Devlin almost felt a pang of guilt at the sound. Almost.

"Many members of my crew need access to this room for my maps or navigation equipment. Most are aware that I'm interested in learning more about my fate and I trust that they will refrain going through my personal things. Regardless, I would prefer that these pages didn't reach the prying eyes of those who are in the king's employ."

"But you can't trust that I won't share them?" Fenna huffed. Her gaze returned to the journal and bored into it as though it had done her a grave injustice.

Devlin couldn't help his callous chuckle. "You're standing here, are you not? Seems as though I had the right mind to ensure their safety."

The waves slapping against the keel was the only sound between them for a long minute. Devlin waited, his curious stare roving Fenna's face. He wanted to know what she was thinking, what emotions zipped through that body of hers. He wanted to know how to bring that defiant, brash spark back to her swiftly falling expression. She bit her bottom lip, as though in deep thought, and he fixed his stare to the spot her teeth dug into her flesh.

"Where are they, then? The pages. What did you do with them?"

Devlin regarded her for a series of pattering heartbeats. It normally took quite a bit of coaxing to allow his teasing to surface, but with her, it came uncomfortably natural. "Come with me, I'll show you."

He rounded the desk, the clunk of his boots loud and heavy in the quiet of the night. He made a show of walking too close, allowing his hand to brush against her wrist, feeling the heat of her skin mingling with his. Fenna took a step back, a deepening flush on her cheeks.

"Where are you going?"

Devlin glanced over his shoulder when his hand rested on the knob of his cabin door and spotted Fenna's shifting silhouette. Her hesitation sent an aching spike through his chest and he absentmindedly rubbed at it, as though he could identify its cause with a simple touch. "You asked where the pages are. Are you coming or not?"

Fenna's deep inhale whistled through her nose. "As long as you aren't planning anything...untoward." By the shift of her eyes over his shoulder, Devlin knew that she was thinking of the bathing tub now sitting empty in the corner of the cabin. He thought of it often.

"On my honor." He placed a hand over his heart and dipped his chin to his chest. A wave of wicked relief pulsed through him when Fenna tilted her head upward and swept past him, crossing the threshold into his cabin. "Over by the back windows, beyond the serving table."

The soft footsteps were blunted when Fenna crossed the worn rug, but Devlin wasn't paying mind to it now. He tugged the key to his cabin from around his neck, hung on a simple leather cord, and promptly locked the door behind them.

"I don't see anything," Fenna said, exasperation winding her tone. "Are you sure you put them here?"

"Positive, love. Let me help you." Devlin paused at the foot of his bed, where he had placed the spare spyglass Loma had borrowed earlier in the day. He handed it over to Fenna when he reached her.

Her frown only deepened as she looked down at it. "What—"

Devlin cut her off by placing his hands on her shoulders and turning her to face the floor to ceiling windows. The sea was an ominous dark and he could barely tell where the horizon and the water parted ways. The stars, bright when they escaped the confines of the misty clouds, reflected off the wake trailing the ship.

"Place the spyglass to your eye," Devlin started, leaning so close that his breath ruffled her hair. A shiver worked down the back of her neck, her skin prickled and tight. He swallowed back the sudden pull to grip her hips and bend her over the table. "And look long past the waves from the ship. If you squint your eyes and angle your head to the right, you might be able to spot their ashes floating three leagues back from us."

Fenna whirled within his grip, so close to him that her anger-filled exhale rippled the laces of Devlin's tunic. "You're unbelievable," she stated, shoving the spyglass into his chest, hard enough that a hollow *thump* sounded. She pushed past him as Devlin let out a joyous, barking laugh and wrapped her hand around the knob of the door. The frame merely rattled at her yank, the door refusing to yield to the lock. "Let me out."

Devlin hooked a thumb around the leather cord, lifting his hand to reveal the key he had tucked back beneath his tunic. "And allow you to rummage through my things as soon as I fall asleep? I think not." He let the key fall to his chest as he leaned against the foot of the bed, crossing one ankle over the other.

Fenna scoffed, shaking her head. "You promised nothing untoward."

Devlin held up his hands in surrender. "I've kept my hands as much to myself as I dare." He tossed the spyglass onto his bed, where it bounced against the furs and sheets layered there. "But you can't fault me for being cautious."

"Let. Me. Out." Fenna punctuated each word, the command seething and riddled with fury.

Devlin pushed off the edge of the bed, reaching up to grasp the collar of his tunic. He pulled it over his head in quick succession, balling it up and tossing it into the corner of the cabin. He was never one for clutter, abhorred it to his core if he was being honest, but Fenna's blanched expression and unfocused gaze was enough of a prize. He stood before her, breeches slung low on his hips and chest bare of any linen, as she attempted to avert her eyes for a touch too long before finally turning away completely.

"You need to dress. This is completely—"

"I'm going to sleep," Devlin announced, peeling off his boots and letting them fall to the floor. Her eyes widened, as though the sight of his stockings was going to send her over the edge of an unseen precipice. "You can choose to stay awake if you wish, but the weather tomorrow will require my expertise at the helm."

"I— I can't stay here!" Fenna blurted, blinking rapidly. Her hand carved through her hair, tugging at the strands loose from her braid. "I have nowhere to sleep, I—"

"You are staying here," he replied, sitting on the edge of the mattress, "and there is plenty of room for us in my bed." His cheek dimpled with the force of his grin.

She openly stared now, and Devlin felt a little light-headed with her wide, hazel eyes gouging into his very soul.

"I'm not sleeping in the same bed as you," she finally stated, her hands trembling at the force of her clenched fists. "That's not— I'm not—"

"Take the floor then," Devlin retorted with a bite of impatience that made Fenna flinch. "It's no matter to me where you sleep, as long as I know you're here." He paused to grasp the leather cord from around his neck and didn't miss Fenna inflate with hope as she eyed the wooden table at his bedside.

Instead, Devlin wrapped the cord into a knot and stuffed the entire necklace, key and all, down the front of his breeches. He jolted when the cool metal settled against his groin. Fenna gaped, her mouth opening and closing like a fish out of water.

"Just so you don't get any ideas." He paused, peering over at her through his lashes as he slid into bed. "Or, get as many ideas as you like. If I wake with your hand down my front, it'll make me a happy man indeed."

Fenna sat in the armchair with a rasping huff, the old frame groaning under her weight. Her gaze stalked across the room, planting glares of incredulity at the books on the table, the windows, the mattress, and, finally, him. She stayed silent, though Devlin could read her expression well enough. How dare any of them have the audacity to exist.

Devlin closed his eyes and took a deep breath in through his nose, the cool scent of the night sea promising a deep sleep. His cutlass was leaned against the back of the armchair she sat in and he wondered...no, *hoped*...that he would wake to her pressing it against his throat. It would be the most exciting thing to happen to him in quite some time.

He nestled deeper into the mattress, sighing with content. He had mastered Fenna at last, brought her to heel in the confines of his private cabin. She was stuck here with him and he was—

Chirk

Devlin cracked his eyes open, narrowing them against the golden glow that now bathed his private cabin. The armchair groaned again, nearly swallowing the rustling of parchment pages. "What are you doing?" he asked, tempering the instinct to suck a tooth. He didn't need her to know of his rush of irritation.

No doubt, she would find it amusing.

"Reading," Fenna replied curtly. Parchment rustled again.

"Reading, what, exactly?" Devlin demanded through gritted teeth. He shifted to peer down the edge of the bed, only to find her nose-deep in the creases of his journal with her legs curled underneath her. She had pulled the stack of books closer to her. The flame of the candle perched on the table, newly lit, danced happily at her side. He didn't give her the chance to answer. "Why are you reading my journal?"

"Seeing if I can find anything of interest to me." She lifted her hand to tuck a strand of auburn hair behind an ear before turning another page. "If I'm to be stuck here for the night, may as well make use of it."

"Don't you think I would have gone through every page of the books on the table before allowing you to be in here for any length of time?"

Another page turned. The sound was grating.

"You surely cannot expect me to comment on what you do or do not do before locking me in your quarters," Fenna said, a sharpness to her tone despite her seeming desperation to remain even-keeled. "That being said, I'm quite sure that you aren't nearly as smart as you believe yourself to be." A soft smile appeared on her lips.

Devlin tossed the sheets and furs from his body and clambered out of the bed. Fenna watched him with a cat's curiosity that made his agitation soar as leaned over the table and snatched the candle from the brass holder. "Hey—" she started quickly, but Devlin paid her no mind. He marched to the windows and unlatched one before throwing the lit candle into the dark, rolling wake of his ship. Without saying another one, he latched the window into place and returned to bed.

"That seemed rather unnecessary," Fenna said from the shadows of the cabin. The journal snapped shut, much to Devlin's chagrin. "You certainly don't appreciate having your intelligence questioned. Consider that fun little fact noted."

The preening, self-satisfied tone her voice had taken on made Devlin wonder if it was worth locking her in his cabin after all.

Chapter Thirteen

Fenna

The night had been long. Fenna spent it curled in a half-way decent armchair that, she was sure, had once been stuffed correctly. The cushions were worn down and the seam at the top of the backing had split away from the frame. But it was better than throwing away her pride and crawling into bed with Devlin Cato.

She didn't have much left, but she still had that.

Fenna watched with seething breaths and roiling anger as the captain slept soundly in the comforts of his bed. It was the one time he looked peaceful, his lips parted with soft snores and locks of hair falling against his brow. She wanted to take the journal from the table and beat him over the head with it, for nothing but to pull him from his slumber.

She refrained, though the thought crossed her mind many, many times.

By the time the sun had peaked from beyond the horizon, dyeing the sky in streaks of deep orange and pink, Fenna was exhausted. Her eyes felt puffy and, no matter how hard she tried, it was becoming increasingly harder to keep them open. She was unwilling to let herself get a lick of sleep until she was in the safety of her hammock later that night...or afternoon, if she could help it.

A sharp rap against the door sent Fenna flying out of the seat, a gasp escaping from her throat. Her very nerves felt flayed open and raw from how tired she was, and the sound of the knock was like a cannon blast to her chest.

"Did you not sleep?"

Fenna inhaled, deep and slow, to keep herself from lashing out at Devlin. "Of course I didn't sleep." It hadn't worked.

Devlin merely grunted in response as he lifted his palms to rub his eyes. "You're grumpy when you're tired." He pulled back the covers to sit on the edge of the bed before Fenna could respond.

Fenna let her gaze roam his hunched figure as he tugged his boots on. He looked warm and well-rested, red creases indenting his chest from being wrapped in the covers all night. For reasons unbeknownst to her, she wanted to trace them with her fingers, then with her tongue— she shook her head. What was wrong with her? It was morning, which meant she could slip out of the cabin any moment.

Devlin plodded to the door, pulling the key from beneath the waistband of his breeches. "I'm a little disappointed to find this, that's for certain." He winked and her core, despite her fatigue, clenched in a traitorous response. "Booker. To what do we owe the pleasure?"

Fenna peered over a shoulder and surprise briefly flit over the quartermaster's face when his eyes connected with hers.

"A rip in the mainsail, captain. Iris spotted it on her climb. We've prepared to take it down, but we need it fixed before the storm hits. The clouds already gather on the horizon."

With the news, Fenna turned her attention to the windows bordering the back of the cabin. Indeed, on the right side of the framed glass, a heavy darkness had begun to block the soft light. The sea was tricky— Fenna didn't know how far off the storm truly was— but she managed to catch the looks of concern Booker and Devlin exchanged.

Devlin cursed under his breath, running his hand down his face and scratching at the shadowed beard that grew there. "Replace Iris with Waller and *make certain* that he leaves the *fion* in the berth. I need him at his steadiest. Tell the crew to hoist the spare sail until Iris has the other patched."

Booker curtly nodded before turning on the heels of his boots and marching away. The echoes of them through the office quieted with every step until only the rush of the wind could be heard whistling through the ship. On it was carried a charged scent and a warning of violent waters.

Devlin blew out a breath as he flicked the door shut. He ran his hand through the sleep-ridden tangles of his hair as he rifled through a wooden chest at the foot of his bed, pulling out a clean tunic and hastily yanking it over his head. If Fenna thought her raging lust would temper when he put more clothes on, she was sorely mistaken. The sight of his tunic disheveled and untucked from his breeches was one that she was sure was an extremely intimate one. She wondered how many had seen it before.

"Booker will have left breakfast on the desk. You should eat before making your way to the deck."

That heady desire came to a grinding halt.

"Devlin, I haven't slept all night," Fenna moaned, letting her head fall against the back of the armchair. "The deck doesn't *need* to be scrubbed today if there's a storm on the way."

"It's Captain Cato," he corrected, though the corners of his lips tugged up before he buried them behind a pewter drinking stein. He took a large pull of the freshwater, his throat bobbing with every swallow. Fenna couldn't help but track the cut of his jawline. "And it isn't to scrub, though I should have you do it regardless. The crew will be readying the barrels to collect the rainwater."

She huffed a sigh as Devlin placed the stein back on the table with a dull *thud*. "You'll have me drag the barrels up from the berth in my skirts and stays?"

Devlin's grin only deepened. "I'm sure someone has breeches you could borrow. The work will help you stay awake. Don't dawdle. Booker has been eager to lay his leathers down on the sister of Dasos Terrigan. Your brother sicked himself and ruined Booker's favorite pair of boots three days before abandoning my crew."

Fenna's heart jolted at the sound of her brother's name and she was temporarily dragged from the cabin to the memory of Dasos. Terrified, covered in bloody lashes, and unable to speak. It had shocked her to the deepest recesses of her soul to see her brother like that. And it was the final memory she had of him before boarding the ship.

He still would have allowed you to go.

The statement rang through Fenna like a church bell. The longer she was on *The Phantom Night* the more she wondered if Devlin's words held some truth to them. Would Dasos have traded her? She wanted to think he wouldn't have, that he would have willingly returned to the ship and lived out his life to protect her.

But, there was a tendril of discomfort that snaked its way into that thought. Dasos fled from Devlin the moment he was close enough to land...knowing the captain would have no choice, but to come after him. He had even told Fenna herself that he knew Devlin would.

And Dasos allowed it. He went from port to port, allowing Devlin to burn the cities to the ground and killing innumerable people in search of him. Who was her brother, if not just as bad as the captain? Worse even?

A sharp *thwack* brought Fenna back to the present. She shook her head in a poor attempt to clear her thoughts, but they had already taken root. Grief, cruelly thorned, sprouted like a weed.

"Do you have experience with patching?"

Fenna had barely emerged from the darkness of the office when the question was tossed at her. She swept her gaze over the massive bundle of linen, finally landing on Iris's slim figure perched in the middle of it all. "Patching?"

Iris pinched the linen between her forefinger and thumb, lifting it to reveal the tear that had rendered the sail useless. If Fenna were to guess, the rip was nearly as tall as Delvin. "Patching, yes. Sewing. This tear in the mainsail needs to be repaired before the storm arrives in case we need use of it. It'll take me nearly all day and night to do this alone."

"I— Captain Cato told me that I needed to help bring the barrels up to collect the rainwater."

Iris's brow pinched together before she stood, needle still in hand, and scanned the deck. She lifted a cupped hand to her mouth. "Oi, captain!" Her shout emanated over the heads of the crew. "I'm stealing Fenna!"

Fenna's cheeks flushed as Devlin quickly wrapped a rope around the base of the mizzenmast and approached them. Sweat dripped down his temple and he wiped it away with the back of his hand.

"I need Fenna to help bring the barrels to the deck. I've given her orders." He slid a stern gaze toward her, as though she were the one to request the change in duty.

Iris shifted her weight to one leg and crossed her arms over her chest. Fenna suspected she was the only one who could challenge the captain this way. "And if you want your sail patched before the king dies of old age, I need an extra hand. A female one. The last time I had a man help me, I had to go back and fix everything. Nearly took me twice as long."

Devlin scoffed. "Use Esta."

"She's in the galley peeling potatoes."

"Maud?"

Iris frowned, the corners of her eyes crinkling. "Don't like her."

He opened his mouth, as if to snidely retort, and seemed to think better of it. "Loma?"

"She has fat fingers." Iris lifted a hand to brush her curls from her forehead.

"Ailith?"

It was Iris's turn to scoff. "And steal her away from the important work that is sucking off every man on rest in the berth? I wouldn't want to interrupt that."

The outline of Devlin's tongue poked lightly into his cheek as he let out a sharp exhale from his nose. "What about Cynric? His fingers may be dainty enough for you. Certainly more than Loma's."

Iris's returning smile was tight on her pursed lips. "You can go through every person on this ship, captain, and I will gladly give you excuses until the words *take Fenna Terrigan* are uttered from that perfectly-shaped mouth of yours."

Iris and Devlin regarded one another for a long minute. Fenna stood, unmoving, as the wind lifted the corners of the sail, billowing it off the deck. Tension gathered in the air between them, building like the humidity of the upcoming storm.

"Fine," Devlin finally relented with a shake of his head. "Take Fenna Terrigan."

Iris beamed. "Best idea you've had all morning."

The warning look that flashed to Iris would have made Fenna's blood run cold if it had been directed at her, but Iris was already settling amongst the fabric of the sail once more. That clenched stare softened as Devlin turned his attention to Fenna, lobbing her a once-over that she couldn't quite decipher. Then he was gone, grasping hold of a loose rope and yanking it back into place.

"Come. Sit. It wasn't in jest, I do need your help."

Fenna made her way through the piles of linen, taking a seat next to Iris. "And I thought you preferred to be alone."

Iris snorted. "Being alone is a funny thing. I don't mind being alone, but I don't enjoy being lonely. And this is busy, tedious work. I could use the company now."

Fenna took the needle Iris handed her and bundled a handful of linen into her lap.

"And besides..." Iris trailed off, her accent thickening with her ringing desire to remain nonchalant. "I wanted to hear from the horse's mouth how Captain Cato is in bed. I've heard he's quite the ride."

Fenna choked, coughing on a rogue swallow that tickled the back of her throat. She whirled to face Iris, mouth gaping and eyes wide. "I didn't— we didn't— how did you know I was in his cabin?"

Iris laughed as she threaded her needle through the sail. "Everyone knows, don't be naive. You're not the first person, female or male, to make their way to the captain's quarters. You are the first to not make it back, though. Do you have a magic cu—"

"We didn't do...that," Fenna retorted lamely, stabbing her own needle through the linen. Her mind drifted to his bed, to the wash basin in the corner, how she had pleasured herself there under his direction. He hadn't mentioned it since it happened. "He slept in his bed and I sat in the armchair by the window."

Iris quirked a brow. "There are people aboard the ship who would have killed to be in your position. Captain doesn't allow his dalliances to stay the night."

A sudden and unexpected rush of gratification buzzed through Fenna at Iris's words. "If you want to be a *dalliance*, I'm sure all you have to do is ask."

Iris smirked and the wrinkles in the corners of her eyes deepened. "I have no interest in being a *dalliance* nor does he want that either. I've been serving the captain for nearly forty years now, it would be much like you having feelings for your brother."

Fenna wrinkled her nose.

Iris sighed. "Besides, I loved a man completely for thirty years and that love is still as thorough now as it was then. I don't have the room in my heart for another."

Fenna glanced over to her, studying the wistful smile and the downturned gaze on Iris's freckle-lined face. "You've been on the ship for forty years? Did you— I mean, you must have taken a challenge?"

Iris's distracted gaze lifted to Fenna. "Yes, I did. My initial debt was twenty years. My husband and I challenged him together. I won thirty more. He did not."

Fenna' heart stuttered at her confession and a weight seemed to settle onto her chest. "You— He— And Devlin forced you to remain after killing your husband? That's extremely cruel."

Iris allowed her hands to fall into her lap, pulling at the taut sail settled between them. Her head tilted, brows knitted and lips pressed. "The captain doesn't do any of that. He's a conduit, a messenger of sorts, for Liddros. Our God of the Sea sets the terms and takes his share when the time is done. Did you— did you not realize the captain is cursed to this ship?"

Fenna turned to look at Devlin, who was busy helping the crew hoist the spare mainsail onto the mast. His hair, damp from the humidity, was plastered to the back of his neck. The sleeves of his tunic were rolled up, exposing the forearm tattoos usually kept hidden.

"I— I never really gave it much thought," Fenna finally answered, peeling her eyes away from Devlin's back. "I thought he possessed magic of some kind. He—" She paused, drawing in a deep breath. "What do you know about the Clairs?"

Iris gaze sharpened and her fingertips whitened as they stiffened around the needle. "What are you on about?"

"The Clairs," Fenna repeated, though she knew that wasn't Iris's question. "What do you know?"

Iris let out an impatient huff and shook her head, returning her attention to the sail. "You should ask the captain, this isn't—"

"I don't want to know what Devlin wants with them." That was a lie and, by the deliberate stare Fenna was receiving, Iris knew it too. "I want to know about them. What or who are they?"

Iris said nothing for a long moment, keeping her eyes fixed on the movement of the needle in and out of the linen. Fenna bored her gaze into the side of Iris's cheek, hoping that the woman would become too uncomfortable in the silence.

The ship bobbed beneath, the waves becoming steeper with the coming storm. Clouds, thick and dark, circled the sea. Judging by the color of the sky and the roiling of the water, it was going to be a strong one.

Iris finally sighed, tying a stitched knot into the sail before threading a new silk string cord through the needle. "I don't know much." The wind picked up the edge of the sail and, once again, lifted it from the deck. Both women reached forward to pin it down and Fenna wiped her sweaty, trembling palms on the linen. "I know they're hunted like wild animals. Many are sold out by their friends, their neighbors...gods, even their families. Most of the Clairs recovered are executed by the king and, even though it may not sound like it, that is mercy compared to what awaits the others."

Fenna's mouth went dry. "What awaits the others?"

Iris stabbed the needle through the linen, accidentally pricking her finger. She grunted in frustration as she extracted her finger to suck against the pebble of blood on the tip. "Some are sold to mercenaries and pirates to help in the battles on the sea. They're kept chained in the brig, away from the feeble minded men who may be convinced to let them out. They rot in those cells until they're riddled with infection or the captains find other uses for them."

Nausea crept up the back of Fenna's throat and the sour taste of it coated her tongue. "Have you ever met one? A Clair, I mean."

Iris sat back, leaning against the bulwark behind her. Her eyes became unfocused, as though lost in a memory, before shaking her head. "I did. Once." She cleared her throat. "I suspect I did, anyway. It was the last time we ported and the captain was permitted access to land. The majority of us ended at a brothel in town—"

Fenna flinched at the words, but Iris hadn't seemed to notice.

"—this woman was newly eighteen years old and sat in the corner of the main room with the madame. Though many of the men advanced on her in hopes of purchasing her services for the evening, the madame turned them down every time. She was pretty too, she would have made the madame a pretty coin. They would whisper in the corner together and I would watch as men flitted around the room, suddenly becoming interested in women they had once passed by."

Fenna swallowed. "What kind of Clair do you think she was?"

Iris shrugged a shoulder. "I'm not sure. I don't think I ever caught her name." Her eyes suddenly snapped to Fenna, narrowing slightly against the deluge of sunshine that had broken through the wisps of clouds ahead. "I would keep your questions to yourself, girl. Don't go around asking anyone about the Clairs...or the captain's interest in them."

Rain began to drip against Fenna's hair, blotting the top of her head and running down the back of her neck in thick droplets. And, had she not been completely wrapped up in Iris's story, she would have starred in wonderment at the rainbow that had bloomed before the storm clouds.

Fenna merely nodded, peering down at the linen still bundled in her lap. Her thoughts were running rampant through her mind. From Iris and her long-dead husband, to the well of her own unknown power, to the faceless woman stuck in a brothel as she pulled the mind strings of weak men. And, though she didn't want to think about it, she also considered how long she had with Devlin Cato before he, too, threw her in the brig like the others before him.

Chapter Fourteen

Devlin

The torrential rain blew sideways, lashing against Devlin's face. He struggled to wipe it from his eyes long enough to see down the quarterdeck. Not that he would have been able to see much anyways, the dark skies against the churning sea made for poor visibility. The only person he allowed at the helm with him was Booker, who was combatting the shrieking winds with equal amounts of difficulty.

Devlin had ordered the sails to be tied down, much to Iris's chagrin, before locking the rest of the crew in the berth. If it had been a normal sea storm, he would have authorized some of the men to keep working. But he knew by the swirl of the clouds and the force of the lightning that this was no ordinary storm.

Liddros, God of the Sea, was angry and he was making it known to Devlin that it was with him. Devlin had suspected it for some time now. His dreams had become increasingly more disturbing, waking him with a start at the same time each night. It started with a tingling in his gut and steadily moved to the visions of his corpse, bloated and floating in the sea. When he had locked Fenna in his room the night before, that was the first time he had a dreamless sleep in months.

His plan had been to keep her in the cabin for the one night, but now...now he wondered whether it would be worth her ire to have her there all the time. And he also wondered how many sleep-filled nights it would take before she chopped his balls off with his own cutlass. He had to be honest with himself– he was fiercely curious to find out.

The ship dipped into a valley between the waves, tipping *The Phantom Night* to one side. Devlin gritted his teeth as he slammed his body against the wheel, bracing it against the oncoming wave that would surely wash over the taffrail. Three ropes, previously tied taut to the masts, snapped under the force and whipped with the gale. Devlin knew that Liddros wouldn't sink the ship, he needed those aboard the vessel, but Liddros was not below throwing a god-sized tantrum to show his displeasure.

And he was *very* displeased.

Devlin and Booker had been battling Liddros for hours, alternating at the wheel until the other's upper body became too tired from the constant bracing and gripping. Devlin was soaked to his skin and cold to his very bones.

He didn't know whether his teeth were chattering from adrenaline or the frigid waters seeping into his water-logged boots. He didn't know whether it was day or night, and he still couldn't spot the break of the storm against the horizon.

If Liddros let up his punishment soon, Devlin would be grateful. But he knew the God of the Sea well enough now that it wasn't worth the hope.

Dawn hadn't yet broken by the time the winds died down. The clouds were still tall and dark against the sky, but the sea had calmed enough that Devlin was comfortable placing Loma at the helm long enough to catch up on much needed rest.

But his time at the wheel was just enough to reflect on what he wanted, which was why he took a detour to the grated door that housed the sleeping quarters of the crew.

Devlin tromped down the stairs, his boots squelching out the excess water with every step he took. He dipped his head below the framing and placed a handkerchief against his nose to protect himself from the acrid smell souring the air of the berth. It seemed that even the strongest of men had a hard time holding their stomachs against the wrath of Liddros.

Stepping around the piles of sick that hadn't made it into the buckets, Devlin squeezed through the crowds of moaning men until he sighted the small cluster of hammocks occupied by the women. Esta and Ailith, the brown-eyed beauty Devlin had snagged up nearly ten years ago now, were both pale and clammy, but on their feet at the least. Esta leaned over the side of a hammock, a wet cloth pressed clutched in her hand and a small bucket in the other. Ailith was on the other side, reaching into the confines of the fabric to dab her own cloth against whoever was inside.

Ailith was the first to see him, her glazed eyes lighting up with surprise at his unexpected appearance. "Captain, what can we help you with?" Her voice was quiet and hoarse, an indication that she had spent a decent amount of her own time emptying her belly.

"Where can I find Fenna Terrigan?" Devlin didn't bother with pleasantries. He wasn't particularly fond of Ailith, she had stirred up enough fights amongst his men at the beginning of her tenure on the ship that he had needed to separate her from the others, and he had no interest in allowing her to challenge for more years when her debt came due.

Ailith dropped her gaze to the hammock Esta was leaning against. "She hasn't been well since the start of the storm, sir. She's been like this for hours."

Devlin peeked over the side of the hammock and his stomach twisted at the sight before him. Fenna was coated in a thin sheen of sweat, her skin pale and clammy. Though she was curled as tightly into a ball as she could muster, violent shivers still managed to wrack her body. Someone had placed a wet cloth at the back of her neck and it dripped onto the laces of her stays.

"I'm taking her with me," Devlin announced, diving his hands into the hammock. His forearms tucked behind her knees and shoulders as he hoisted her onto his chest. Fenna moaned with the movement, but kept her eyes clenched tightly shut.

"Captain, she needs rest," Ailith began, but just as quickly clamped her lips together at the murderous gaze Devlin returned her way.

Devlin said nothing else as he navigated toward the stairwell, moving with ease despite the dips of *The Phantom Night* on the sea. The salty air was a blessing and he took in deep, gulping breaths to rid his nose of the stench from below. Tomorrow the berth would need to be cleaned and the hammocks plunged into the sea, but that all could wait. Many of the men would be sick well into the night.

Fenna groaned again and Devlin felt her body tense. *Fuck*. He dropped her legs just in time for her stomach to clench and he managed to turn her head to the side as she vomited onto the deck at their feet. Devlin held her braid tightly behind her, waiting a series of breaths to make sure she wasn't going to sick herself again, before sweeping her up into his arms.

Her eyes cracked open and she tried to blink through the blurry haze of them to focus on his face. "Devlin?"

The corners of his lips involuntarily tugged upward, much to his own annoyance, as he shouldered open the door to his cabin. "It's Captain Cato."

His cabin was a cluttered disaster, though that didn't surprise him. He had expected the broken instruments that littered the floor, the overturned table and armchair, and the misplaced bathing basin. The furs and sheets of his bed had been tossed from the mattress, and they laid in a bundled heap on the damp wooden floor.

Devlin kicked at the overturned armchair until it righted itself, plopping Fenna into it a moment later. She attempted to curl her legs under herself, the beginnings of a tight fetal position, but Devlin grasped her knees and tugged her into a seat.

"I want to lay down," she moaned, weakly pushing at his shoulders, but Devlin ignored her.

Instead, he curled his fingers around the arms of the chair and pulled it toward the back windows, the legs scraping loudly against the floor. He turned away to shuffle through the chest at the end of the bed, extracting a drawstring bag that held the emergency stash of ginger he always kept on hand for this exact reason.

Devlin yanked her knees back down, she had begun to tuck them underneath her once more, before unceremoniously shoving a small piece of ginger between her open lips. "Chew," he said firmly, placing a finger under her chin to lift her gaze toward the windows. "And look at the horizon—"

Fenna turned an unpleasant shade of green and Devlin was barely able to grab an empty water pitcher to place beneath her before she was emptying her stomach once more. She lifted her hand to wipe her mouth, collapsing against the chair with an exhausted groan.

A sigh whistled through his nose as Devlin reached for the windows, opening one just enough for the cool sea air to slide through. Fenna let out a deep shudder when it hit her skin.

"It's freezing," she said, crossing her arms tightly around her chest. "Close the window."

Devlin continued to ignore her. He spun on the heels of his boots, shaking a fur loose from the bundle on the floor, and made his way through the ruin of his room. "Are you going to get sick again?"

Fenna's hazel eyes made an appearance, her brows knitting together. "What?"

"Are you going to get sick again?" Devlin repeated, slower this time. Fenna attempted a sneer at his tone, but it landed on a simple curl of her upper lip. "I'm rather fond of this cover and would prefer it if you didn't coat it in your vomit."

"I— I don't know."

Devlin gestured for her to lean forward, shoving the cover behind her back and wrapping it around her shoulders. Fenna shivered as she tugged at the covers, holding the excess in a ball at her breast. Digging out a second piece of ginger, he held it at her lips, an expectant stare on his face.

"I'm not h-hungry," Fenna stuttered out, another shiver wracking her body. "I'm afraid I'll th-throw it up."

"It's ginger," Devlin grunted, letting the root dangle in front of her mouth. "It'll help with the nausea."

Fenna lifted a trembling hand, taking the ginger between her thumb and forefinger. She inspected it for a long moment and, just when Devlin was going to pluck it up from grasp and force feed it to her, she placed it between her lips and began to chew.

"Watch the horizon," Devlin instructed again, tentative optimism filling a void in his chest at the small flush of color that perked Fenna's sallow cheeks. "Do not watch the waves. You want something steady to focus on."

"I can't even see the horizon," Fenna retorted softly, but her gaze was straight-on nonetheless.

Just the fact that she was feeling well enough to attempt getting the last word was relieving enough to Devlin. The memory of her shuddering and sick in that hammock curled awfully unshakable in the depths of his gut. A sudden wave of exhaustion crested and he fought the pressing urge to lay in his bed, knowing he would immediately fall asleep.

Instead, he righted the upturned table and nestled it against the windows before hopping to sit on the surface of it. The water from his dangling, wet boots drained in fat droplets onto the rug beneath his feet, but he paid it no mind as he zeroed his focus solely on Fenna's pale face. Her eyes lifted to meet his and the sight of them thawed the pieces of his heart that had long been frozen solid.

"What am I doing here?" Her question was quiet, but her gaze pierced through Devlin's very soul and it took him longer than he was willing to admit that he was having a hard time forming words.

"I felt so well-rested after our time last night that I thought we would try it again." Fenna's scowl deepened at his reply, but Devlin went on. "I've had my fair share of sea sickness. I know plenty of remedies for it. Being in the berth is the worst place you can be."

Fenna's stare drifted back to the windows, scanning the scene just beyond Devlin's left shoulder. "There were other men just as sick as I was— am. You didn't bring them up here."

Devlin shrugged. "Many of them have years, if not decades, of experience under their belts. They have their own ways of taking care of themselves during a bad storm and have no need for my coddling. You are barely a month into your debt."

A shadow shuttered behind her eyes. "Are all of the storms quite that terrible?"

"No," Devlin swallowed thickly, looking down at his fingers threaded in his lap, "no, not usually."

Fenna breathed a sigh of relief, leaning back into the thin cushion of the armchair. Silence fell between them and Devlin fought to untangle the web his thoughts had knotted into. *Fucking gods above.* Irritation swelled inside of him, threatening to burst. He couldn't recall the last time a female had his belly in ribbons. Certainly not since his youth, to be sure. Looking back, he didn't think that *she* had ever made him feel this way.

She made him feel other things. Lust and violence were the first things that came to mind. Not...this. This perpetual need to hear her voice, this pull to have the right thing to say, this overwhelming need to have her within the scope of his sight at all times. It was irritating. It was absolutely *maddening*. It was–

"You have dark circles under your eyes."

Devlin flicked his gaze upward, lips parting in surprise when he realized she had been studying him. "Manning the helm during a storm takes more effort than one would think."

Fenna tilted her head. "You should get some sleep before the sun rises."

"I will."

Silence fell again, the steady drip of water sluicing off his sodden clothes the only sound between them.

"Tell me a story then."

Devlin scratched at the stubble on his cheek, his mind searching for a sliver of a crafty response. "What?" is all he managed to come up with and he internally kicked himself for it.

"A story. I've told you one…" Fenna trailed off and Devlin was pleased to see a blush reddening the exposed skin of her chest. He hadn't mentioned the bathing basin again knowing she wasn't ready to discuss it, but he thought of it often. And he had, in fact, bottled some of that water and tucked it into the chest at the end of his bed. "And now you owe me one."

"There once was a man who loved to lick–"

"Not that kind." A spark of amusement flashed across Fenna's features, lighting her up with a kernel of the energy that normally rolled from her. "Just…a story. It doesn't have to be intricate. What was a favorite that your mother told when you were young?"

Devlin's hand wrapped around to the back of his neck, hesitation brimming through him. "We didn't— she didn't— that wasn't the kind of family I was born into." He felt a tug of disappointment at the downturn of her expression. He desperately wished he had one to tell.

"Why don't you take my bed tonight?" Devlin said, sliding from the table. It knocked heavily against the panes of glass with the shift of his weight. "You could use the rest." He held out a hand.

Fenna stared at it for a heartbeat before her eyes darted up. "You should take your own bed. I have my hammock in the berth–"

"Unless you have a burning desire to return–" Fenna's nose crinkled and, in that moment, Devlin knew he had won. He smirked. "I'm still uncertain whether you were feigning or not. How do I know that you just didn't want access to my private books again?"

Fenna blanched before a look of cool indifference settled over her face. "I'll take the bed then." She batted his hand away and a zing of pleasure shot from his fingertips to his shoulder at the feeling of her skin against his. "Alone." Her eyes bored into his at the last two words.

"I'm a man of my word." Devlin settled into the now empty armchair as Fenna crawled into his bed, flinging her boots off with sharp kicks. They clattered to the floor, deep, hollow thumps echoing across the cabin.

"Devlin?" Fenna's voice came a few minutes later when he had already tipped his head back in anticipation of the worst night's sleep he had in a long time.

"Hmm?" He didn't have the energy to correct her.

"Thank you," Fenna said, her voice tender and sleepy, "for taking care of me."

Though Devlin merely returned her gratitude with a gruff grunt from the back of his throat, he was certain he would choose to spend the rest of his existence in an uncomfortable armchair still in his wet, frigid clothes just to hear her say them again.

Chapter Fifteen

Fenna

Fenna slept for the rest of the night and into the next day. She barely awoke to Devlin's movements as he got ready in the morning and she stirred only one other time when the shouts of the crew at the nearest mast infiltrated under the cabin door.

When she finally did open her eyes, it was with a blank expression that quickly evolved into confusion and, finally, panicked unease. She sat bolt upright in the bed, the thick covers wrinkling at the bend in her waist. Her stomach twisted with reluctance at her sudden movement, still tender and sore. She blinked, forcing the sleep from her eyes, as she ran a hand over her brow.

It took Fenna a moment to remember where she was and why she was there. The storm. The horrific bout of seasickness and the two women attempting to soothe her in the aftermath.

Devlin.

Her lungs seized in her chest, tightening to the point of pain when realization of where she was finally sunk in. She was in Devlin Cato's bed, in the mess of his covers. Her boots were perched near the windows, laid in straight perfection against the baseboards. She had a faint memory of flinging them off before collapsing against the mattress and she grimaced when she imagined Devlin picking them up to neatly place them amongst his things.

Fenna swung her legs out of the bed, flinching when her toes connected to the cold wooden floor. The worn rug that had taken up the space was now hanging on a hook in the corner, just another reminder of the lashing rains that seeped through the ship. Her skirts and stays were still damp, and she desperately wanted to clean her teeth. Her mouth was gritty and sour from the hours she spent getting sick.

She briefly glanced down, relief clanging through her when she saw that she, miraculously, hadn't gotten any vomit on her clothes. Tugging on her boots, Fenna crept through the moonlit room and opened the door of the cabin. The hinges squeaked in resistance as a rush of salty air swept the loose tendrils of her hair behind her shoulders. The desk in the office was devoid of any human, captain or otherwise, and Fenna took the opportunity to continue onto the quarterdeck.

Most of the crew had already descended into the berth for the night, save for the few who had been tasked with keeping *The Phantom Night* on course. The mindless hum of chatter rose through the seams of the deck. But as Fenna crossed the ship, aiming for the staircase that would lead to the berth...she lurched to an unexpected stop.

She hadn't been on the quarterdeck after darkness blanketed the ship, usually wanting nothing more than to curl in the confines of her hammock and sleep the night away. Tonight though, her energy was freshly renewed, and the moon reflected off the calm waters like a mirror. It illuminated the deck in a cool glow that threw the masts and sails into sharpened relief.

And the stars.

Fenna had never seen so many stars before. They spackled the black sky, as though a painter had flicked gold paint from his brush again and again and again. Some glittered and pulsed, while others shot across the ether before burning out into nothingness.

She had seen stars back home, though certainly not to this extent. The torches lining the streets of the town worked to block a fair number of constellations that attempted to peek through. The best place to view the stars were at the cove, *her* cove, but one risked a turned ankle or a tumble into the cold waters trying to navigate the coast. That was a lesson she learned the hard way and it was one her parents reminded her of when she wanted to visit at night.

Fenna slowly lowered herself to the deck, adjusting her skirts to allow her legs to cross underneath them. She had studied constellations through some of the books in Algie's bookshop and she rifled through them, narrowing her eyes in concentration.

"What are you doing out here?"

Fenna started at the voice, so absorbed that she hadn't realized Devlin walked up behind her. She glanced over a shoulder to peer up at him, her eyes dropping to the steaming mug clutched tightly in his hand.

"Broth," Devlin answered her unspoken question. "Courtesy of Oswin Vance in the galley. It isn't much, but it should make sure your stomach stays settled. I was on my way to bring it to you, but—"

Affection pinched at her heart as Fenna took the mug from Devlin. The steaming liquid smelled savory, replacing the salty scent of the sea against her nose, and the warmth of the mug at her palms made her realize how cold she was. She shivered as she took a small sip and the taste of simmered vegetables burst against her tongue.

Fenna sensed Devlin's hesitation, his boots shifting just behind her lower back. She glanced back over her shoulder, quirking a brow at him. "I'm looking at the stars. Care to join me?"

Devlin's head reeled back and his lips turned down in thought. "Why would you—?"

She reached her hand back and wrapped her fingers around his wrist, tugging him toward her. His eyes widened when he stumbled, unsuspecting, down to the deck. He caught himself with a fist and Fenna bit her lip to keep from smiling. He settled, slowly, and it seemed as though he were unsure of how, or where, to sit.

Fenna watched him with amusement, taking another slow sip of the broth. "When was the last time you sat on the deck of your ship without having a job to do?"

Devlin stilled as he pulled on the front of his breeches, giving himself more room. Another gust of wind shuddered the steam rolling off the mug, flapping the sails noisily into the night. "This is nonsense," he finally said, resolving to pull a knee toward his chest to rest his forearm on it.

"This is beauty!" Fenna admonished, sweeping a hand out to the endless darkness before her. "How many times will you be here at this very moment? When will you see that shooting star again?" She tracked one with a pointed finger, letting her hand fall to her lap once it fizzled out.

Devlin considered her for a long, silent minute. "You must be feeling better."

Fenna sent him a humored grin. "I feel human if that's what you mean."

Silence fell between them, but from the corner of her eye, Fenna watched as Devlin tilted his chin toward the sky. She set the mug onto the deck and another raucous shout of laughter reverberated from below.

"When I worked at the bookshop, my employer let me borrow a book about the stars," Fenna started, taking in a deep breath. The chill of the air bit at the inside of her nose, settling into the deepest regions of her chest. When Devlin's arm brushed against hers, she heated. "There was one that always stuck with me. It's about a woman, the most beautiful woman the continent had ever seen, who lived in the sky. She loved to spend her time dancing and, one night, she was spotted by a hunter. The hunter decided he wanted her and disguised himself as a hawk to lure her down from the heavens.

"The woman fell in love with his kindness and they were happy for a long time together. One night, she looked into the sky and saw the vast darkness where she once danced. Seeing her sadness, the hunter gifted her with his own wings. Every few months, she would leave the continent and dance in the sky. That's why you can only see those stars during the cold season."

Fenna turned to regard Devlin and nearly reeled back at the sudden closeness at which she found him. At some point during her story, Devlin leaned closer, using his hand behind him as a brace. His breath tickled against the top of her cheek and, for the moment, she forgot how to breathe.

They were quiet– the charged energy between them growing with every passing second. Tension clashed with a thrumming desire to erase the inches between them. Fenna became acutely aware of how her heartbeat drummed in her chest, how her fingers ached with the need to reach out and touch him, and how the laces of her stays were uncomfortably tight around her.

Fenna's tongue darted out to wet her lips and Devlin's gaze dropped there. For a brief second, Fenna was sure he was going to kiss her. And she was sure she was going to let him. She wanted to, had thought about the first kiss they shared to the point of near obsession, and she would have been lying to herself if the memory of it didn't make her restless. She didn't think about the storm or that she had been eager to scrape any knowledge about the Clairs from him.

Under Devlin's scrutinizing gaze, one that was filled with promise and darkness and passion, Fenna was alive. His crooked, wicked grin stoked a fire in the confines of her belly that she was having a hard time extinguishing. And she wasn't certain she wanted to.

But this Devlin? The one who stared at the stars with her, brought her hot mugs of broth after a night of seasickness, and drew out the pieces of her that she had long since stashed away? Fenna knew that she could spend the next twenty-five years of her debt learning the inner workings of this Devlin.

The realization was jarring and exciting. Daunting and dangerous. Unsettling and filled with a wild, untamed heat. It was what her mother had told her about, what her father had said she deserved nothing less of, and what her brother had comforted her over when the boys at the learning house relentlessly teased her.

Dasos.

The thought of her brother dashed through her mind, soaking her spine in a cold chill that washed away any lingering, heart-stopping wants.

That Devlin had her brother whipped. Had killed three men before her very eyes and left their bodies to rot in the heat of the sun. Was the captain of a specter ship that demanded the souls of innocent sailors in return for a handful of years at sea. Had ordered her town to be leveled if only to find one wayward man.

It was important, Fenna knew, that she didn't try to separate Devlin into different people. He was dangerous and he was cruel and he was passionate and he was thoughtful. And until she knew that she wanted to be wrapped up in all of the things that he *was*, Fenna knew it was best to keep her distance.

Fenna cleared her throat and shifted away from Devlin, allowing the briny breeze to sweep between them. Hurt flickered across his face, but it was masked by indifference just as swiftly.

"That's not how we tell that story," he countered with a jut of his chin toward the sky.

She took the bait, curiosity peaking, as she picked up the mug of broth from beside her. It had cooled in the minutes since she set it down and the mug no longer heated the palm of her hand. "How do you tell it then?"

"We don't. We know the stars are nothing more than a set of navigational tools. The gods don't care about us and they certainly don't care about a dancing woman in the sky."

A painful tightness narrowed Fenna's throat and she struggled to swallow around the lump that had formed there. "Well I think there are mysteries in this world that we aren't meant to understand. Don't you?"

Devlin's scoff was cynical. "I don't think there are any mysteries in this world."

Fenna's grimace remained and she took a slow sip of the broth. "You can look at me, knowing what I am, and still think that?" She sent him a leveling gaze. The empty stare he returned pebbled her skin. "I want to know about the Clairs."

"You read that journal entry. You already know about the Clairs. Better yet, why don't you use that little *gift* of yours and—"

"Are you angry with me?" Fenna asked, and her confident stare shrank into a long, pained one before she finally broke away. The interruption was quiet, barely heard over the wind in the sails and the waves against the ship, but it caught his attention nonetheless.

Devlin started. "I'm— I'm not—"

"You are," she countered. She tapped the mug with her forefinger, sucking in a sharp breath. "I didn't have someone to...teach me. I wasn't allowed to use my gift. But the thoughts of others just came to me and it..."

Devlin blew out a breath and scanned the star-speckled sky, his eyes squinted in thought. The clean cotton scent of his tunic intertwined with the next gust of wind. "You're lucky. I've spent fifty years trying to find a Clair who can...it doesn't matter. Most end up at the gallows before long, unable to control themselves as children." He peered over to her. "The fact that your parents didn't immediately turn you in the moment you showed yourself— they were good people."

Fenna didn't bother to agree. She knew what her parents had risked, even when she didn't know what she was. She knew magic was outlawed and they had just as much of a chance as she did to be hanged. "Why are you looking for a Clair?"

Devlin shifted on the deck, leaning forward to rub a finger along his lower lip. "Never you mind that," he finally said, much to Fenna's dismay. He squared his shoulders to face her. "There aren't many on my ship who you'll be able to hear, I suspect. Many have had their guards up for decades, an Audient being on my ship aside. You should learn how to use your gift."

Fenna furrowed her brow. "Why?" Discomfort snaked up her spine and she steeled herself to keep from trembling. "So you can force me to use my gift for your ship? To help you plunder, murder, and—"

"You need to protect yourself." His voice dropped, low and urgent. "There are men who would sell you to the continent for a bowl of fresh stew—"

"Why do you keep them as your crew then?" Fenna retorted, shooting him an accusatory glare. She waited for one of the overnight sailors to walk by before continuing, paranoia spiking through her chest. How long would it take for these men to sell her? To find a way to notify the continent? Parsons Nottley would have. How many else are here watching?

"I made my choice a long time ago, and I no longer have the ability to make them now." Devlin pushed himself to standing, reaching a hand down to help Fenna to her feet. "You'll work with Iris, but not tonight. Tonight we both need to rest."

Fenna slipped her hand into his and allowed him to haul her to his feet. "I do need to change from these skirts and stays." She paused to pinch at the petticoat before smoothing the linen back into place. "It'll be nice to sleep in my hammock."

Devlin smirked, amusement flooding his darkened eyes. "What hammock?"

She stilled, her hands closing into fists that whitened her knuckles before whirling to face the captain. His smirk widened as he scoured her features. He didn't...he *wouldn't*... Devlin crossed his arms over his chest, the sleeves tugging upward to reveal the tattoos circling his forearms. Fenna ignored the inscriptions and the way they seemed to absorb the light from the moon.

"What did you do?" Fenna demanded, poking a finger into the crook of his chest.

"I moved your things from the berth." Devlin shrugged, reaching forward to clap her hand to his chest, pinning it in place. He took a step forward, closing the gap between them.

Fenna flushed, but refused to step away. Her chin lifted, eyes narrowing into a glare.

"You made your choice," he repeated, though this time, he directed it to her. "And I've taken your ability to make them. You'll sleep in my cabin from now on, because you shouldn't be with the others, because I can't trust that I won't wake to you rifling through my things, and because I want you to." He leaned closer and his breath tickled the shell of her ear. "And I always get what I want." His thumb brushed along her bottom lip, parting her lips.

Desire bolted through Fenna, striking her fast and hard, and startling her into stumbling backward. She barely moved, still tucked against Devlin's muscled body. She struggled to suffocate the rising tension that was shifting the very air around her. Heat coursed through her blood, heating her from within.

Would she spend every night for the next twenty-five years there? Or, at the very least, until he found someone else to fill his time with. With a hitch of fear, Fenna finally wondered how long it would be possible to resist him if there was nowhere for her to run.

CHAPTER SIXTEEN

FENNA

The cannon boomed in the night, jolting the ship and echoing into the distance of the sea. Fenna imagined it bounding off the horizon and slingshotting back to them, a warning that returned full force. The crew were nearly vibrating with excitement, each man clutching a cutlass in their fist.

Fenna hadn't yet witnessed a boarding and had been strictly instructed by Devlin to *stay in the cabin*. "It's not proper for a lady to see such an act," he said the night before as he settled into the armchair across from the bed. He had received his own correspondence in the changing of the wind and a searing pain against his forearm. She hadn't been allowed to see that either.

But Fenna's need to see the happenings of a boarding, and how Devlin worked his own gift, quickly overtook any need for self-preservation. She snuck into the storage compartments below the berth in the hours after finishing her cleaning and managed to steal a pair of breeches and tunic. She figured they would still be too big on her waist, but they fit better than anything of Devlin's could have.

A shiver of anticipation rang up Fenna's spine with the next cannon blast and the deck shook with the force once again. Shouts, urgent and riddled with fear, called through the thick fog that hung heavy above the waters beyond the ship. The flames from the torches could barely be spotted through the curls of misty air, casting *The Phantom Night* in a ghostly darkness.

"Fire the third," Devlin said from the helm, a clear order that Fenna heard even from her place in the center of the masses.

The crew began to move, the men at the gunwall slinging grappling hooks tethered with thick ropes above their heads. They clanged against the wooden bulwark of the unseen warship and Fenna tightened her grip on the cutlass in her hand. She had never held a cutlass before and it was surprisingly heavy in her hand. She dipped her head to her chin, tucking the stray locks of hair that escaped from underneath her tricorn hat behind an ear.

A third cannon sounded, the deafening noise piercing the haze like a sharp knife. From the muffled splash, Fenna knew the shots weren't meant to hit the warship, only keep it in place. Devlin crossed from the helm, hoisting himself onto the gunnel by the rigging, and scanned the shadows before him. For a brief moment, Fenna wondered what he was looking for, but his sharp whistle interrupted her thoughts.

"Board in the smoke," he called out.

Low jeers and chuckles reverberated all around her, and Fenna was jostled from side to side as the men streamed forward. She was careful to keep her eyes down and her chin tucked to avoid detection, but it seemed that none of the crew were paying her any mind. They all had a singular focus, and what that was became clear enough as soon as she got close to the side of the ship.

The ropes attached to the grappling hooks disappeared into the fog, pulled taut between the two ships. The sea was eerily quiet, and an unpleasant wave of uncertainty crested through Fenna in the next breath.

"We're headed to the galley," a voice whispered to another behind her. "Captain ordered the sacking of the kitchens, the storage quarters, and the gunnery. Three men aboard are in need of his...services. Leave the water, though. Captain is questioning contamination."

"Will we be expecting new members of our crew then?" the second man replied as Fenna was shoved forward once more. Her stumble was barely noticed.

"Don't be stupid," the first man murmured. The zing of his cutlass scraping against the wooden deck followed in the silence. "Captain Cato isn't like the others. He gives the men a choice and no one is fool enough to take on this life."

"What do you mean?"

Fenna perked her ears, straining to continue listening to the men behind her. Ahead of her, another man hauled himself forward and turned his back to the sea. He lowered himself off the side of the ship, scrambling back to hook his knees over the taut rope. He scuttled into the fog, using his hands and knees to scoot along the make-shift bridge. He disappeared into the darkness and a bone-deep chill erupted at the base of her spine.

Fenna had climbed the tall cliffs of the cove a countless number of times, but this...this took a different kind of strength that she wasn't quite sure she had.

"I heard a rumor the last time we were in port. You know, when we were supposed to pick up that ninny of a man and landed his sister instead–" Fenna swallowed, curling her chest inward to hide any lingering indication that she was, in fact, the sister. "There's a second captain, one who's been spotted north of here, and he doesn't allow for..."

Shouts of surprise interrupted the man's tale and Fenna's head darted up at the snap of a rope. Two men careened into the sea below, garbled splashes echoing up the passage between ships. Laughter rose through the crew at the sight. Fenna was elbowed by the man next to her and the force of it sent her stumbling into a meaty shoulder. She peered up for the briefest of moments before tucking her chin once more, recognizing the man as Jefford Bing, a gunnery man who assisted with ammunition.

"Can't imagine Fenwick's happy about that," Jefford said with a shake of his head. "He tries to stay out of the water if he can help it."

Fenna merely grunted a response, but was lost for words when Jefford climbed onto the side of the ship and stepped overboard, his body disappearing with a swirl of the misty haze.

"And he's a showoff, that one," the man behind Fenna said. "He'll climb the netting of any ship just to prove that he can."

Fenna licked her lips as she shakily pulled herself onto the gunnel. Her palms were slick with sweat as she sheathed the cutlass at her waist. With trembling hands that shook the rope, she clutched at the thick, fibrous braiding and swung a knee to hook over top of it.

"Any day now, lad. We're all getting closer to death just watching you," a man called from the deck, sending another round of jeers and chuckles her way.

With a deep breath that seized her lungs in an icy grip, Fenna began her crossing along the rope. *One hand beyond her head, pull her knees forward. Second hand beyond her head, pull her knees forward.* Her back and shoulders shook with the effort, each of her movements jerky and cumbersome. It wasn't long before *The Phantom Night* disappeared into the thick fog, leaving Fenna alone in the darkness.

The silence pressed into all sides of her and nothing, save for her ragged breathing and the crashing waves against the ships, penetrated the unnatural quiet around her. The air was cool and damp against her exposed skin, and it took a single gust of that wind to blow the tricorn hat from her head. It tumbled toward the sea, but Fenna squeezed her eyes shut so as to not track it falling away from her. Her braid hung loose, swaying like the rope in the breeze, and the mist settled in thin droplets against her hair.

She froze, unwilling to continue onward and unable to go back. Frigid dizziness bubbled through her, narrowing her vision into pin-points. Her hands and knees slackened against the ropes, threatening to send her plunging into the water. She imagined the needles of cold biting her, the burning clamp of it surrounding her limbs. She imagined being pulled downward by the churning currents, struggling to surface.

Time stalled; seconds or hours or days could have passed as she hung there, suspended above the sea.

Finally, Fenna sucked in deep, gulping breaths, allowing the briny mist to sink into her chest. Her vision focused just as the fog cleared above her, separating to reveal a strip of stars against the night sky. She narrowed her eyes on the brightest, blinking star and willed herself to move.

She thought of nothing but that star as she clawed her way across the rope. She listened to the water and pretended the slap of the waves were crashing against the rocky terrain in the cove. She breathed in the air, heavily scented with used gunpowder and waxed wood from the ships.

Fenna swallowed a yelp when the top of her head slammed against the bulwark of the warship. Hands wrapped under her arms, hauling her aboard.

"Come on, boy, there are others right behind you. You need to move faster if you— *of the old gods...*"

Fenna whirled, wide-eyed, to face Booker Colby. A vein popped at the peak of his forehead, half covered by a lock of blonde hair, and throbbed with each clench of his jaw. His glassy stare assessed her for a long moment before he grasped her upper arm and pulled her to the side.

"The captain is going to have your head," Booker hissed, "and I'm not going to be the one to tell him you're here. You need to go back. Now."

Fenna let out an impatient huff, hitching a scowl on her face. She tore herself from Booker's grip, hands and knees still trembling from the scramble across the gap. She still didn't quite feel as though she had come up for air, but the irritation sliding through her was a welcome relief from the bone-chilling fear.

"He's not my keeper, I can—"

"No, he's your *captain*," Booker retorted, jutting his chin toward the mainmast of the warship, where a yellow flag was posted high above the sail. "It's too dangerous for you to be here and—"

A pistol shot rang out, followed by sharp shouts that reverberated across the deck. The jostling of metal on metal clanged around her, with more of Devlin's crew appearing from the shroud of fog that encased them. A cannon boomed under their feet, sending the ship reeling to the side. Booker made to grab her, but Fenna dipped under his arm. His fingers scraped against her tunic as she narrowly avoided him, sprinting head-long into the smoky battle on the deck. Booker swore loudly, lurching forward to chase after her, but Fenna was lost in the crowd a heartbeat later.

Fenna navigated the two crews with ease, unsheathing the cutlass from her waist. Her braid bounced between her shoulders as she ran, eyes skimming along the outer wall until she found what she was looking for. A stream of Devlin's men descended the steps below the ship, their bootsteps heavy. She snagged a lost tricorn hat from the deck as she moved, plopping it on top of her head and tucking her braid underneath the band.

The scent of the ship turned eye-wateringly sour with every step Fenna took below deck. She pulled the seam of the tunic over her nose and mouth, her throat tightening with the struggle to keep her own sick at bay. Laughter echoed through the narrow hallway and she turned into the closest open room to hide in the shadows. Royden Alby, the leader of the deck scrubbers, stalked by, an oak barrel slung over a shoulder and two decanters filled with amber liquid clutched in the other hand. His ascent up the stairs was slow and he twisted to the side to fit through the hatch before disappearing into the mist that rolled across the deck.

Fenna blew out the breath she had been holding and slid back into the hallway, creeping down the passage. The bustle from the deck quieted the longer she walked on, but the acrid smell only grew stronger. She nabbed the hat from her head and placed it over the bottom half of her face, as she took another set of stairs deeper into the hold.

The excitement of being aboard a warship, one so similar to the ship Dasos had signed onto, quickly evaporated when she passed a large room, laden with swaying hammocks. Vomit slid across the floor with every stomach-turning plummet of the ship, seeping into the tar-filled seams of the framing. Fenna pressed on, in search of something that would make the trip worth the while.

The warning creak of the ship was as loud as the cannons booming above her, but Fenna felt an odd squirm of discomfort low in her belly. Where she expected sailors to be hastily repairing a leak in the outer wall, there was no one. Where she thought the crewmen of *The Phantom Night* would be heaving the crates and barrels to the deck, they continued to sit, untouched, in storage. She halted in her steps, glancing down one end of the long passage to the other.

For a number of seconds, all Fenna could hear was the thundering of her own heartbeat and the distant shot of pistols. Then...a faint moan. She tilted her chin toward the noise, straining her ears over the sounds of hollow footsteps in the decks above. There it was again...a faint, misery-filled moan.

Fenna was off, gliding down the quiet passage. The hat against her face filled her nose with salty sweat and pungent body odor, but it was better than the foul stench that stained the hallway, stale and unmoving. She glanced into every cabin she passed by, each as empty as the next, until she reached the end of the ship.

Gods, it hurts...Samael...please...

There was a gut-wrenching tug just behind Fenna's navel as she peered around the doorframe. It was dark, save for a small flame dancing within the iron-framed lantern, and what little she could see was densely veiled in shadow. A small bed was tucked in the corner, an unmoving lump nestled under the linen covers. The lump moaned again as a second figure appeared from the shadows and Fenna flattened against the wall as it passed.

A series of creaks echoed through the otherwise empty space as she peeked back in, stabilizing herself against the wall when the ship lurched with another cannon blast. The figure placed a bucket onto the floor, water sloshing over the side, as it settled onto the stool next to the bed.

"You don't have much time left."

Fenna's heart pattered dangerously in her chest, so loudly that she was sure the two men inside the cabin would hear. Devlin took off his tricorn hat, exposing the kerchief tied around his loose hair. He slid the kerchief from his head and dipped the fabric into the bucket at his feet. Water sluiced off the edge, running onto the floor in rivulets that coated the toes of his boots.

Please...Samael... "Have...mercy..."

The last two words were said aloud, the man's weak voice cracked and strained. It wasn't until then Fenna realized she had been hearing the dying man in her head; pleads of a quick death to take away the pain and suffering. The man's empty gag was muffled against the linens covering him and Devlin leaned forward to place the wet kerchief against the man's pallid, clammy skin.

"I'm here to offer you time." Devlin rested his forearms on his knees and, though Fenna could only see his back, she imagined the intense stare that furrowed his brow and downturned his lips. She could see it like it in her mind's eye like it was her own reflection she was looking at. "I'm here to take away the pain you feel now. To put it off until Liddros has decided it is time for your judgment."

Bone rattled against bone as the man's teeth chattered together and it melded with the sound of the dice rolling in Devlin's outstretched palm.

Samael...please...take me to her...let me find her...

The ship creaked once more as Devlin soaked the kerchief, replacing it on the back of the man's neck. "I don't condemn you. I can only allow you a debt that must be paid in full, but it may buy you enough time to settle your life and say a proper goodbye to your loved ones."

The man let out a weak chuckle and a trembling, gnarled hand emerged from the blankets. Fenna's lips parted in surprise as the man tapped Devlin's wrist three times, as though in comfort, before folding his fingers around the dice still in his palm. "I know...what you...are...captain..." The man managed to wheeze. "And I...pray...that you...find...solace...soon...too..."

Devlin hesitated for a moment before resting his hand on top of the gnarled one. "I hope for the same, Captain. Journey well through the deep. We'll meet again one day."

Fenna reached for the dying captain and his labored breathing, pushing through the layers of his tired mind with ease. *You'll be with me soon, my love. Come home to me. Come home to me.* She threaded the tendrilled words like a mantra through his mind, convincing him to let go, convincing him to move on.

The old captain let out a wet cough that sounded painful against his throat, but his mind opened to her in wonderment.

Hettie, Hettie, Hettie...I'm coming, my love...I'm coming.

Another set of creaks snapped down the passage, louder than the firing pistols above her. And, before Fenna could react, a large hand clapped across her mouth and yanked her away from the door frame.

Chapter Seventeen

Devlin

Devlin pulled the stained linen over the old captain's ashen face. He sucked in deep breaths, despite the stale smell of room, and absently toyed with the pair of dice still in his hand. Something unseen sat on his chest, weighing him down until his heart began to ache, as though someone had taken a sharp knife to each individual vessel.

Frustration clattered through him, pounding against his ears and hardening his stomach into knots. It was a pinched tension, a growing pressure that forced him to replay the scene of his own death again and again and again.

How Devlin had stood over *her* dead body. How he had begged and pleaded for *her* soul. How it had been on deaf ears until...

A prickling on the back of his neck pulled Devlin from his thoughts and he looked over his shoulder, unsurprised to see the figure standing amongst the shadows. At first glance, the figure appeared to be a man. His dark hair was shoulder length and pulled into a bun at the back of his head, loose locks framing the sharp angles of his face. When Devlin looked closer, though, he knew the man was much more.

There was an aura that surrounded him, a silent power that Devlin knew not to tempt. He was a fraction too tall, a little too good looking, and the muscles that strapped his shoulders were a smidge too defined.

"Liddros," Devlin mused, squaring his shoulders to face the god that stood before him. "To what do I owe the pleasure?"

Liddros pushed away from the wall, his boots scuffing heavily against the wooden floor. He bore no weapons in the belt at his waist, merely folded his hands at his front as he approached the middle of the cabin. The action was not lost on Devlin and a shudder coiled at the base of his neck.

"I thought the storm I sent was enough of a warning for you." Liddros paused to stare pointedly down at the body of the old captain. "I mustn't have made much of an impact."

Devlin crossed his arms over his chest. The sleeves of his tunic pulled away from his wrists, revealing the thick swirls of black that had been tattooed on him the moment he accepted the proposal from Liddros all of those years ago. "Your storm was well received, as you know—"

"And yet you allowed three men to pass beyond my reach, placing their souls in the hands of my brother," Liddros snapped. Devlin's spine straightened in silent reply. "You don't work for the God of Death, you work for me."

Devlin shook his head, gesturing toward the shrouded captain behind him. "He was old, there were no years left for him—"

"And that is for me to decide, not you." Liddros stepped forward again, his frame towering a few inches above Devlin's. His hand shot forward, clamping tightly around Devlin's throat. "I've been patient with you, captain. I've allowed this ridiculous game of yours to continue while other captains take what is mine. You will bring me fifty souls to show your worth."

Energy cascaded from Devlin, as though Liddros were siphoning it directly from his core. Devlin glanced down to where the pair of dice was still clutched in his hand, horror rocking through him as he watched the back of his hand begin to desiccate before his very eyes. The skin thinned, twisting into the consistency of old parchment that barely covered the brittle bones and thick tendons.

"My patience wears thin," Liddros hissed as he released Devlin, who stumbled away, gasping breaths sawing his throat. "I need Time to give to the king. We both require the souls of those lost at sea. I know that your mind serves you well."

Devlin shook his head in an attempt to rid himself of the memories, but they crashed over him like a rogue wave. The captain who had fought to the death, a heart-sized hole in his chest where Devlin had torn it out. The women who could no longer taste food and were never satisfied, no matter how much *fion* they ingested. The men who laid on the rocky shore, crying and begging for a death that would never come. And the children...the children...

Liddros's grin was neither comforting nor amused. "I thought you would remember." He paused and Devlin felt the god's icy stare penetrate through to his very bones. "And you should not forget again. The consequences of it will be severe."

Devlin steeled his gaze, daring to lift his eyes toward the god still before him. "You've taken my life. You've taken my choices. You've taken my soul. What else is there for you to steal from me?"

Liddros tilted his head, contemplation spilling over his features. "I've gifted you my power in exchange for Verda's life." Devlin's belly lurched at the sound of her name, a name that had not been spoken aloud in decades. "A life that she no longer wished to share with you, but there is another who comes to mind."

Devlin's eyes narrowed. "Speak plainly."

Liddros smirked and took another step forward, now close enough that his honeyed breath ghosted over Devlin's face. "Aren't you curious why the debt didn't take to Fenna Terrigan? Haven't you wondered why you feel a pull toward her? An uncontrollable urge to—"

Devlin shook his head, clenching his molars so tightly that they ground together. "Verda was—"

"Verda was nothing," Liddros interjected with a short tone that made Devlin's hair stand on end. "Verda was a loose cannon who you gave everything for and who allowed you nothing in return. Humans don't feel the ones they are bound to, the souls they are tethered through realms and time...but you aren't human any longer, are you, Devlin Cato?"

Devlin went quiet, his mind acutely aware of his tunic against his bare skin and the pistol that weighed down the belt around his waist. The solid thumping of his heart pulsed into his fingertips. He thought before that he had been struck stupid at the first sight of Fenna, but he knew it went deeper than that. He felt her *everywhere, at all times.* In the way her smell surrounded and suffocated him, how his cock twitched at the moaning stretch she let out when she woke. His need to know her favorite book and to tangle his fist into her hair.

"I can't have her," Devlin finally said, searching Liddros's haughty gaze. "I can't have her like this. If she didn't—if the debt didn't take—"

"She will age and she will die, yes."

Devlin barely suppressed the urge to clutch the front of the god's doublet. "I need time, I need...you have to let me go. I need— I need—"

"You had time," Liddros scowled. His hand darted out to grasp tightly on Devlin's forearm, yanking it into the space between them. Even in the veiled shadows, the markings seemed to devour what light was left in the cabin. "You gave yourself to me and you know what needs to be done for the return of your soul."

Devlin's swallow was thick as his desperate stare glided over the room, looking for something...*anything*. "Sacrifice. It takes a sacrifice for me to be free of this burden." His eyes darkened, narrowing into slits. "I won't subject her or anyone else to that."

Liddros smirked. "You mention her, which tells me that you already know. That's the choice you've made." His silhouette shimmered into a haze as he began to disappear into the depths of the cabin. "Bring me fifty souls, Devlin. You know the consequences if you don't. You have two weeks."

Devlin was finally alone. The shout of frustration that clawed up his throat bounced off the walls as he lunged forward to grasp onto the iron lantern still seated on the bedside table. He flung it hard into the corner of the cabin, where it crashed against the wall. The candle hissed when the flame was extinguished and Devlin was cast into darkness.

His chest heaved with the force of his breath and, for a moment, he only listened to the *plink* of water leaking from the ceiling and into the small puddles on the floor. He cursed Verda for tangling him in her disastrous web. He cursed Liddros for appearing when he had, for marking him...chaining him. But, more importantly, he cursed himself for allowing it all to happen.

A sharp scream made Devlin still, his shoulders going taut as the strings on a fiddle. A scream during a raid wouldn't have bothered him, wouldn't have given him second thought. But this one...it hooked in the spot behind his navel and tore at his instincts. It was unmistakably female, the pitch of it too high for even some of his gentler sailors. And the flash of auburn hair he swore he saw in the crowd...

"*Fenna!*" Devlin yelled, sprinting from the cabin and twisting into the hallway. He halted just beyond the threshold of the door, pausing to listen beyond the ongoing cannon blasts and clatters of sword against sword. The ship creaked as it bobbed in the waves, letting out a troubling groan.

Scuffling, as though boot heels frantically scraped across the floor, sounded above him. Devlin took off, the tip of his cutlass dragging against the wall of the narrow hallway as he drew his pistol from his belt. He took the stairs two at a time, bolting onto the next deck.

"Fenna!"

The second shriek was shrill and filled with terror, but it was cut off just as quickly as it sounded. Devlin waited, his heart thrashing against his ribcage. He felt nothing, not the pain in his jaw from clenching or the numbness in his hand from how tightly he gripped the firearm. His mind was focused into a single thread of consciousness. Fenna.

He was sensitive to every sound as he crept down the hallway. Every slap of the waves against the hull, every tiny claw against wood as the rats skittered through the pools of water...he envisioned it was her body careening into the sea or streams of her blood that bifurcated the deck under his feet. His very soul fractured at the thought of it.

A shadow flickered at the next door, a darkened silhouette that flashed across the threshold. Heavy footsteps and a muffled protest followed, along with a sharp slap of flesh against flesh.

"Keep her quiet," a voice harshly whispered. "We don't want him to come before we're ready—"

"This is madness," a second voice retorted, his tone leaking with anxiety. "We don't know if this will even work. If this ship goes down and she dies with us–"

"This will work," the first male interjected. Boots scuffled against the floor once again. "I know this will work. She wasn't standing outside of the captain's death bed for nothing. She was watching *him*."

Devlin stepped into the door frame, scanning the scene in front of him. Three men, each with their backs turned to the hallway, stood in a semi-circle around Fenna. Two with cutlasses clutched tightly in their hands, the last adjusting a kerchief he tied around her mouth. Fenna glanced over their shoulders, her bulging eyes unblinking as they landed on Devlin.

"What was your plan, then?" Devlin asked nonchalantly, as though commenting on the poor weather. He managed to steady his trembling hands by tracing the outline of the piston's barrel with a finger. "Kidnap a woman? Hold her down here while your ship overcomes with plague?"

The three men stiffened before whirling around. Devlin leaned against the door frame, slowly and deliberately studying each man. The one to the left was portly, his shirt a size too small and his pants a size too large. There were holes in the toes of his boots and his hair had begun to thin, most likely due to the diets sailors were required to keep.

No, not him.

The man in the center was wiry and lithe with a mop of blonde hair that hid his tall forehead. His expression was harried and feral, but not in the way Devlin preferred his crew to be.

No, not him either.

The man to the right was a fraction smaller than himself. He stood his ground despite the cutlass clasped tightly in his hand still trembling. He appeared edgy, almost twitchy, but his stare was arrogant and cruel. Cruel like a man who would use a woman as a bartering chip, Devlin mused.

He'll do nicely.

Devlin lifted his pistol, cocked back the flintlock, and pulled the trigger. The *bang* was deafening in the small space and, for a moment, the men looked around at each other in nervous relief. That was, until the man in the center fell face-first to the floor, blood spilling from the gunshot wound in the middle of his forehead.

The kerchief around Fenna's mouth sucked in with the deep inhale she took and shock opened the faces of the other two men. Devlin didn't move from his lean against the frame, but holstered the pistol in the next breath.

"Now, will one of you strapping lads tell me what your plan was or shall I guess?" Devlin paused to flick his eyes between the two men still blocking Fenna from him. A wild impatience rose inside of him in the silence. "Well? I don't like to be kept waiting."

"We found the girl outside of the captain's cabin," the portly man spouted, a thin sheen of sweat forming on his brow. "We thought— he thought— this ship is going to sink—"

"We want to bargain with you," the man on the right interrupted. Devlin swung his gaze over to him, brow arched in question. The man reached back and tugged Fenna forward, her eyes widening, if possible, even further. "We know this ship is sinking. It's taken far too much damage. And we know what you're here for, *Specter*."

Devlin clasped his hands at his front, attempting to give off even an ounce of power that radiated from Liddros. By the way the sweat was now rolling down the first man's temples, it was working. Devlin cocked his head. "None of my cannons have made contact. I wasn't going to sink your ship, just take the sick, but I'm certainly going to sink it now. You've tested my patience."

The second man drew his cutlass up, positioning the razor edge at her throat. Rage pounded through Devlin, heating his blood with every pulsing beat of his heart. "We want you to let us go," the man said, jutting his chin toward the hallway. "We want to get on a lifeboat and leave this ship, whether you sink it or not. We don't want the plague. No death, no pleading for time. You accept and we will let the woman go free."

Devlin dipped his head back and forth, as though in deep contemplation. "No," he responded simply, pushing his shoulder from the frame.

The man holding Fenna pressed the blade deeper into her neck and Devlin watched a trickle of blood cascade into the hollows of her collarbone. "No?" the man scoffed, shaking his head. "You are outnumbered, sir. There are two of us and–"

In the next heartbeat, Devlin grabbed the dagger he strapped near his cutlass and flicked it across the room. It lodged with a deep *thunk* into the sweating man's sternum. The man stumbled forward for two steps before sinking to his knees and collapsing into the pool of his colleague's blood. The two bodies shifted as the ship rocked to the side. Fenna lost her balance, stumbling further into the cutlass. Her cut deepened.

"You were saying?" Devlin asked. He took shallow, calming breaths to keep himself under control.

"I–I can kill her right now," the man managed to sputter out as the ship rocked again. A cannonball blasted through the hull, close enough that Devlin heard the wood splintering in its wake. Booker must have gotten fed up with the crew as well. Devlin almost smiled. "I'll do it. I'll cut her throat and then you'll have nothing."

Devlin took a single step forward, his boot slicking with the pooling blood. "You're going to let her go," he said softly, a dangerous glint entering his tone. "Because there are far worse things than death."

With a lunge, Devlin struck. He unsheathed the cutlass in a zing, swinging it upward with all of the force he could muster. The blade connected, metal against bone, and he knew he made his mark when the man dropped to the floor and let out an agonized bellow. The hand, still clutching his own cutlass, lay at Fenna's boots.

The man continued to scream as Devlin gestured with two fingers for Fenna to walk forward. She barely gave the man a glance as she passed, keeping her eyes fixed on Devlin. He reached for her, his hands clasping tightly around her upper arms.

"Are you— why didn't you stay on the ship?" His words turned biting, an instant regret when tears pricked at the corners of her eyes. He reached up to untie the kerchief around her mouth, letting it fall to the ground between their feet.

"I just wanted to see. I just wanted to—"

"Captain?"

Devlin looked over his shoulder, readying to run his cutlass through the next man who looked at Fenna the wrong way. He only relaxed a fraction when he saw that it was Booker.

"Captain, the ship is sinking. I've ordered the retreat, this inferno is disgusting. We've cleaned out the gunnery and the—" Booker stopped, leaning to the side to peer under Devlin's arm. "What happened here?"

The man at Devlin's back let out another battered moan.

"Booker, take Fenna back to my cabin. Lock her in and stand guard until I get back."

"I want— I can't— I want to stay with you," Fenna said quickly, her eyes searching and desperate.

Devlin stroked her cheek with his thumb, satisfaction ringing through him at the shiver that went down her spine. Liddros's words clanged through him...*bonded through realms and time*. He took in a breath, forcing his hand back to his side. "You'll go with Booker and you'll get off this ship. I have work to attend to."

It took all of his will to brush past her and, though he felt her eyes boring into the back of his skull, he didn't turn around. Her footsteps disappeared as Booker ushered her down the hallway and, only in that moment, was Devlin truly able to relax. He bent to a squat next to the man, whose glare could have poisoned a well of water if he tried hard enough.

"Just kill me," the man spat, the nub of his arm tucked tightly into his chest. Blood leaked from between his fingers, rivulets of red running to his elbow. "I will not be part of your crew."

Devlin's returning smirk was callous. "I will not kill you. As I said, there are far worse things than death."

The man blanched, lips parting in shock. "You can't take me without my consent. I have a choice–"

"Others have bartered with that choice, because I allowed them to have that choice," Devlin seethed, darting a hand out to clasp tightly around the man's open wrist. He let out a shout of pain. "You no longer have that. You will sit in the brig, surrounded by nothing, but rats and your own waste. When you come close to death, whether that be by your own doing or nature's, I'll revive you myself. You'll be down there so long that only Liddros will be able to save you. If he even remembers that you're there."

The man's eyes widened, fear flashing through.

"Welcome to *The Phantom Night*," Devlin said, hauling the man to his feet. "However long I want to keep you alive is your debt."

CHAPTER EIGHTEEN

FENNA

Murmured voices floating in from under the locked door pulled Fenna from her thoughts. Her dark, regret-filled, self-loathing thoughts. She had come so close to death, the small slice along her throat pinched as a reminder with every turn of her head. She quickly brushed the tears away from her swollen, red-rimmed eyes and took a shaky sip of water from the cup still on the table from breakfast.

Fenna tensed as the lock clicked open and heavy boot steps entered the cabin. She didn't turn around, decidedly keeping her eyes trained on the wake as *The Phantom Night* sailed further from the wrecked warship a league away. But she felt Devlin's eyes digging a hole into her spine when the door swung shut behind her. The cabin was silent; the strained air between them impenetrable. Fenna couldn't be certain she was even breathing.

"I told you to *stay on the ship*," Devlin started through gritted teeth. She could hear the seething anger with every punctuated syllable. "I told you to stay in this cabin where you would be safe."

"It isn't going to be possible for you to reprimand me any more than what I've already said to myself," Fenna said quietly, wrapping her arms around her chest. Her hands still trembled.

Devlin's sigh whistled through his nose. "Why?"

"Why what?"

"Why would you do that? You don't have experience with swords or pistols. You have no skills with fighting. Why—" He trailed off as his tone became increasingly more frantic. He took in another deep inhale. "Why would you do that?"

Fenna swallowed, thought just barely. "I wanted to see what it was like. I— I read all of the books. I knew all of the stories—"

"This is real life, Fenna! This isn't a damn story."

Fenna whirled around to face him, opening her mouth to scathingly reply, but tears pricked at the corners of her eyes at the sight of him. His tunic and forearms were stained with blood, his clenched hands still bore the cutlass. Though the blood on the blade had long dried, she imagined it dripping from the tip as he navigated the warship. His hair was disheveled, as though he had been ripping his hands through it. And suddenly, Fenna could no longer stop the deluge of tears that streamed down her cheeks.

Devlin's shoulders loosened as she cried and the nerve-wracking quiet that poured out of him only made her sob that much harder. The cutlass clattered to the floor and Devlin crossed the room to wash in the basin near the table. His hands were cool and damp when he reached her, clasping them gently around her shoulders.

"What's the matter?" he asked softly, wiping her cheeks with his thumbs. "This isn't about those men. You climb my ship enough that I know you suffer from the inability to regulate any self-preservation." He paused, bending down to look her square in the eye, his hands still cupped against her face.

Fenna sniffled. "I'm just tired, that's all." She attempted to pull away, but Devlin held her steadfast in his arms.

"No, you're not. Try again, but with more eye contact this time."

Her eyes brimmed with tears again and mortification bloomed hot when she realized they were dripping onto his thumbs. "It's just– you were right. I wasn't meant for this." She snuck her hands between his, covering her eyes with her palms. Her entire body shook with each shuddering breath.

Devlin's hands lowered to the crooks of her neck, pinning her loose locks of hair against her skin. "Tell me what you mean."

Minutes passed before Fenna was able to calm herself down long enough for words to be discernible. And Devlin waited patiently, the tips of his fingers curling and uncurling in a soothing pattern against the tops of her shoulders. She took in a long breath, lifting her eyes to the windows that lined the cabin. The warship was merely a slim column of orange-lined smoke in the distance.

"I'm weak," Fenna finally lamented. She felt drained and heavy, a soreness creeping into her lower back that she couldn't quite identify. "Those men saw me as weak...your crew sees me as weak...you—" She paused to swallow and she could have sworn needles had taken root in her throat. "I went on the ship, because I wanted to prove that I can. Because I know you didn't think I could handle it. And...and you were right."

At the very least, she had stopped crying. All that was left was her gummy eyes, blurred vision, and a rising desire to sink into the bowels of the ship and never resurface. She was somehow hollow and heavy at the same time. And she didn't dare slide her gaze over to meet his.

Devlin said nothing as he led her across the cabin, plunking her on the side of the bed. She sank into the mattress, allowing her knees to knock into one another. She barely felt the sharp dash of pain that shot up the back of her thighs. He observed her for another string of heartbeats, his persistent stare grating at her raw nerves.

He turned away from her, seemingly having decided she wasn't going to bolt for the cabin door, and grabbed a folded wash linen from his trunk at the foot of the bed. Fenna kept her eyes trained to her lap, studying the cotton threads of her breeches, as he submerged the linen in the basin. Water streamed from the hem as he squeezed the excess out before kneeling at her front, taking one of her wrists into his hand.

"I never thought you were weak," Devlin finally said, running the cloth up her forearm. She hadn't realized the sleeves of her tunic were glued against her skin, dried blood the adhesive. "Quite the opposite, actually. It takes an incredible strength to step in for those that they love."

There was a light quiver of doubt in her stomach, one that was accompanied by the shake of her head.

"You don't have to believe me, but I speak honestly," Devlin continued, dragging the cloth up to her collarbones. He was gentle around the base of her neck, where the cut still throbbed. "I told you that I kissed you that day, because I liked fierce things. While that's certainly true, I left out a valuable piece. I couldn't fathom someone as beautiful as you wielding that level of unshakable kindness in the face of danger. And that, Fenna Terrigan, can never be considered a weakness."

Fenna's eyes lifted at his words and her heart shuttered when they connected with his seafoam green ones. Her skin tingled where the feather-light touch of his fingers brushed against the column of her throat.

Looking back, Fenna didn't know who closed the space between them. Whether it was her or him or the two of them together. In the end, it didn't seem to matter anyways, because patience was no longer a virtue that she wanted to possess. All she knew was that she wanted

Devlin Cato so badly that she ached to her very bones. She wanted to be filled by him in every way possible.

Devlin's fingers were in her hair, her own threaded into the cotton of his tunic, tugging him impossibly closer to her. His tongue grazed at the seam of her lips and she parted with a soft moan that only seemed to amplify his own blistering need.

The kiss was dizzying and charged, a dance of tongue and teeth and skin that Fenna needed more of. Her nipples pebbled against her shirt as she hastily untucked his tunic from his breeches. Devlin tore his mouth away long enough to pull the tunic over his head, letting it fall into a pile near her feet, before descending on her once again.

Fenna couldn't keep her hands off of him even if she tried. She had read all sorts of passages that involved sex, had studied every word out of lustful curiosity. But she had never imagined it would be like this.

A flush worked up Devlin's muscled chest. Fenna wanted to trace the outline of it with her tongue. To make a new constellation from the freckles on his skin, one that was hers and hers alone.

Devlin slowed as he deepened the kiss and, for a fraction of a second, Fenna's mind cleared of all thought. It was just him that she tasted, him that stroked her tongue like it was the last thing he would ever devour. His hand skimmed down her chest and he pulled a moan out of her when his hand cupped the swell of her breast, his thumb grazing over a taut nipple.

"You're— you've never—" Devlin asked, leaning away to study her. Fenna wondered if she looked as messy and tousled as he did.

She shook her head. "No, no I've never—" She trailed off, self-consciousness thrumming through her. "Is that...is that a concern?"

Devlin's smile was devastating, as was the dimple that quirked the corner of his mouth. "Never." He skimmed her throat with the tip of his nose, planting soft kisses in the column of her neck. "Tell me what you want. I want to hear what you're comfortable with."

"Everything," was her immediate reply and Devlin chuckled, the ghost of his breath pebbling her skin. "I want everything."

His hands slipped lower, fingers dancing along the band of her breeches, and her blood heated to a boil. He plucked at her own tunic, wide eyes staring up at her in question. She nodded slowly, heart thundering a needful song against her sternum. His hands were slow as they glided over her spine, lifting her shirt over her head. Her back arched into his touch, her nipples dragging against the bare of his chest.

Devlin's lips replaced his hands, his tongue teasing her collarbones, then lower, laying wet kisses against the curve of her breast. He sucked gently on her nipple and a moan tumbled from her when he scraped it between his teeth. He quickly stood, releasing her from his mouth, and the cool air against her warm skin was a contradiction that she didn't bother to try and understand, she just knew it left her wanting.

Fenna's own skin felt too sensitive for her body as a shiver of desire bolted down her back, coming to rest at the base of her core. Her inner thighs slickened at the sight of Devlin's naked torso silhouetted against the light of the moon and his heavy-lidded stare boring into her own. He was just as desperate as she was and power, euphoric and satisfying, rose inside of her.

Devlin sunk a knee between her thighs and clasped a hand around the back of her head, tilting her neck back as his breath fanned along her swollen lips. Fenna gasped and he took the opportunity to kiss her again, sweeping his tongue against her own.

"I've had a never-ending, unquenchable need to taste you since the moment I laid eyes on you," he rasped against her mouth, threading his fingers tighter into her braid. "I can't think about anything else. I wake up in the middle of the night wishing my tongue was between your thighs. Please, tell me that I can."

Aching want pulsed, pushing away any worry that she wasn't enough. "Yes, please, yes."

A guttural groan escaped from Devlin's throat, low and husky. His lips pressed against the hollow of her throat, the valley of her breasts, the curve of her waist as he made his way down the front of her body. Hands skimmed and ghosted along her sides, prickling her skin and leaving her panting.

He tucked his thumbs into the band of her breeches and tugged, the fabric pulling over her hips and thighs. They were discarded, along with her boots and stockings, into another pile on the floor. Utterly forgotten.

Fenna's heartbeat was in her throat, vibrating down her bones and catching into the tips of her fingers and toes. She was naked before him, her first time being naked in front of anyone, and she tried not to squirm at the thought. But, from the darkened pleasure that flooded Devlin's eyes as he roved her body, that was exactly how he wanted her. A fiery desperation flamed inside of her, coiling in the apex of her thighs.

Devlin knelt at the side of the bed and Fenna stilled, watching intently as he hooked a thigh on his shoulder, baring her to him. "Do you like me on my knees before you?" he asked, leaning forward to caress her inner thigh with his lips before nipping at her. Fenna couldn't help the whimper that bubbled up from the heat of his breath against her sex. "Because I rather enjoy the view."

"Devlin," she gasped, back arching off the bed as Devlin descended on her.

He chuckled as he lapped at her entrance, but that laugh turned into a groan of desire as he clutched at her thighs and yanked her to the edge of the bed. Fenna was open-mouthed and panting as he slid his tongue inside of her, reaching upward to tweak her nipples. Her eyes clenched shut and her hand shot down to tangle in his hair. He deepened his kiss against her and Fenna felt another shot of arousal as she glanced between the valley of her breasts to see Devlin watching her, studying her.

He pulled his mouth away, a mewl of frustration whining out of her. "It's Captain Cato," he said with a devilish grin. A finger slickened along her slit, pressing gingerly between her thighs. Fenna bowed off the bed again as Devlin slowly slipped that finger inside of her. "Gods, you're so tight," he groaned, letting his forehead fall against her hip. He left a trail of kisses down her thigh as he curled his finger, pressing against her front wall. Fenna trembled, painfully at first, but easing to unimaginable pleasure as he carefully, patiently stretched her.

Once Fenna had begun to move against him, begging and pleading for reprieve, Devlin slipped a second finger in. Gods, she was so full. She was...everything. Her skin tightened around her as heat began to coil, sharp and fast, in her belly. Devlin laid a flat hand against her hip, holding her in place as he lowered his mouth to her clit. His strokes were firm and punishing, open-mouthed and wickedly perfect.

Fenna's body trembled as Devlin coaxed her to the edge of the cliff. Then, she fell. Devlin pulled unhurried and consuming convulsions out of her as she gripped at his shoulders, at his hair, at the linen covers that spanned the bed. Time stopped, stretching from one moment to the next. Fenna's breath caught in her throat as her inner muscles clenched around his fingers, as her arousal coated his chin. She saw the stars, she saw the constellations that she begged to form with him, and, for that moment, she allowed herself to tumble into the darkness beside him.

Devlin withdrew his fingers from her when she finished, leaving her unexpectedly hollow and empty. With widened eyes, she watched as he lifted his fingers to his mouth and sucked her orgasm off of them. His mouth quirked into a grin once more. "Just as I thought you would taste."

Fenna's core clenched as she sat up and Devlin stood from his position on the floor. His hardened length tented the front of his breeches and she didn't bother to attempt hiding the curious gaze she gave it. Her body finally began to calm, the dizzying pleasure subsiding.

"I won't take you tonight," Devlin said, bending forward to bracket his fists on each side of her hip. He kissed her, soft and slow. She tasted herself on his tongue, something she never thought would be so...sensual. "You'll be sore tomorrow." He planted kisses along her jaw, to her ear, and down the side of her neck.

Fenna reeled back, her brow furrowed. "What about you?" Her gaze dropped pointedly to his groin, where he still stretched the fabric around his hips. She imagined taking him in her mouth and she heated at the thought.

"Tonight was for you." A kiss to her ear. "I want you consumed and utterly breathless." A kiss on her shoulder. "I want you needing and begging for me." A kiss on her breast. "And when I do take you." He lifted his head to kiss her lips once more. "I'm not going to want to be gentle." He pulled away, his intense stare scrutinizing her. "And you're not going to want me to be either."

Chapter Nineteen

Devlin

"If you aren't going to pay attention today, then I don't know what we're doing this for," Devlin heard Iris snap for the fifth time in so many minutes. He barely hid his smile as Fenna sheepishly mumbled an apology that seemed half-hearted at best. He knew what she was looking at. He had felt her stare against the spot between his shoulders as he stood at the helm with Loma and Booker.

Devlin desperately wanted to return that stare, to show her that all he had been thinking about was the way she tasted, how erotic it was to have her clenching around him. No matter how many times he had spilled his own seed in the confines of his office, it hadn't been enough. But he swallowed back the urge when Liddros's words came to the forefront of his mind.

Fenna would age and die. Devlin would not.

And it took every piece of his being to pull himself away from her. They would have time, of course, but only limited amounts of it. Devlin knew it wasn't worth putting her through the horror of life at sea. More importantly, he knew that he wasn't worth the horror of life at sea. Subjecting her to that was more than he could take. There was no path forward for them, not one that didn't involve a sacrifice.

Unless...unless Devlin could find another Clair; one with the gift of knowledge that might be able to tell him where to turn, where to look. He had been searching for nearly one hundred years. He just didn't have another hundred more.

"The birds aren't acting right, Booker," Loma was saying as Devlin returned his attention to the two at the helm with him. Eye pressed tightly against the spyglass, her face was scrunched as she scanned the horizon. "There's another storm brewing somewhere around us."

Devlin's chest constricted as Booker scoffed, shaking his head. "You can't know that," he responded, dropping his stare to the compass in his hand before adjusting the wheel to the left. "Birds?"

Loma glared, dropping her spyglass to her side. "There are more ways to tell the weather is changing without hearing the first rumble of thunder amidst the darkened clouds." She didn't add *you bilge rat* at the end of the sentence, but Devlin knew her favorite insult hung loudly unsaid. "Mark my words, Booker, there will be another storm by the end of tomorrow night."

"If there's another storm by the end of tomorrow night, I'll lick your useless cunt myself—"

"Eat my ass, Booker Colby—"

"Quiet," Devlin barked, irritation rifling through him. Loma and Booker immediately clamped their lips shut, but by the tense silence behind him, he had a distinct feeling they continued to glower at one another.

He slid his gaze over the nearest sandbar, watching the seaweed drift on the current past it. Crabs scuttled over the rotten fish carcasses that had washed onto the sandy slopes. The sickly sweet scent of decay and algae wafted along the salty breeze as Devlin took a deep breath in.

Loma was right, of course. The seabirds that typically nestled on the mainmast were oddly startled, bristling their feathers and refusing to settle. A fair few had already taken flight toward the continent, seeking shelter in the safety of the harbors and bays that littered the shoreline still out of sight. It was certainly unusual considering the only coverage was the wispy, white clouds that lazily drifted across the otherwise clear, blue sky.

The cold season was one of the worst seasons for sea storms.

"Booker, have the crew batten down the hatches and have Waller confirm that the guns are tied down," Devlin finally said, shifting away from the side of the ship. He didn't miss the smug grin Loma sent Booker, one that had Booker's face grow red with anger. "Loma, take in the mizzen sail and turn course toward the storm when you see the waves take form."

Loma lifted her chin and crisply nodded toward Devlin. *See?* She seemed to say to Booker, raising an eyebrow before she slunk toward the quarterdeck in a deliberate, cat-like walk.

Booker frowned, his narrow-eyed glare fixed on her back as she left. He raised his hand to rub his neck, peering toward Devlin. "What of your prisoners in the brig?"

"What of them?" Devlin asked, angling a sharp gaze onto his quartermaster.

Booker dragged his hands through his hair, rocking back and forth on his heels. "It's a rare thing that we have them aboard," he started slowly, his fingers plucking at the dirt that stained his tunic. "While I have my doubts about Loma's storm prediction, keeping them in the brig during a storm seems like a waste of man-power, and—"

"They stay in the brig," Devlin cut in firmly as he pushed up his sleeves. His mouth dried at the sight of his tattoos curling in tight swirls around his forearms. They had darkened since his visit with

Liddros and he couldn't help but envision being swallowed whole by them. If Booker noticed the shift in his demeanor, he didn't comment on it.

"Captain, those are able-bodied men and—"

"They stay," Devlin repeated, slower and steadier this time. He moved toward Booker, invading the space his quartermaster occupied, his jaw set and brow tight. "In the brig. If they get swept off the ship, or worse, decide to throw themselves from it...I lose any and all leverage I have over Liddros."

Booker blanched, rapidly blinking as he reeled his head back. "You mean to keep the men on the ship as weight against the God of the Sea?" He glanced around, lowering his voice as though Liddros himself would overhear. "Have you gone mad? There is no bargaining with him, there is only—"

"He will bend when I offer him concessions. Fourteen concessions, might I add."

Booker shifted on his feet, discomfort flashing across his face. "What has the woman filled your head with? I thought we were look-ing for a Cognizant, one that could find a way to break this fucking curse without a human sacrifice. You always said—"

Devlin's hand shot out, clasping tightly on the front of Booker's tunic. "We are out of time to look for a Cognizant. Clairs have been in the wind for centuries now."

Booker tore himself away from Devlin's grip. "We have centuries to look," he hissed through gritted teeth. "I became your second in command, because I knew you would never stand to sacrifice someone for our sins. That you would give the men a choice in their lives, in their years." He paused to scoff, taking a step back, and realization dawned on his face. "We don't have centuries, do we?"

Devlin couldn't quite swallow his pained grimace. He curled his hands into fists before straightening them again and he was contrite to notice they were trembling. "No, Booker, no we don't."

Booker was quiet for a long moment, biting at his already short fingernails. "There have been rumors on the ship," he began slowly, glancing uneasily around the stern deck, "that stemmed from some of the men who spent time in the region we picked her up at. Rumors of a girl with...odd abilities."

Devlin wished Booker would stop talking. He didn't think he had the ability to lie to his quartermaster, not after all of these years.

"What is she to you?"

Devlin sighed dejectedly, a sensation of numb emptiness dropping into his stomach. "Never you mind what she is to me," he muttered, scrubbing a hand down his face.

That response seemed to only enrage Booker further. "Is she one of them?"

The question was so pointed that Devlin knew he could no longer afford to evade an answer. He took his time, running a finger along his lower lip as he thought. "Yes and no," he responded slowly, his stomach tensing with the growing desire to order Booker to the crew. He knew that would only fuel the resentment currently building behind his friend's eyes. He took a steely breath and continued on. "She isn't a Cognizant, but I suspect her to be an Audient."

Booker's features widened and brightened. "Captain, this changes everything—"

"This changes nothing," Devlin clarified with a stiff shake of his head. "She didn't know what she was until weeks ago. She doesn't have a handle on her own gift." He dropped to a whisper, so low that Booker had to lean in to hear him over the shouts of the men drawing in the sails. "And if the king is notified that we are harboring a Clair, the entire might of the continent's navy will come down on us."

As if by design, Iris clapped out, "Fenna, for Liddros's sake, pay attention when you do that. I thought you slipped a knife between my fucking eyes."

Booker watched Fenna from over his shoulder, assessing her with a bitter smile, and Devlin knew he had won...for the moment. "Clairs are impervious to the gods, then? Is that why she doesn't carry a debt?"

Devlin opened and closed his mouth, unsure of how to answer. "I— don't know. There's quite a bit at play that is hard to understand."

Booker squared his shoulders to Devlin, tearing his gaze away from Fenna. "And the men in the brig?"

"An offering," Devlin said, leaning a hand against the wheel. The pull of the current straining the helm was familiar to him, and it helped to ground his thoughts. "Nothing more."

Booker let out a long breath. "I'm not thrilled with it, captain, you know that. But I trust you." He snorted humorlessly. "I trust you more than Loma. The birds are telling her a storm is incoming? Please."

Devlin was sure Booker was eating his words. By the morning, the wind had churned the sea into a torrential swirl of powerful currents that threw the ship around like a child's toy in the bath. As the afternoon approached, the air grew thick with moisture. The charge that ran through it was enough for Devlin's hair to stand on end.

Some of the men watched in awe as black built against the sky and the rainfall became so pronounced that it streaked the clouds into a haze that blurred the horizon. The other men watched with trepidation and increasingly clammy skin, making sure ropes were secured to the masts to tie around their waists in a moment's notice. Even those who had pledged their years to Liddros did not want to be thrown overboard.

The storm was on them by the evening and Devlin felt his bones vibrate with the force of the thunder shaking the deck beneath him. Though the winds whipped and the rain pelted down on them hard enough to plaster their hair to their heads, it wasn't nearly as bad of a storm as the last one.

Devlin thought of Fenna and briefly wondered if she was covering his cabin with her sick. He pushed the thought out of his mind, bracing against the helm as *The Phantom Night* dipped into a valley between waves. Water crashed onto the deck, sweeping over the men, flooding into their boots and drenching up to the hems of their breeches.

"I like my cunt licked slow," Loma shouted to Booker over the shrieking winds. She didn't bother to hide the cock of her head or the look of superiority that radiated through the rain. "You can push your tongue inside of me and—"

The rest of her statement, as well as Booker's responding string of curses, was lost as the ship careened down a cresting wave and slammed against the sea. The jarring violence of it knocked several men off of their feet, sending them tumbling through the slick of water still blanketing the quarterdeck. Their bellows of panic ricocheted off the masts, reverberating up to Devlin loud enough that his attention was peeled from the helm.

A handful of the crew were struggling against a rope, attempting to yank the sail back into submission. A gale blew and they scattered, boots slipping against the wet wood.

"Take the helm!" Devlin shouted to Booker, who stumbled past Loma to brace against the wheel. "I'm going to the quarterdeck."

The ship rocked again as Devlin took to the stairs and he gripped the railing hard enough that splinters pinched against his palm. He rushed toward the mainmast, sure-footed and steady despite the maelstrom around them.

"Captain! We've got a handle on—" a man named Locke Wither shouted through the downpour, wiping the briny water from his eyes with the back of his wrist. He didn't finish as the wind pulled against the sail, ripping the rope from his hands. Devlin shot forward, grasping the corded fibers and hauling a foot against the trunk of the mast to keep him in place. He pulled down with all the strength he could muster, his muscles straining and tense.

"Tie it down!" Devlin called back, squinting through the deluge that pounded against every inch of him. "Against the—"

Crack

A rope snapped from the mast behind Devlin and there was just enough time for a shout of warning to permeate through the claps of thunder before his back burned. He clenched his eyes shut against the pain, stars bursting behind his lids. By the luck of the sea, Devlin held onto the rope in his hands. The rain slid through the tear in his tunic and down his bare skin, stinging the open wound. He knew without a doubt the flailing rope had caught him in the back.

Shuddering breaths sawed through his flared nostrils. His limbs trembled and cramped as he struggled to regain control of his body.

"Captain! Oh, gods..."

Booker was at his side in the next moment and Devlin assumed he saw the accident from the helm. "Loma is at the wheel. I've got this. You need to clean up your wound."

"After the storm," Devlin managed to say through gritted teeth, though his shoulders had already begun to hunch and his breaths came in panting gasps.

"Your back is gone, captain," Booker yelled over a clap of thunder. Lightning flashed before him, brightening the dark brown of his eyes. "Liddros might not let you die, but recovering from blood loss isn't going to be a damn promenade, even for you."

Locke Wither stepped in, hoisting the rope from Devlin's hands. "I've got this one, captain. Go. It's just a storm."

Devlin hesitated for another moment, but Booker pushed him toward the cabin. He groaned as he bent at the waist, the full amount of his pain flooding him at full force. There was someone under his arm as the ship rocked to the side and his stomach flipped with nausea as they led him toward the stern.

He took in one more shuddering breath, his vision narrowing into black tunnels and his mind blurring with dizziness before darkness finally pulled him under.

CHAPTER TWENTY

FENNA

"What happened?" Fenna demanded, lifting her skirts to cross the room. She kept her hand firmly planted on the table as a member of the crew led Devlin into the cabin. Despite the seasickness rippling through her, she swallowed back the sour taste of vomit clawing up her throat to tear the covers from the bed. "Put him here."

Devlin was unceremoniously dumped onto the mattress, his flayed back open and profusely bleeding down his sides. He was unconscious, his breathing still labored yet even, and he let out a low groan when his back stretched with the sudden movement.

"Sail rope snapped," the crewmember said, straightening to a stand and pushing his wet, wind-swept hair from his eyes. "Caught him unexpected in the back. He fainted on the walk here." The man hesitated, water sluicing from the hem of his tunic and pooling at his feet. He glanced out of the window, where rain still lashed against the glass panes, and slid his gaze toward Devlin. "Do you require anything else? I need to get back to the deck."

Fenna's eyes went wide. "Wh—I'm sorry. I don't—" But he was already gone, the cabin door banging shut behind him with another rock of the ship.

Fenna was numb, her mind blank as she bit her bottom lip, frowning down at Devlin. The mattress was already stained red with no indication that it was going to stop on its own. She shuffled forward, gripping the edge of the bed to keep from falling over. The edge of the bed where he had...she softly shook her head.

He had been avoiding her, even though she had still been ordered to share his room, and she knew it. The feeling broke a piece of her that she hadn't realized was there.

Fenna sucked in a deep breath and took a moment to think. She read a book once. Well, skimmed it out of curiosity really. It was a lifetime ago now; when the bookshop was empty, the tea was made, and she had nothing else to do. She didn't realize it was about wounds and slammed it shut with a turned stomach.

She peered around uneasily, ignoring the tenseness in her shoulders at the sight of Devlin's bloody back. She needed alcohol to clean the wound, that much she could remember. The captain didn't drink much, or often, but Fenna had seen an old bottle of *fion* kept hidden in the top drawer of his desk. The cork had begun to disintegrate and the glass was covered in a thick blanket of dust, but it might do the trick.

Fenna stumbled out of the cabin, slipping and sliding toward the desk. Water had begun to seep in, leaking under the seam of the door. Shouts echoed across the quarterdeck, followed closely by ordering bellows from Booker, as the wind careened through the ship. But she ignored that too.

She kept her mind solely fixed on the task at hand. Get to the desk, grab the *fion*, and somehow make it back to Devlin's bedside without breaking the bottle...or her neck. The ship dipped once more, sending Fenna pitching into the corner edge of the desk. An involuntary hiss of pain shot from between her clenched teeth as she rubbed at her hip, sure there would be a marking there by morning.

The contents of the desk clattered around as a large wave crashed against the small window. Fenna winced, half-expecting the panes to give way. When they didn't, and the knots in her lower belly retreated just enough for her to move again, she reached for the top drawer.

The bottle of *fion* was tucked in the back, behind an old, faded compass, a set of well-used quills, and a few of the brass instruments that typically resided on the shelves to her left. She rifled past them, grasping the neck of the short bottle and pulling it from the drawer as the ship rolled again. Stumbling back, Fenna managed to keep herself from falling over by clutching onto the heavy chair that sat behind her. The glass bottle clanked dangerously against the desk.

As soon as the ship righted and jolted forward, the tucked sails still pulling taut with a gust of wind, Fenna was off. Using the shelves lining the far wall, she stumbled her way back into the cabin, collapsing onto the edge of the bed. The lashing rain had slowed and, though the waves still churned along the wake of *The Phantom Night*, the clouds above them had begun to break apart.

Liddros, she hoped it would be over soon.

The glass bottle looked even older than Fenna originally thought it was and it took her a few minutes to pry the cork from the opening. Blood still trickled from the wound at a disconcerting clip, but she blotted most of it clean with a stained rag. The laceration was deep enough that she spotted bone and fibers from the rope had embedded into the flesh.

Fenna hesitated, the *fion* held just above his back, the mouth of the bottle tilted downward. Amber liquid sloshed within the container, but still, she held steady. Doubt settled in her mind, tightening her ribs and quivering her fingers. She had only skimmed the pages of that book, and she wasn't entirely sure what she was holding was *fion*. She shook her head and steeled her spine.

Either this would work or it wouldn't, but she did know the wound required cleaning. Devlin kept still for the first few seconds that the *fion* dripped onto his back, but as the ship rocked in the direction the mouth of the bottle was facing, the alcohol doused the wound like a waterfall.

Devlin's eyes flew open as a shout of pain escaped his pursed lips. He didn't seem to know where he was, his stare scanning wildly around him as though trying to get his bearings. His back pushed upward with his panting breaths and his knuckles whitened when his hands clenched around the linen blanketing the mattress. He writhed as Fenna patted the wound dry with a second stained cloth and his gaze finally slid to her, his brow sheen with salty rain and sweat.

"Where am I?" he asked stiffly, a stinging tremor lacing his tone. "What happened?"

"You got hit in the back by a broken rope," Fenna said. She attempted to keep her tone neutral, but she felt a rising grate of irritation within her. It was the first time Devlin had looked at her in days.

His movements were stiff, though seemingly from anger rather than pain, as he tried to push himself off of the mattress. "Thanks for the assistance, but my crew still needs me." There was a hardened edge to his voice, but it still didn't hide his agonized grunt. His nostrils flared as his wound split, the flesh Fenna just cleaned coating with blood again.

"Lay down," she snapped, leaning forward to shove his shoulders to the bed, "you're in no condition to help your crew." Her stomach gave a traitorous lurch at the feeling of his bare skin beneath her fingertips, but she pushed it aside. "You'll likely just get in the way. You passed out and had to be carried here after it happened."

"I'm not going to die," Devlin scoffed with a roll of his eyes.

"You may not," Fenna retorted, padding the linen against the flayed border of his wound, "but it'll still make a terrible recovery if this gets infected from the fibers stuck in your back."

Devlin's stare lacked any of the warmth he had shared from the nights before and he turned to fix his gaze on the wall at the head of his bed. "Pick them out then. I certainly don't have all day."

Fenna sucked a tooth as she leaned over his back, carelessly pinching a thread between her forefinger and thumb, and plucking it from his wound. He hissed a string of curses under his breath, whirling his head back around to glare at her.

"Carefully," he barked, his mouth drawn and his expression sour. "I may not die, but I can still feel what you're doing."

Fenna stood from the edge of the bed, tossing the dirty rag onto the floor. She knew he would hate it, he hated clutter. "I'm doing the best I can. I have no healer training and here you are..." She trailed off to take a deep, angry breath. "I don't know why you're pushing me away, maybe you got what you wanted from me. But I can avoid you for the next twenty-five years, if that's what you want."

She took a step away, but before she could take another, a hand wrapped tightly around her wrist. She glanced down, her surprise shifting into hesitation, and she fastened a mask of indifference over her face before lifting her gaze.

"No," Devlin mumbled, his voice thick. The column of his throat bobbed when he swallowed. "Please stay."

Fenna's heart thudded as she stared down at him, studying the hunch of his shoulders and the vacancy in his green eyes. She stayed where she was, an expectant lift to her brows. Devlin let out a deep sigh, one that emptied his chest completely. "You're right, I have been avoiding you," he went on, releasing Fenna's wrist from his grip. "I— it's complicated."

Crossing her arms over her chest, Fenna continued to glare down at the captain, pushing back any feelings of sympathy for the wound in his back. "That's not good enough."

Devlin gritted his teeth as he shifted and blood poured from his wound again. He collapsed to the mattress in a huff of irritation. "Would you accept that my past and the curse on this ship are tangling things between us in a way that makes it nearly impossible to unravel?"

"No."

He sighed again, though this time, the skin pinched at the corners of his eyes. Exhaustion seemed to sweep over him and his gaze darted around the room, as though he expected an unknown force to save him. Fenna knew that look, the one where she wished a hole would open up and devour her, and she was unhappy when an aching tug of empathy swelled within her.

"I— I had a partner once...a woman," Devlin started, though he trained his gaze on the view of the sea behind her. "Her name was Verda. I— over one hundred and fifty years ago I was a lieutenant on a warship that served the king's grandfather. She was originally a barmaid who sold herself to the galley to pay off her father's debts. We ignored one another for a while, but those sorts of attractions always come to the light."

Fenna shifted from one foot to the other, biting her inner cheek as he went on.

"It was good between us for a few weeks, but Verda had a...blood-thirstiness in her that wasn't easily satiated. She would beg the captain, my brother, to port on days of executions, because she wanted to watch." His gaze turned inward, eyes squinted, as though he were struggling to recall a memory long suppressed. "It turned into a game for her, one that always ended with us in bed together. It didn't take long for the executions to no longer hold her attention and she turned to the men in the brig for entertainment. She was...relentless and I couldn't help but become tangled deeper into her web of highs and lows."

Fenna's stomach churned, so similarly to the sea beyond the windows. The rain had finally cleared and all that remained was the streaks of water that ran in rivulets down the glass. Tall, gray clouds still littered the sky and shimmering light peeked through the layers, reflecting brightly off the white foam crests of the waves. The shouts of the men were muffled through the closed cabin door, though they seemed far less distressed now that the gales had passed.

"The warship hit a reef that stripped a hole into the keel; there was nothing we could do. When that happened, Verda was in the galley and the knife that was near her slid from the table, catching her in the side. I was scouring the ship while the men evacuated into the row boats, eventually finding her down in the kitchens covered in her own blood. I— I begged for a god, any god, to save her. I promised that I would do anything. And one answered."

"Liddros," Fenna said quietly, shaking her head as she sank down onto the edge of the mattress.

"Yes, Liddros. He made me a deal. My soul in his employ in exchange for Verda's healing." Devlin scoffed, and then grimaced at the pull of the muscles in his back. "I was a fool."

Fenna reached out to grab his hand and he glanced down at it in surprise. "You aren't a fool for wanting to save the woman you loved."

"No, I was a fool for thinking that she would stay with me when I did. She showed me who she was and I didn't believe her." He tightened his grip on her hand and her heart quivered in response. "I was not the only one who was involved with her. You remember how I said my brother was the captain..."

Fenna blanched, her lips parting. "No. They wouldn't— she didn't— your own brother?" She thought about Dasos and her quivering heart slammed to a stop. "How could they?"

Devlin smiled, but it didn't quite reach his eyes. "As I said, Verda was relentless. She could get any sick sap to do what she wanted, when she wanted it done. There wasn't much one could do against it."

Fenna contemplated him for a moment before withdrawing her hand back into her lap. His eyes dropped, pinging back-and-forth between his empty palm and hers. "Did Liddros tell you how to break the curse?"

Devlin stilled. "No, he didn't," he finally said, his tone slow and carefully crafted. There was enough hesitation in his voice that Fenna narrowed her eyes onto him. "I wanted to find a Cognizant, a type of Clair who can sort through future threads to see different outcomes. I— Booker and I have been searching for over one hundred years."

Fenna tilted her head to the side, increasingly aware that her need for information was blossoming fast and hard within her. "I don't know how I can help, but I want to." She leaned toward him to look at his wound. The blood had stopped flowing, leaving it thick and clotted within the split of his flesh. Gently, she reached forward and plucked another fiber from the gash.

Devlin stiffened, clearly awaiting the pain, before he relaxed enough to shake his head. "There is nothing you can do. I will continue to sail these seas long after you pass on from this life."

"Not unless I challenge for more years, right? I could do that. I could stay here with you and help find more Clairs to break your curse." She pulled another fiber from his wound and he hissed under his breath.

"Fenna, your debt didn't take."

Her head flinched back, hand stilling just above his shoulders. "What do you mean?"

"I— Liddros, he didn't accept your years. You are not bound to me like the others are."

Fenna glanced around, searching the cabin for answers as though the worn rug under her feet or the pitcher of water on the table would be the one to provide it for her. "I'm not bound to you? Does that mean I can go home?"

Devlin's swallow was loud and thick. His chin dropped to his chest and a sigh emptied out of him once more. "Yes, that means you can go home if you wish to."

Her hand flew up and she clutched at the laces of her stays, twirling them around her fingers. The thought of seeing Imogen, of sleeping in the bed she had been birthed in, of slipping her toes in the waters of the cove, and climbing to the plateau that sat high above the rocky shoreline. An air of readiness shifted in her lungs and she licked her lips, almost tasting the hope upon them.

Then, Fenna thought of the members of her town and how they had tormented her. She thought of the wavering looks, how parents would scuttle their children to the other side of the square to keep them away from her. She remembered the jealous glares from the women and the lustful thoughts from the men, how she couldn't stop them from infiltrating her mind, no matter how hard she tried.

She looked down at her hands, the bubble of hope now gone. Her shoulders drooped and she couldn't help the grim twist of her mouth as she slid her gaze toward Devlin. She hadn't realized he was watching her.

"And Dasos? What happens to him if I return home?"

Devlin sighed, scraping a hand down his face. "As long as you remain on this ship, I will consider his debt paid. But the moment you leave, I will be forced to find him. Liddros will force me to find him."

Fenna nodded, pushing herself from the edge of the bed. She walked toward the windows, studying the waves, the reappearance of the gulls, and the break of the storm clouds now off in the distance. She breathed in, smelling the waxed wood and old parchment that was Devlin, and blew out the breath through her mouth. Resolve straightened her spine.

"Then I'll stay here," she finally said, turning to look at Devlin over her shoulder. "I'll stay here and finish out his debt. In the meantime, perhaps we can find a Cognizant that will know a way to break your curse."

Devlin was quiet for a long minute and, for the first time, Fenna was having a hard time reading the look he angled toward her. Her determination wavered, leaving her wondering whether he was going to tell her that he didn't want her to stay.

Instead, he let his chin tilt toward the ceiling, the locks of his dark hair nearly brushing against the flaying flesh that split his back. "Your brother didn't deserve you," he finally said, "but I am sorry that I didn't give you the chance to say goodbye to him."

Fenna curled into the armchair that night, a book splayed open in her lap, allowing Devlin space to heal from his injury. But she woke the next morning, warm and confused, to find herself in the bed and nestled into his chest with his arm wrapped protectively around her waist.

The book had been placed on the table, dog-earred at the exact page she had fallen asleep.

Chapter Twenty-One

Fenna

"Give us a story then, love," a man named Atwell Ramsey said to Fenna, shooting her a wide, toothless grin that was nearly as bright as the afternoon sun above them. He untangled the rope as he looked up at her, his eyes squinted against the brightness of the sky. Sweat gathered in the contours of his skin and the intense rays glistened off his tanned, oily face. "We want to hear another one."

"Another one?" Fenna laughed, adjusting herself on the overturned crate she used as a seat. "What could you possibly want to hear another one for?"

She was lighter than she had been in days. Perhaps it had been waking that morning to find that Devlin moved her into his bed at some point overnight. It could have been the steamy kiss they shared moments later, one that heated her very core. Alternatively, the sun was warm on her skin and it cast her auburn hair in a golden glow. The salty breeze was calm and, for the first time, she was enjoying the gentle rocking of the ship against the sea.

"Begging your pardon, miss," another man named Dane Rassler interrupted, wrenching on a rope to hoist a sail into place, "but maybe you'll tell us about the Blood Singer?" He grinned sheepishly. "I quite like that one."

"It's not romantic at all," a third man, Nyle Asema, complained, sweeping a glare toward Dane. He paused to take a long gulp of water from the pouch resting at his feet. "And Butcher had nightmares for three days after she told it last time."

"It's not my fault he didn't listen to the story," Dane argued, tying the rope off before wiping the sweat from his temple. "If he did, he would have known that the Blood Singer is afraid of water and he would have been perfectly safe on the ship."

"The Blood Singer isn't real—" Fenna started, but she was interrupted by Atwell.

"I like romance stories just as much as the next bloke, but if we only wanted to listen to stories that were romantic, then we would never expand our critical skills beyond what our brains are currently capable of."

What. Fenna furrowed her brow, opening her mouth to speak once again.

"If we are going to debate about the ethics of expanding our critical skills, then shouldn't we be discussing our roles in repeating stories rather than being told new ones?" Dane replied breathlessly. He snagged the water pouch from Nyle, his thick neck tilting back to take a drink.

"Fenna just read a chapter from the captain's personal books that said it took multiple readings for someone to gain the ability for repetition." Nyle snatched back the water pouch and tied it to his waist, where it bounced off his slim thigh. "Therefore, she can tell the same story to us multiple times before we understand the true scope of its meaning."

"I—" Fenna began again, wanting to interject that she was willing to tell more than one, but she was interrupted yet again.

"I can accept the argument for multiple readings, but it doesn't take a Cognizant to explain to you that romance stories don't require much thought."

"Romance stories give us proper insight into our perceived notion of communication with our partners and renew our belief that life has meaning beyond ourselves," a fourth man, Greeley Fitch, jumped in.

Atwell and Dane stared at him, their mouths ajar and their brows furrowed. "You don't know that. You don't even *have* a partner," Dane bit out, his words nearly swallowed by the flapping sails under the renewed sea breeze.

"*You* don't know that," Greeley said, exasperation marring his tone. By the tilt of his head and the jut of his chin, Fenna thought he appeared mildly offended.

"You've been on this ship for fifty fucking years, Greeley," Atwell stated, folding his withered arms over his chest. "Of course we know that."

Greeley narrowed his eyes, pinching his features. "Then I'll be ready for one, because I'll have known the importance of putting in the hard work to build the correct foundations."

"You're all fucking idiots," Iris called from above. Fenna looked up to see her tawny, freckled face peering over the side of the crow's nest. "Every single one of you."

"What say you, Iris?" Dane shouted toward her, crinkling his nose as he squinted an eye shut to fend against the bright sun. "Romance or something different?"

Iris was quiet for a moment, contemplating. "I— I did enjoy hearing the story of the Blood Singer." Dane sent a mollified look to Greeley and Nyle. "But that doesn't mean that I would dislike hearing a romance story."

Nyle bowed his head in a silent prayer of thanks to Iris.

"You've made monsters out of them," a quiet voice said in Fenna's ear.

Fenna started, having not heard footsteps whisper across the deck. She glanced up, surprise flickering over her face when she saw Esta silhouetted in the golden afternoon light. "I've only been reading to them while they work," she replied, stiffening as she leaned away. She couldn't pinpoint the reason why, but defensiveness bricked a wall at her back.

Esta's smile was small as she lowered onto the overturned crate next to Fenna. "I just mean they've never been interested in things like this before." Her hands clasped in her lap. Fenna took a moment to study her long, thin fingers and full lips. She knew that Esta and Devlin had been together in the past. A bolt of jealousy flashed as Esta spoke again. "Most of the men signed onto the king's navy as young boys to assist their family's bills. They never learned to read or write, this is all they've known. You've given them a gateway into new worlds and new ways of thinking that they wouldn't have access to otherwise."

Fenna glanced back at the men, who were still in the throes of debating one another on the importance of romantic literature. "And what do you think?" she asked, swinging her gaze to Esta.

"In my past life, I taught in a learning house in the capital," Esta replied softly, a wistful and longing gleam entering her eye. "I made my choice to chase a sailor I met across the sea and I must live with it now. But all of these years later, I still harbor hope that the men of our world will take an interest in reading like I once had."

Fenna's heart twinged as she plucked at a crease in her skirt. "The characters in the books I read were my first friends. I didn't have many of those in the town I grew up in, but I had my books. I worked in a shop after aging out of the learning house. Reading and storytelling are a part of me. I don't think they'll ever fade."

Esta's hair ruffled in the breeze, brushing over her bare shoulders. "I should hope not. Even those of us in the shadows have come to enjoy hearing you tell them."

Fenna was unexpectedly struck with an intense sense of recognition toward Esta, one that only a woman to a woman could share. "You know, Devlin has quite the trove of books himself. I'm happy to give you some recommendations. If you feel the urge to read again, I should say."

Esta seemed pleasantly surprised, the corners of her lips lifting. "I can't imagine the captain would be pleased with his personal books being passed around the crew."

"You may be right," Fenna said with a returning grin and a shake of her head. "I doubt he realizes that I've snuck half of his books from the shelves to read when he thinks I'm cleaning."

Esta studied her for a moment, her eyes darting across Fenna's face. "He knows," she finally said. She stood from her perch on the crate as Fenna sent her an incredulous stare. "I should get to the galley to assist with dinner preparations. Coleridge wants to make fish stew for the men tonight, but he isn't quite as willing to ensure all of the bones have been removed from the fish."

Fenna nodded as Esta squeezed her shoulder, the tapping of her boots fading toward the staircase that led to the decks beneath the ship. She returned her attention to the men at her front, who were sending her expectant looks. "What?" she asked, curling a stray lock of hair behind her ear.

"We've decided that it's high time we allow you to tell us a new story," Atwell said, though by the grumbling eyerolls from Greeley and Dane alike, she had a feeling that it wasn't a belief that was shared.

Fenna barely contained her snort of laughter. "And did you decide on what kind of story?"

"A romance," Nyle said, vindication thrumming through his tone. "Though we're happy to have it be secondary, if need be."

"No fucking stories, you all have been gallivanting on the captain's ship long enough!"

The men groaned their responses as Loma marched towards the group, an apple in her hand. She took a bite, the juice running down the thick of her chin, as she surveyed every one of them individually. She didn't quite meet Fenna's eye. "Hard to starboard, captain's orders. The mizzen sails need to be released to catch the wind."

"Hard to starboard?" Greeley asked defiantly. "The continent is hard to starboard. Where could we possibly be going?"

Fenna lifted her gaze to Loma, who seemed to actively be avoiding her eye contact now. "If you want to question the captain, be my guest. He says hard to starboard, so we hard to starboard." Loma crunched on the apple one final time before tossing it over the side of the ship. She spun on the toes of her boots and marched away, taking the stairs to the helm two at a time once she reached them.

Unease wriggled like a worm in the pit of Fenna's stomach, prickling the back of her scalp. She pressed her lips in a tight line, absent-mindedly biting the bottom one. Loma was manning the helm herself, Booker nowhere in sight. While that was an odd sentiment on its own, Fenna also realized that she hadn't seen Devlin on the deck in a few hours either. It was fairly normal that he assisted the crew with the ropes or studied a map over Loma's shoulder.

Something wasn't right. Fenna wasn't able to shake the feeling of it.

She headed toward the captain's quarters, stepping into the shadows of the narrow hallway that led toward the office door. It was shut, though not latched, and Fenna was inches away from pushing it open when angry voices trickled through the gap between the door and frame. She paused, hand resting on the grainy wood and tilted her head to better hear.

"She is a distraction, captain," Booker said, his voice seething and angry. There was a sharp slap of parchment being tossed onto the desk, followed by a deep sigh. "Liddros is going to become impatient again. We need to act on this—"

"There is no distraction to be had, Booker. I apologized before about my abrupt change in plans, but I truly believe—"

"Not three days ago you were saying it was imperative that we sacrificed the men in the brig to Liddros. That it would buy you time and the ability to break the curse. Now, I was hesitant when you said that they were the ones to do it, but you've never given me a reason to not trust you."

Fenna blanched, shaking her head, and her spine turned to ice beneath her skin. The men in the brig? Surely he didn't mean...Devlin couldn't have... She wracked her brain, trying to think when the last time she had ventured that deep into the ship was. Certainly not in the last few days. Even so, she actively avoided the brig like it was plagued. Lanterns barely lit the iron-clad cell, making it hard to navigate. The musky, rotten stench of stale, pooled water and rats only added to the hair-raising aura.

Devlin sighed and Fenna imagined him pressing his fingers to his temple, the way he did when he was frustrated. "I cannot keep her on this ship and sacrifice those men to Liddros, I just cannot. Even if that means—"

"Even if that means subjecting the rest of us to this ship? You aren't thinking clearly, captain."

"You were more than willing to be subjected to this ship the moment you became my quartermaster. And you've been at my side for nearly one hundred and twenty-five years now. What has changed?" Devlin snapped.

"You changed!" Booker pushed back. A chair scraped across the wooden floor. "The captain I knew would have never allowed a woman to take on the debt of her brother, would have never locked her in your cabin overnight, would have never–"

"There are pieces at play here that you do not understand," Devlin interrupted. Though his tone was firm and final, Booker pressed on.

"Then help me understand them." When Devlin said nothing, Booker sent a whistling sigh through his nose. "I believe it is high time we bring Fenna back to the continent. You've had your fun, captain. Take the last few days to have whatever time you need with her cunt, but I think it's best that we—"

There was another scrape of wood against the floor, a crack of bone, and a cry of pained indignation.

"You will not speak about her in that way," Devlin raged. "You will not...you will..."

Fenna could feel the tension from outside of the room, the silence thick with it. She placed a hand over her mouth to quiet the ragged breaths sawing her throat in half.

"You're in deep shit, Devlin."

It was the first time Fenna had ever heard Booker call him anything other than captain. And the sound of his name on Booker's lips only furthered the tug of discomfort behind her navel.

"More than you know." One of the men inhaled before Devlin spoke again. "Parting with Fenna would be akin to ripping out my own heart and tossing it into the sea."

She froze, her heart hitching to a stutter in her chest. Surely she had misheard him. She took a small step back, wincing when the deck creaked beneath her feet. Neither man seemed to have noticed.

"That is what you said about Verda," Booker replied, though his tone was softer than it had been a few moments before. He sniffled and there was a brush of linen against linen, as though he had taken a rag from his pocket. "One day you will have forgotten about her. It will take time and it will hurt like the gods have damned you. But it will happen."

"We are bonded, Booker," Devlin said quietly. Fenna heard the anguish ripple through his words. "There is no forgetting her. There is only her."

Silence, save for Fenna's heart, pounded a devastating beat in her ears.

"There's no such thing," Booker rasped. "It's a myth, told by the gods and saved for creatures that left this world long ago. You misunderstood him, there isn't a possibility—"

"Liddros told me himself," Devlin cut in. The desk groaned, as though he had leaned his fists onto it. "Since I am imbued with a fraction of his power, I have the innate ability to sense a bond. As he put it, since I am no longer human." He paused to scoff. "Though, so far that has meant I can't seem to go more than a half a day without seeing her and the thought of her leaving puts a hole in my fucking chest."

Booker blew out a breath. "Then you know what your choices are, captain. You can choose to let her go and the crew can track down Dasos. Or, you can choose to sacrifice the men in the brig and potentially break your curse. What are you willing to do in order to keep her at your side?"

Fenna wasn't sure she wanted to hear the answer. She took another small step back, readying to flee from the narrow hallway and back onto the quarterdeck. The ship lurched forward, the sails of the mizzenmast having finally opened and caught the wind. Fenna stumbled into the cabin door, throwing it open and sending her tumbling onto the floor.

"Fuck."

CHAPTER TWENTY-TWO

DEVLIN

There were very few moments in Devlin's life when he didn't have words to describe how he was feeling. He prided himself on the education his father insisted he have and his above-average ability to articulate himself. But, as he stared at Fenna from across the cabin, he found himself at a complete loss.

"How much of that did you hear?" he asked, finally breaking the silence between them. Silence that had been deafening since the moment he removed Booker from the office and damn near dragged Fenna to his private cabin.

"A fair chunk of it, I imagine," Fenna replied, though her gaze was determinedly fixed on the late afternoon sky. Orange had already begun to streak across, outlining the thick, white clouds in gold.

Devlin carved a hand through his hair, grabbed a fistful of it, and then released it with the breath he had been holding. "What does a fair chunk of it mean, Terrigan?"

The tips of Fenna's ears turned a shade of red he was sure he had never seen on a person before. "The men in the brig. Booker's insistence with me leaving the ship." She cleared her throat, dropping her gaze into her lap to watch her threaded fingers. "Something about a bond."

His heart thumped in his chest and down into his fingertips. His mind was in pieces, fogging his self-assurance. He lay awake for days following Liddros's confession, he had thought of this moment again and again. Yet still...he had considered, and then hurriedly decided upon, dropping her off at the furthest port he could and then sailing to have his crew track down Dasos.

That was, until her wide hazel eyes peered up at him from her fall on the floor, locks of auburn stuck within her long eyelashes. He wanted her, fully and desperately, but he believed keeping his knowledge to himself would be easier. Cleaner, even. Gods, now that she knew...

Devlin never felt this need with Verda. He was sure he cherished her the best that he could, even now when he knew how it felt for his entire heart to be overflowing with someone else. But, how he felt for Verda paled in comparison.

He was intoxicated by Fenna. Her cedar sweet scent, the way she cocked her head when a rushing challenge flashed through her eyes, how her eyes roamed over a book illuminated by the lantern late at night, the look of pure awe when she stared up at the stars. A vile wave of self-loathing coasted through him when he realized what he had done with those men from the warship and he was hoping to hide it from her, to release them before she had a chance of finding out.

But...Booker was right. What would he do to keep Fenna at his side? Absolutely anything was the resounding answer. He would do anything. He would sacrifice a thousand men, and burn the world to the ground in the process.

And what would be left for her if he did? Would she even look at him the same? Devlin knew the answers to those questions, too. He needed to make a choice, one that he was certain would end with him alone, no matter what he did.

Devlin darted his gaze over to her and he thought his chest would cave in when he realized she had been watching him. The deep breaths he took in did nothing to calm his erratic, racing heart. "Do you know what it means?" It took every bit of his remaining courage to ask and he already dreaded her reply.

"I read a book once that detailed the myths and legends surrounding the gods," Fenna started. She began to pace, her boots skirting over the worn rug that paralleled his bed. "The gods gifted humans with the ability to find their soul bond, considering their short lives in comparison. They could sense one another, but...the god of the underworld retracted it when he staged a mutiny. It fell into myth and..." She paused, her swallow so pronounced that Devlin watched her throat bob. "Liddros told you this?"

"In the flesh."

Fenna nodded her head and began to pace again, seemingly losing the ability to stand still. "How long?"

Devlin felt a pebbling shiver crawl up his neck as he opened and closed his mouth, unable to form a single word. He scrubbed a hand down his face, glancing around the cabin for something, anything to help him. "Fenna, you have to understand that—"

"Devlin." Her tone was short and she squared her shoulders to him. "How long?"

He closed his eyes, ignoring the tightness that gripped at his lungs. "Since the warship," he said, letting out the breath he had been holding. "Liddros came to me, very angry that I had refused to offer the captain a spot on my crew. He told me then."

Fenna went silent, clamping her mouth so tightly that her jaw tensed. Insecurity screamed through Devlin as she studied him and he was certain time had stopped. He fought to overcome the throbbing desire to flee from her scrutinizing stare.

Devlin had never run from a fight. He had never fled in battle or when death looked him in the eye. But he wanted to run from this, from her, from where this conversation could lead to. He almost laughed and managed to temper it. He would be a coward if he ran and a fool if he stayed.

"You knew, then…you knew before we— before you—" Fenna stalled, but took a lurching step forward. It seemed almost involuntary.

Devlin forced himself to keep eye contact with her. "Yes, I knew then."

Her breath hitched in her throat as her tongue darted out to wet her lips. The glisten of them against the golden sun made his cock twitch and he traced their outline with a slow, roving gaze.

"What do you want with me, then?" Fenna asked, steeling her spine as though it helped to gather her nerves. Her fingers were trembling and she was trying her best to hide it, curling them into a fist. "If you've known, you must have thought it through."

The corners of his lips curled upward at the sight of her flush dipping under the seam of her stays. He couldn't help that his focus lingered on the swell of her breasts or the curve of her delicate neck. "Everything," he said, steadying his stare on her and repeating the words she had spoken to him. He took a slow step forward, his boot falling heavy against the floor. "I want everything with you." He could see her pulse slamming against the side of her neck as he reached forward, skimming his hand up the curve of her back.

He knew that this would end in heartbreak. He knew that he was not meant to have Fenna in this life…probably the next one, too. And he knew that if she didn't leave this room, then he would be buried in her long into the night.

Devlin's fingertips threaded in her hair, tilting her head back until his breath ghosted against her cheek. "Tell me to stop," he whispered, pleading with her. His cock rested on her lower belly and, from the way she leaned into him, he knew she could feel it too.

Fenna blinked and warmth spread through him at the raw innocence of her. For the span of a heartbeat, Devlin thought she was going to step away. Instead, she pressed further into him, eyelashes fluttering as she scanned his face, until their lips were less than an inch apart. Her scent flooded his senses, drowning him...remaking him...his fingers dug into her hips, pulling her closer.

"And if I don't want you to?" she asked, her voice soft and assuring. She reached between them, allowing her hand to slide up his chest, and tugged on the laces that held the top of his tunic closed. "What if I want you to show me how you feel, rather than tell me?"

With a groan, Devlin snapped. He closed the gap between them, slamming his lips onto her, firm and demanding. He was tired of holding back from her, tired of fighting. And if this was the only opportunity to have her, then he was going to take it. His tongue stroked hers, a dance of need and longing and teeth and skin.

"I've been driven to near madness by you," he said, yanking at the laces of her stays, letting them fall to the floor. "Having you in my bed." He licked up the side of her neck, nipping at her jawline, as he ran a finger along the waistline of her skirts. He found the loop of laces keeping them in place, untying them with a deft curl of his knuckle. "Seeing your smile, watching you interact with the men on the ship...fuck."

Fenna was panting beneath his hands, standing in front of him in nothing but her shift. She had shucked her boots from her feet with the deposited skirts and Devlin's responding groan at the sight of the sun lighting the vee between her legs nearly had him falling to his knees.

Their lips collided again and Devlin ran his tongue along the seam of Fenna's mouth. She widened for him in an instant, her hands pulling and pleading for the removal of his own tunic. Devlin bent down, grabbing her at the back of her legs and hauling her against him. She wrapped her legs around his waist, the shift lifting to reveal the smooth skin of her upper thighs. He felt the heat of her core pulsating against his cock, separated by the fabric of his breeches. And, in that moment, Devlin hated nothing more than them.

His world narrowed to her kiss, the way her mouth moved against his, the taste of her filling him. *Mine.* The thought burst through the thinly veiled layer of control he still held. *Fenna Terrigan is fucking mine.*

And Devlin knew what he needed to do. What it was going to take to keep her here, with him, in his bed.

Chapter Twenty-Three

Fenna

Her mind was blank, her focus stolen by the pirate captain who had penetrated every dream, every thought, every piece of her. His hands scalded her skin, rubbing and squeezing. Heat flooded the spaces where his hands had been, turning her to liquid molten beneath his touch.

Devlin spun, depositing her on the table with enough force that wood scraped against the floor and the rounded edge of it crashed against the window pane. The plate, utensils, and empty stein clattered to the floor. She started as her bare skin bit against the cool surface, her shift still bundled around her waist. His mouth trailed wet, hot kisses down her neck and into the hollows of her collarbone.

Gods, she wanted more. She needed more.

His chuckle skittered down her spine, burning her. Fenna hadn't realized she said those words out loud. Teeth grazed over the top of her shoulder as his hands left her hips. Her eyes flew open at the sudden rush of air, but locked on the heated green of his. She leaned against her hands, spread out in a fan behind her, as he grasped onto the backs of her knees and lifted her feet to flatten on the table.

Devlin stood back, blowing out a long breath as he surveyed her, bared and open before him. Fenna couldn't have felt embarrassed even if she wanted to. His stare heated her core, darkening as she let her knees fall to the sides.

"Touch me," Fenna said quietly. She reached down with a hand to pull the shift over her head and his eyes widened as they landed on her breasts, roving over the puckered skin of her nipples. "You said that you would be the one to do it." Her breasts swayed as she discarded her shift to the side. "Do it."

Devlin cursed under his breath, clawing a hand through his hair again. He stepped forward, his hips nestling between her knees as he leaned over her body. The calluses of his hands tickled her as he ran his palm down her front, through the valley of her breasts, and settled onto her lower belly. His thumb grazed south, pressing against the apex of her thighs and sweeping through over her sex. Fenna let her head fall back, a moan tumbling from her lips as he pushed the tip of his thumb inside of her, curling it against her front wall.

"So wet," he mused, removing his thumb to lick her arousal from the end of it. "Fuck, Fenna, you taste so fucking good."

Devlin drew his hand away from her belly, his touch leaving her long enough for him to delve a single finger into her. Fenna gasped a whimper, stars bursting on the periphery of her vision at the sweet pain of it, edged with a pleasure that she was sure she would never find again. Because it was him. It was him doing this to her. And she couldn't stop. Her legs spread wider as he began to move his hand, the heel of his palm brushing against her clit with a devastatingly delicious pressure.

"You own me," Devlin said and Fenna raised her head to look at him through half-lidded, hazy eyes. His stare was clear, wickedly so, as he watched her. Her gaze slid from his, falling onto where his hand was fucking her, where his hand glistened with her arousal. His finger stroked deeper inside of her, his breath deep and steady. "And nothing could buy me back from you. I am completely…" He pushed deeper, eliciting a moan. "…and utterly…" He curled his finger. "Yours."

Fenna's lips parted and Devlin's eyes dropped to her mouth. Pleasure coiled in her belly, teasing and unrelenting. He leaned forward to kiss her, his tongue stroking in the same motion as his thumb against the swell of her clit. She shuddered and rocked her hips, the beginnings of her orgasm roaring to life as though it were a living thing within her. She was flushed and falling, her heart hammering a beat against her chest that she would never recover from. All she could do was moan and mewl and circle her hips against the palm of his expert hands as he swallowed her groans, returning with deep moans of his own.

Come for me, Fenna. I can feel you. Gods, you're breathtaking.

He hadn't spoken the words, but Fenna heard them just as clear. Her back arched until her nipples were caressing his tunic. That coil that had tightened into a spring within her unleashed, bursting through her and scattering the constellations they had built between them. She was jagged and raw and pulsating. Her hands clutched at his biceps flexing with every skilled stroke of his fingers.

"I– I need you," Fenna managed to sputter, her chest rising and falling rapidly as Devlin withdrew his fingers from her, leaving her empty and wanting. So wanting. She ran her hands up his chest, crumpling the shirt under her fingers and tugging it over his head.

Devlin descended on her again, shoving his hands beneath her and hauling her up to him. She wrapped her hands around his neck and her legs around his waist, writhing against his bare skin. She moaned as her sex pressed against his warmth and she tilted her head back as he licked up the thin layer of sweat that had broken out over her. Her hands roamed over his back, memorizing every dip and crevice of the muscles that rippled with every step he took.

This was a mistake, she knew. But she no longer cared. She was his and he was hers, even if it was just for the coming years, months...or even for just the moment.

Fenna fell, her back hitting the mattress with a small bounce. Devlin knelt between her legs, gazing down at her. The sun reflected off the sea behind him, casting him in a golden light. He could have been the god of the sea himself. He leaned forward to brush his lips over hers and she felt the rigid length of him, still encased in his breeches, against her inner thigh.

Awareness blanketed her. The thud of her clambering heart and the flowing pulse of need between her legs fought for her attention. The sound of the waves against the ship filled her ears and she suddenly felt...shy. Fenna struggled to pull air into her lungs as he pushed down his breeches, freeing his cock.

Devlin sat back on his heels, his gaze boring down on her with an intensity that made her squirm. His dark hair fell over his brow and, though Fenna had the sudden desire to tuck them behind his ear, she kept her fingers clenched in the covers. He ran his hand over the side of her breast, his featherlight touch worshiping the curve of her waist and the dip of her groin. She sucked in a breath as his thumb slipped between her folds, caressing her.

"Devlin," Fenna gasped, bowing her back off the bed to incline her hips toward his touch. "Please, I need— I want— just you."

His answering grin was devastating. He gripped her hips, pulling her toward him until the backs of her thighs rested against the tops of his. He leaned over, pressing a scorching kiss to the underside of her breast, nuzzling it. Kisses peppered over her nipple, nipping at her collarbones, before his tongue slanted against her own, slow and deliberate. She whimpered, toes curling when the throbbing head of his cock prodded her sex.

Devlin slid in an inch, falling over her until his hips sat in the cradle of hers and his forearms bracketed her head. There was a heaviness that fogged her mind and a ragged gasp crawled up her throat when he pushed in another inch before stilling again. The stings of pain were followed by waves of unimaginable pleasure, filling her. He groaned, his biceps and shoulders shuddering with the effort it took to hold still, to allow her to adjust to the feeling of him.

"Are you—" He started to ask, his voice trembling and strained.

"Keep going, gods, please—"

Her mouth opened as her chin tilted up when he surged in another inch. It was too much, it wasn't enough. She had barely recovered from her first orgasm and her core was roaring to life again, energy coiling like a building wave threatening to crest.

Devlin groaned again as he kissed her, his tongue dancing with hers as he stretched her, moving deeper and deeper. Unyielding. She gasped as he rolled his hips, seating himself firmly within her.

"Gods, Fenna," he rasped, circling his hips and stabbing his fingers into her hair. "Fuck, we were made for each other." He pulled out a few inches before sliding into her again, his strokes long and punishingly sweet. The pain that had pinched deep in her core gave way to boiling heat as she relaxed her muscles to let him in further.

"Yes," Fenna pleaded as he thrust quickly into her, seemingly unable to keep himself still and slow any longer. Both of them groaned and Fenna's skin pebbled, the sensitive bumps exploding over her arms and down her back. "Please." She didn't know what she was begging for, only that Devlin needed to give it to her.

His eyes darkened as he reached behind them, grasping her knee and folding it toward her chest. His smirk spread, wicked intent flashing on his face as he punched into her, circling his hips to keep the pressure along her clit. It was glorious and filthy and all things him.

"Hold onto me," Devlin growled in her ear, withdrawing only to sink into her again. "I told you I wasn't going to be gentle."

Fenna clasped her arms over his shoulders, gripping her fingers into his flesh. She knew it would bruise, hoped it would. She wanted him marked, wanted everyone to know that it was her who sent him tumbling over the edge. "And you were right," she retorted, hooking an elbow around his neck to pull his lips onto hers, "I don't want you to be."

A startled cry was pulled from her when he thrust inside of her and she rocked her hips toward him, meeting him stroke for stroke. He wasn't gentle, his cock pistoning into her, deep and hard. They jolted along the bed and Fenna threw up a hand to keep her crown from slamming into the headboard. Devlin shifted, kneeling back enough that he was able to grip her hip with one strong hand, forcing her to return to him after every punishing thrust.

He was careful when he pushed her knee to the side, opening her wider for him. "Look at us, Fenna. Watch my cock as I fuck you." Fenna dropped her gaze, the sight of her jiggling breasts and the slide of his wet shaft sending another bolt of arousal down her spine. Devlin let out a guttural chuckle when her muscles flexed against his length, tightening around him.

Moans and groans and the slapping of sweaty bodies filled the cabin. Devlin let out a low hiss, dropping his chest over her body and nipping at her earlobe, running his tongue along the shell of her ear. It was feral and fast, stealing Fenna's breath from her lungs. She savored it, still wanting more, still wanting him deeper. They weren't close enough, she needed to feel every flex of his body, every quiver of his muscles.

Devlin reached his hand between them, his palm sliding along their slick bodies, to thumb at her nipples. "Tell me you're mine," he rumbled, his tone on the edge of a beckoning prayer. "Tell me that you're mine, no matter what happens." His hand slid lower, his fingers pinching her clit, rolling it between the pads of his thumb and forefinger.

"I'm yours," Fenna cried out as her body barreled toward her second orgasm. Her head tilted back, but Devlin gripped her chin and forced her back to him.

"I want your mouth as close to my ear as I can get it," Devlin groaned, his thrusting becoming more and more erratic as his cock swelled inside of her. "I want to hear you come, I want your breath on my neck, I want to commit the sounds you make to memory."

Fenna's breath hitched and, for a moment, the ship stopped moving. It was just him and her and time no longer mattered. She fell. Nearly unbearable pleasure ripped through her body as she tightened around him. Her teeth sunk into the tops of his shoulders to muffle the scream that tore from her throat. She surrendered to it, allowing the waves to flood her again and again.

Devlin roared, his thrusts deepening at a savage pace, growing rougher. He came undone above her, his body trembling with the intensity of his own orgasm. Fenna watched him with spellbound obsession, relishing in his loss of tightly kept control. He pulsed within her, lashing her with his heat, as her inner walls continued to clench him.

As soon as she relaxed and her body ebbed away from the flowing pleasure, Fenna gasped as though coming up for air. Devlin collapsed onto his back next to her, his chest heaving with panting breaths. She felt empty without his cock stretching her and the sudden rush of air cooled the mix of their orgasms painting the inside of her thighs. He threaded his hand through her rustled hair, pulling her into him and planting a rough kiss on her swollen lips.

"I don't...I'm not.." Fenna started before taking a deep breath. Devlin's fingers danced along her bare side, lazily stroking her. "Is that...normal? That, between us. Is that—" She didn't know what she was trying to ask, though he did.

Devlin sighed through his nose, lowering a hand to clasp hers. "No, no Fenna, it isn't usually like that." His hand left her hair to cup her face, his thumb running along her jawline. "That was...it was...I don't quite have the words to describe it."

Perfect. Fearsomely so. Even that description seemed hollow.

"Did I hurt you?"

Fenna swallowed, shaking her head. "No, no you didn't hurt me." Her fingers strayed down his abdomen, tracing the outlines of his muscles, the vee of his groin. He groaned as her touch skimmed the half-hard curve of his cock, and a knot of pleasure twisted in her core when it began to harden, surprising her.

"Peace, love, give me peace." Devlin nipped at her bottom lip, dragging it between his teeth.

Fenna smirked, pulling herself forward to straddle his hips, and his cock dragged along her sensitive folds. He didn't seem to mind. His hands roved her hips, his thumb already slick with her growing arousal as he pressed it against her clit. Those constellations were rebuilding, stars prickled at her vision.

"Devlin," she said softly, rocking against his length.

There was no hesitancy in his grip. His jaw ticked as he grabbed the base of his cock and thrust up into her. The heat of him seared her and pleasure bolted up her spine. They both groaned as Fenna began to move, slowly at first, before setting the same punishing pace he had used on her.

CHAPTER TWENTY-FOUR

DEVLIN

"Gods, Devlin, yes," Fenna moaned, her hands fanned and braced on the headboard.

The night had been long, with sleep interrupted by tangled limbs and scorching kisses. The morning sun had begun to break over the horizon, the sky filled with shades of pink and orange. The undersides of the clouds, thick and white, were outlined in soft light. He didn't know if it was the morning moisture beading on her skin or sweat from the night's activities, but he didn't care.

Not when his tongue was delving between her legs.

Devlin clutched at her hips, prodding her knees further apart with his elbows. She sunk deeper onto his face, his mouth nipping and sucking. Her fingers grasped at the edge of the headboard, sinking into the crevices and curves of the pattern carved into it. Her hips rocked against him, scraping along the hard line of his chin, and he could feel the muscles of her sex begin to quiver on his tongue.

His palm scraped up her belly, holding her steady. His tongue lapped at her, his thumb roaming down to caress the apex of her thighs. She tried to circle her hips, but he held her at bay and he smiled against her when she let out a frustrated cry. He pushed a finger into the tightness of her swollen sex and she broke, fast and quick, when he curled it against her front wall.

Panting, Devlin watched as Fenna looked down the front of her body to find him peering up at her, his eyes wickedly dark as he drank from her. Her smile was lazy and wide as she tilted her head back, riding his face as though she had done it a million times before. And, *gods*, how he fucking loved the sight of it.

She collapsed against him when her body finally relaxed and Devlin reached up to twist her off of him, lying her flat against the bed and pinning her down by his hips. He prodded her entrance with his cock and he felt her shift beneath him to allow her knees to part, opening for him.

A knock rang through the cabin, shaking the door in its frame. "Captain? We've got news."

Devlin groaned, dropping his head against her shoulder, leaving open mouthed kisses in the crook of her neck. She stifled her moan in his chest as her hands tightened around his back. He took in a deep breath, smelling sex and the briny morning dew that was caught in her hair. For a moment, Devlin was sure he was going to unravel himself from her arms and answer the call of his men. A better idea came to mind.

He punched an unexpected thrust forward, seating himself inside of her with one punishing stroke. "I'll be there, Booker," he called over his shoulder, clapping a hand over her mouth to muffle her sudden groan. He smirked as her eyes rolled back with pleasure. "Ready the sails and gather the men from the brig."

"Yes, captain."

He rolled his hips, dragging them upward until she writhed beneath him. Grinning down at her, he kept that hand tightly over her mouth as he angled his head to graze his teeth over her nipple. He pulled away from her as her skin pebbled under his touch and she smiled up at him, nipping the pad of his finger when he removed his hand from her mouth.

Devlin's grin faded as he stilled to look at her, his cock seated inside of her. Fenna drew her eyebrows together as concern flashed over her face. He bracketed her head with his forearms, lifting a hand to run his fingers through her tousled hair. He needed to see her, needed to study her features and memorize every line of her face. A wave of bewildering affection crested over him and his stomach jolted inside of him when he realized what it was.

He had known for some time that he felt like this toward her, but he wholly intended on ignoring it, refusing to put a word to it. Love. It was frightening and euphoric and...he tried to swallow it back as he darted his gaze up to connect with hers, but his heart would no longer allow him to ignore it. Love roared to the forefront of his mind, wedging into its rightful place.

Fenna's grin faded, as though sensing the shift in his demeanor. His eyes wandered in the depths of her hazel ones, getting lost in their kindness and warmth and gentleness. She was here, she was here with him and she was looking at him like that. Something cracked in his chest as he leaned down to kiss her, a slow and deep one that had his lungs squeezing the air from inside of him.

Devlin reached back to wrap her legs around his waist before rocking into her, pulling her as close to him as he could. He pulled out just enough to slant his hips and slide into her, repeating the movement with slow and passionate thrusts. The angle of his cock kept a thrilling pressure on her clit and he felt her muscles tightening around him.

Fenna moaned into his mouth, a sound that he wanted to bottle and store away with the water he still kept in his trunk. One that he had, in fact, poured into his hand to fuck himself with. She whimpered underneath him as he seated himself again, rolling his hips until she began to shudder. She sucked in the breath he had been releasing as she groaned and Devlin felt her orgasm clamp around him, milking his shaft and barreling him toward the edge of pleasure.

His thrusts deepened as his cock swelled inside of her and he roared into the hollow of her collarbone as he found his own release. Panting as he tried to draw breath, his shaft still pulsing. He trailed firm kisses on the nook of her shoulder, the spot below her ear, her jawline, at the corner of her eye, and, finally, her lips.

A few minutes passed before he had caught his breath, but when he did, he pulled out of her and rose from the bed to retrieve the cloth draped into the small washing basin. Fenna was quiet behind him and he glanced over a shoulder to see her playing with the threads of the linen covering her lap. She looked thoroughly fucked, her hair in a tangled mess and several bite marks on the swells of her breasts, and a surge of satisfaction clattered through him.

But it was her pinched chin and clouded gaze that had Devlin doubling back to study her. "What are you thinking about?" he asked, walking over to the trunk at the foot of his bed and taking a clean pair of breeches from inside. He tugged them on, tying the laces to hold them around his waist.

Fenna's stare lifted to land on him, furrowing her brow. "What are you going to do with the men in the brig?"

Devlin sighed, rubbing his hand on the back of his neck. She had tried to ask a few times overnight and he had been able to persuade her toward other endeavors, but now... she looked at him expectantly. "They belong to Liddros. I'm only returning them to him."

Fenna swallowed, dropping her gaze back into her lap. "Is that what you meant when I overheard you talking to Booker? That you were going to use the men to break your curse?"

Devlin turned away to pour water from the pitcher at his bedside into the stein on the table. He was stalling, he knew he was. He took a long pull from the cup, feeling the cool water slide down the back of his throat. Licking his lips, and still feeling Fenna's stare between his shoulders, he squared his torso to face her.

"Yes, we're going to use the men to break the curse. It's the only option we have—"

Fenna shot out of bed, bundling the covers around her breasts. Devlin tensed as she approached, nearly flinching back at the intensity in her narrowed eyes, but he stood his ground. He donned a mask of indifference, taking another sip of water that nearly went into his lungs.

"There are other options," Fenna said, reaching out to grab his forearm. "There are the Cognizants, we could find one. We— we could—"

"We're out of time, Fenna," Devlin retorted. Pulling his arm from her grasp, he lifted his hands to place them on her shoulders, fingers digging into the flesh of her back. "Liddros, he— we're out of time. We're out of options." His hands left her shoulders as he leaned down to pull a tunic off the back of the wooden chair behind her. "This is something that might not even work, but I have to try. I–"

"You don't have to try, Devlin," Fenna argued, stepping in front of him as he stooped to tug on his boots. "This is wrong. Subjecting innocent men to this...to him is—"

"Those men are far from innocent." Devlin straightened to full height, towering over her. "Most sailors aren't."

"But those men owe nothing to you or Liddros. They aren't dying, they don't owe you a debt." She paused, her chest heaving as though she had run a long distance. Her eyes narrowed, if possible, even further. "What is the sudden rush? You were more than happy to give others the choice before. What—"

"You happened!" Devlin snapped. "You—" He had to stop to take a breath, to regain control of the anger threatening to power through him. There was a rushing in his ears that had nothing to do with the sea wind and her pulse thrummed beneath his fingertips. He hadn't realized he reached out to grab her wrist until then.

Liquid fire burned in his veins. *Didn't she understand? Why didn't she understand? He was doing this for her.* Her eyes widened and a jolt of awareness had his heart leaping into his throat. She had heard him.

He sighed, withdrawing his hand as though she had burned him. "This is our only chance, Fenna," Devlin said. "A chance to be together, to have a life together, to—" His stomach twisted and he thought he was going to be sick. "Liddros has determined that my time is done."

Realization dawned on her face, replaced by a misery that paled her skin. "No. No, that can't be true. We— you said that we were bonded that we—"

Devlin lifted his hand to cup her face, but she swatted it away. He hesitated, hand still in the air, before curling his fingers into a fist and letting it drop to his side. "We are bonded. That doesn't do anything to break my curse or the curse on this ship." He sucked in a breath. "If I don't sacrifice those men, if Liddros doesn't accept them, there is no way forward for us in this life."

Fenna swallowed hard, the column of her throat lifting with the effort. She glanced through the windows. The sun had risen above the horizon, receding the shadows in the cabin and casting her face in a fiery glow. Devlin recalled the night they met, when the air smelled of blood and she looked at him as though she were ready to run him through with his own cutlass.

She turned to face him, that same look on him again.

"This isn't about me or about us," Fenna said, shaking her head. Her eyes rimmed red, pricking with tears in the corners. "You were happy to give the men a chance until now. What happened with Liddros? What aren't you telling me?"

As though she believed he couldn't, or wouldn't, be truthful, Devlin felt her claw into his mind. Those tendrils were no longer soft and furling, once reminding him of smoke. Now, they were sharp and lethal. A knife slipping between his eyes, unlocking him by force; pulling and wrenching and snatching.

Devlin blindly reached out, one hand flat against his brow as though he could press the aching feeling from his head. He managed to catch her around the upper arm, startling her enough that she retreated, scraping on the way out. He let out a yelp of pain as she stumbled back, letting go of the linen cover held at her breasts. Shaking his head to clear his vision, he tried to focus on her, but merely saw the hazy outline of her naked body.

"I told you once before, Fenna Terrigan," Devlin panted, taking several steps forward to corner her behind the table. He shook his head again, brain still pounding against the front of his skull. "Do not ever use your gift on me."

"Tell me then," Fenna seethed, stabbing a finger into his chest, "tell me what will happen to you if—"

"I will become nothing," Devlin finally yelled, so loud that it echoed through the cabin. It quieted in the office and narrow hallway that led to the quarterdeck, leaving him to believe that some of the crew heard his outburst. Fenna stilled, but he was already raking a hand through his hair. "Everything that I am will cease to exist, but I won't be allowed to die. And neither will the crew. We will become nothing more than mindless skeletons, unable to eat, drink or sleep. You may have already seen some of the crew suffering. May have noticed that they take little pleasure in those now, that they can walk in the sea without taking a breath."

"How do you break the curse? I know that you know. Tell me the truth." Fenna's words were sharp and demanding, much like her gift had been.

Devlin's gaze roved her face, desperately studying her, memorizing her. "A sacrifice," he bit out, shifting his feet apart to try and work out the sword's edge he was resting on. "A sacrifice of the one thing that means the most to you."

Fenna's eyes widened and she took a step back, her lower back thumping against the panes of glass behind her. "You mean me?"

"Yes," Devlin replied, staring into the sea over her shoulder. He was powerless– to her, to Liddros, to himself. He felt empty, hollowed out, as though someone had taken a spade and dug a hole straight through him. "I mean you. Unless I can find fifty souls in the next week to join my crew." He scoffed. "It's impossible to find fifty souls in a decade who will take on the debt, let alone in two weeks, and I was not willing to allow him to break me."

Fenna's gaze was cutting. "You lied to me. You told me that you didn't know how to break the curse—"

"I am not willing to sacrifice you," Devlin said, his voice heating once more. "You truly believe that I would be able to live with myself if I killed you in order to be free of this ship? I would rather spend the rest of my existence, however long that may be, as a husk of myself if that means you stay safe."

"And what about me?" Fenna shot back, crossing her arms to cover her breasts. "You truly believe that I would allow you to sacrifice fourteen men in my name? How would I live with that?"

"We would be together," Devlin retorted, pressing his lips together. "We would have a chance in this life to—"

"I would never ask you to do that for me. And I would never allow you to do it." Fenna bent down to pick up the linen, covering herself once more. Her curled lip and pained expression told him all he needed to know. "If you decide to sacrifice those men, you are doing it for you."

Numbness broke through him, a tightness that refused to loosen squeezing his heart. He knew this had been a mistake, knew that getting involved with her would lead to a heartbreak that he wouldn't recover from. And still, he didn't think it would hurt this much.

"Overboard! Man overboard!" A voice shouted from the deck. Scrambling footsteps beat along the wood, reverberating through the seam in the door. "Pull the ropes, men, lower anchor!"

"I can't make this anymore clear to you," Devlin finally said, reaching for the sheathed cutlass leaning against the armchair. "I would do anything for you. I would run through every man, woman, and child that stood in my way. I would burn every city, every forest, every mountainside to get to you. And I would do it without hesitancy and without regret."

Fenna sucked in a breath, lifting her chin away from her chest to lock his gaze with hers. "Then that is the burden you have shouldered yourself with. But I cannot participate in it, no matter the depth of my feelings for you."

Devlin nodded, but said nothing. What was there to say? He knew he would lose her, one way or the other. Liddros himself had made that perfectly clear. Instead, he steeled his spine and walked from the cabin, ignoring the screaming voice in his gut telling him to fall on his knees before her and beg for forgiveness for what he was about to do.

CHAPTER TWENTY-FIVE

DEVLIN

Devlin stepped into the rising sun, the morning fog in the process of being burned away, and marched past the huddled group of men in the middle of his ship. They watched him with apprehension, their faces streaked with mud, shit, and blood, but he paid them no mind. They would mean nothing to him in the end—in a matter of minutes if it were up to him.

His crew worked tirelessly to lower the anchor, to pull in the sails, to reach the sailor floating amongst a pile of wreckage bobbing in the crashing waves. They sailed near a cove close to the continent, empty and long since abandoned. The high arches of rock, dappled with shafts of light slipping through the clouds above them, rippled under the water that crashed on the shoreline. The tide was low and he could spot the sea creatures clinging onto the jagged, wet shore.

He chewed on his lip, taking note of the floating barrels, the half-sunken mast, and the water-logged deck, cracked in half. Something was wrong, something was—

"We hauled the man aboard, captain," Booker said, his eyes gleaming despite the thick smears of white cloud that slid across the sun. A shadow bloomed over *The Phantom Night*, casting the crew in gray. "He's coming to now. He's—" He trailed off and Devlin felt Booker's stare against his cheek. "What are you thinking of?"

Devlin's brow furrowed and he lifted his hand to rub his temple, his jaw clenching. "There are problems in these waters, Booker." At the look of confusion from his quartermaster, he nodded his head toward the wreck. "Look at the ship. See how the barnacles and crabs have made their beds on it? See how the paint has long peeled and there are layers of salt lines against the bow?"

Booker surveyed the wreck as though seeing it for the first time and shook his head. "This wreck isn't new. Where are the other men? There should be bodies, hundreds of them."

Devlin swallowed back his wariness, aware of the crew's eyes that were passing over them. "No, this wreck isn't new." He swung his gaze over to his second-in-command. "Where did that man come from, I wonder? The next port is sixteen leagues from here."

Booker unsheathed his sword, the zing of the metal and the glint of it against the morning rays garnering more attention to the both of them. "Shall I go find out for us then?"

Devlin barely managed to conceal his frown as he nodded. He took a step forward to rest his forearms on the gunnel, studying the wreckage again. Liddros hadn't led them here, there was no calling on the wind that pulled him toward the cove. They had happened upon the wreck...had happened upon the man floating in the water.

He didn't like coincidences, certainly didn't believe in them. He had already ordered the anchor to raise, for the sails to be hoisted into place. Perhaps the man had gotten lost, had fallen into the water trying to explore the old ship. That didn't sit right with Devlin either.

A cannon boomed, splashing dangerously close to the keel. Devlin's head jerked upward, scanning toward the bow and landing on a tall mast peeking above the rounded cliffs before them. A second cannon boomed, the puff of smoke curling like a warning above the deck. "All hands on deck!" he yelled, pushing from the gunnel and running to the helm. He took the stairs two at a time, sliding past Loma, who was turning the wheel as far to the left as she could. "Ready the guns, starboard side!"

Men streamed from the lower decks, fixing the laces of their breeches and pulling on their boots as they went. A chaotic mess of ropes, chains, and rolling cannonballs broke out over the quarterdeck, the air heavy with fresh gunpowder and sweat. Excited surprise hovered over the crew like a blanket, their wide grins and hooting yells echoing into the cove.

Devlin grabbed his spyglass from Loma's hip, pressing it to his eye and focusing the dial. The ship was small, forty guns at most, but that most certainly meant it was fast. He swung his gaze up to the flag, his amusement giving way to blaring anger.

"What is it, captain?" Loma asked, taking back the spyglass and hoisting it to her own eye. "I haven't seen that look since— a mercenary ship?"

The flag was unmistakable. Half black and half white with a painted red lion in the center. The mercenaries were ruthless, most of them employed by the crown, but some of them...some of them took the best contracts they could find. And Devlin could only imagine what this one cost.

"Cannons at the ready!" Booker shouted as he hauled himself onto the gunnel, his hand wrapped tightly around one of the ropes that held the mast in place. He looked expectantly to Devlin, awaiting the order.

Devlin nodded his approval. "Fire."

"Fire!"

"Fire guns!"

The Phantom Night rocked with the force of the blasts, the cannons shooting backward as the iron balls flew from the barrels. Most of them went wide, Devlin and Loma still attempting to direct the ship into the best position, but one managed a direct hit to the hull and the sound of splintering wood ricocheted back to them. The blow wouldn't sink the ship; Devlin hoped the hole would, at least, slow it down.

"Load guns!" Booker yelled as the crew clambered forward, hauling cannonballs into the barrels and pouring fresh powder into the priming vent. "Load guns, men!"

From the corner of Devlin's eye, auburn hair glinted in the sun. His stomach dropped to his boots as cannonballs blasted through the air, both from the mercenary ship and *The Phantom Night*. Fenna ducked amongst a stack of crates, covering her head as fragmented wood flew through the air.

"Fenna!" Devlin yelled over the helm. "Fenna, get back to the cabin!" He could see the fear in her eyes from the stern deck, could see the tightness of her shoulders and the trembling of her hands. "Lock yourself in and do not come out for any–"

"Captain, the ship continues to close in on us," Loma said, pulling Devlin's attention away from Fenna's huddled form. "Are they daft? If they come any closer, we'll blow them all away!"

Devlin scanned the sea as Booker yelled "fire!" and the ship jolted once more, the breeze suddenly thickening with the scent of sulfur and metal. Though the fog was long since gone, black smoke hung suspended above the waves, dimming the horizon against the haze. That head of auburn hair peered out from behind the crates, but ducked once more when another cannonball whistled near feet from her, splashing into the water just beyond the ship.

"Order the sails adjusted to bring the ship around portside, Loma," Devlin said, bracing the wheel against his body, upper arms trembling with the force of keeping it in place. "I don't know—" Through the bleary furls of smoke, Devlin saw it. A second mast, peeking just beyond the first, with mercenary flags billowing with the wind.

The first ship wasn't there to fight them; it was there as a battering ram, meant to stop Devlin and his crew from giving chase to the second. The man floating amongst the wreckage was merely a trap and they had been lured into anchoring.

Devlin swore as another set of cannonballs whistled through the air, blasting through the mainsail and snapping a thick ladder rope that secured the crow's nest in place. It wobbled dangerously atop the mast, Iris grabbing hold of the railing. She flung herself over the side when it steadied, clambering down the other side of the rope with the swiftness of a much younger sailor.

"Fire! Fire at will!" Devlin yelled through the smog, watching with wide eyes as the first mercenary ship crept closer and closer despite the damage it had taken. "Sink the ship! Sink that ship!"

The crew worked to load the cannons, blast after blast after blast stinging the air, but it was too late. The ship rammed into the starboard bow at nearly half-speed, sending the crew scattering across the deck as *The Phantom Night* tilted at an alarming angle. Crates, cannonballs, and spare coils of rope slid across the deck, slamming into crew members and deflecting off the three masts. Devlin was knocked to the side, hitting the deck with a loud oomph. The metallic scent of blood and high-pitched screams filled the air, most from his men that had been closest to the spot of impact. The ship finally righted itself.

Devlin hauled himself up, yanking his cutlass from the sheath at his hip with a zing. The crew of the mercenary ship clawed and climbed their way aboard The Phantom Night, cutlasses drawn and determination plastered on their sweaty, soot-covered faces. The clattering of metal on metal was sharp and resounding, seemingly ringing all the way to the blue sky overhead, and it wasn't long before pistol shots joined in.

Devlin planted a hand on the railing of the stairwell, taking the steps three at a time. He landed with a hollow thunk against the quarterdeck, raising his cutlass and slicing down a mercenary crew member with a devastating stroke. Blood spewed from the man's throat and he dropped with a cry that twisted into a wet gurgle a heartbeat later. But Devlin was already moving.

The men from the brig were the first to be slain, their broken and bloodied bodies still tied with rope. Crew members tripped over their sprawled limbs, landing amongst the pile of corpses. Blood ran like a wide-mouthed river across the deck, pooling into the seams of the wood.

Devlin cut down man after man after man, leaving a trail of bodies that even Samael, God of the Dead, would be proud of. But he didn't stop. Not when a pistol shot whizzed by his ear, not when a rogue dagger split his upper arm open, and not when his lungs began to burn, a tightness that he attributed to the haze and the surging battle at hand.

"Captain!" a familiar voice shouted, drawing Devlin's attention passed the mainmast. He thrust his cutlass into the gut of the man in front of him, yanking it free in the same smooth movement. Nottley grinned at him, face streaked with a mix of red and brown, locks of hair glued to his temples. "I told you, captain, not to leave me on that island."

Devlin lunged forward, shoving through the crowd to the taunting man standing on the gunnel of his ship. *His ship.* Violent, uncontrolled rage boiled inside of him, thrumming in his veins and bolting down his spine.

Nottley laughed as he swung his cutlass down, barreling it into Devlin's. The brutal clash shook Devlin's hands, rattling the bones of his forearms. Time stopped and stretched as he gazed into the cruel eyes of his former crew member, the battle around them narrowing to a roaring silence.

"We've been tracking you for days, Devlin," Nottley yelled over the fray, swinging onto the quarterdeck, his boots landing with a thud that was just as quickly swallowed. "Years aboard your ship was useful, it seems, when it came to selling the information to the captain of this mercenary group. He was very interested to hear what I had to say."

"How did you get off the island?" Devlin seethed, deflecting a blow from Nottley with his blade. "I left you with two bodies in the middle of the sea."

Nottley grinned, his cheeks blooming to a rosy pink beneath the layer of dust, and there was a twinkle of mischief in his eye that made Devlin's stomach squirm. "Swam to retrieve the pistol from the reef and dried out the gunpowder. Managed to flag down a passing warship by firing the gunpowder on a tree. Told them a sad, sad tale of a ship wreck and my daring escape." He swung his cutlass up and Devlin deflected it once again. "Made it back to the continent a couple of weeks later."

Devlin slashed his blade and Nottley jumped to the side, the edge of the cutlass snagging a thin line into his tunic. "I'm not sure what you told the mercenary," Devlin breathed out, cutting his blade through the air again. "The valuables aboard *The Phantom Night* won't amount to the cost of two crews."

Nottley lurched forward, slicing his cutlass into the space between them in an attempt to catch Devlin off guard. Devlin merely leaned to the side, allowing the blade to slide by. "That's where I'm sure you're wrong, captain. Do you remember Dasos Terrigan? Because I certainly do. I never forget a face." A deafeningly loud shot from a pistol rang out, too close for comfort. "He was at the port I traveled to, shouting to anyone who would listen about the specter ship who stole his sister. I listened to his tale, I listened to him jabber on and we decided to find a mercenary together, for my revenge and for Dasos to retrieve his poor sister."

Devlin grew cold, despite the heat of the sun baking the back of his neck. Sweat trickled down his shoulder blades, leaving a thin trail of moisture that cooled his skin with every gust of salty wind. "Fenna is nothing to him and is nothing to this ship, except for a member of this crew. Did you tell the mercenary why you were marooned? Why I left you on that gods damned island?"

"It didn't matter to the mercenary, not when I could provide a method of tracking you and Dasos assured his sister's gift."

The gleam in Nottley's eye made Devlin's stomach roll.

"I have no idea what you mean," Devlin spat, narrowly avoiding another swinging blow from Nottley.

"Yes, you do, captain," Nottley replied, his grin splitting his face from ear to ear. "You know exactly what I mean. And while you and your crew have been busy with the throwaway men of this ship, my employer is happily searching for her. I'm sure she'll make a pretty penny for the crown, even if it sends her to the gallows."

Devlin stared, unblinkingly, at Nottley as the blood rushed to his ears, whooshing in the canals as though he were in the midst of a windstorm. He had long moved past wanting to merely kill Nottley. He had told Fenna, not even two hours before, that he would kill every man that threatened her. He was going to destroy Nottley beyond recognition.

He watched Nottley for a moment, biding his time long enough to learn the foot movements of the man attempting to circle him. Coiled rope to their left, splintered planks to their right, the body of a mercenary man nearest the stern.

Nottley lunged first. Though a sailor through and through, Devlin realized that Nottley had a grave disadvantage. And he clamped onto that weakness, cutting his blade through the air as Nottley lifted his arm high enough to expose his flank.

Devlin's motion was fluid as he slashed his cutlass against Nottley's ribcage, splitting the man's side down to the bone. Nottley howled, curling to the side to protect his injury. Devlin struck again, slicing upward to sever Nottley's hand at the wrist. Blood spurted from the stump, cutlass and hand falling to the deck, coming to rest in a pool of red.

Nottley crumbled to his knees. His shoulders were hunched as his intact hand clutched the bleeding stump to his chest, his mouth agape in a silent cry. He rocked back and forth, shudders racking his body.

"Kill me," Nottley said through gritted teeth, turning his whitened lips and glassy gaze up to Devlin. "It was a mistake to let me live before. Do not make it again."

Devlin smirked, crouching in front of the man. "I'm not going to let you die, that's far too easy." He took in a deep breath as Nottley glared at him with reproach, a challenge darkening what was left of him. "I commend your soul to Liddros–"

"No!" Nottley screamed, spittle flying from his open mouth.

"And may he have not a single lick of mercy on your soul."

Nottley went rigid, his back straightening as though Devlin had jammed a rod down his spine. The veins in his neck popped under his paled skin. He began to desiccate, the thick tendons becoming more and more pronounced as the water was sucked from his body. His skin turned paper thin, filling into the hollows of his cheeks and eye sockets, outlining his skull. And, finally, Nottley's corpse fell to the side.

Devlin stood, turning to survey what damage *The Phantom Night* took. The majority of the mercenary's crew were dead, their bodies littering the deck. Due to the curse, he knew he wouldn't have lost a single member of his own crew and he briefly wondered if the mercenary's crew knew they were on a one-way mission. The others that remained alive had been captured, held captive and trembling by the blades of Loma and Iris.

"The masts are still upright, though the rigging and the sails have been dismantled," Booker said, his chest heaving. He lifted his hand, picking a large bit of sinew that had stuck to his hair. "No doubt to allow the second ship a means of escape."

"Did the second ship make contact?" Devlin asked, sweeping toward the bow to peer over the side. The battering ram of a ship had sustained enough damage to slow it down and, while it had hit The Phantom Night with enough force to tilt it, it seemed there was minimal loss to the hull. It could be patched, at least, and she would still float.

"Most of us were occupied, captain," Booker replied, though he bobbed his head back and force. "Waller swears he saw the second ship flank us and Dasos came aboard, but–"

Devlin whirled on the toes of his boots, wild eyes scanning toward the stern, toward the cabin where Fenna was supposed to have been. "No," he muttered under his breath, his heart squeezing painfully. "No, no, no."

"Captain?"

He stormed across the deck, narrowly avoiding slipping in a pool of blood, and entered the office. His things had been scattered from the desk, tossed haphazardly across the room from the force of the cannons and the ramming of the ship. The desk was overturned, the drawers open and the items within askew.

But that wasn't what made him plead to a god, any god, for help.

The cabin door had been ripped from its hinges. The table flipped onto its surface, the unused dishes lying haphazardly on the floor. The armchair was on its side, a rip in the left seam as though someone had slashed it with the edge of a sharp blade. Blood flecked the covers, the worn rug, and trailed toward the window, where a hand print was smeared across the glass.

And Fenna was gone, only strips of linen from her skirts left behind.

Chapter Twenty-Six

Fenna

"**S**he fucking *bit* me."

Fenna spat another glob onto the shoe of her captive, the metallic taste of blood still coating her tongue. She fought hard when the men broke through the cabin door, had screamed and kicked and punched. It was no use against three brutishly large sailors, one of whom had grabbed her and made the ill-timed mistake to press his hand over her open mouth.

She clamped her teeth around the flesh of his palm, biting down so hard that a chunk of his hand had come off. Blood filled her mouth and his scream filled Devlin's cabin. She tried to run when he released her, but one of the other men caught her by the skirts. The fabric had torn, but not before he wrapped a thick arm around her waist and hoisted her over his shoulder.

"Quit your whining. Captain wants her in the brig, take her below."

Fenna thrashed in his arms, scrambling to grasp the railing of the stairs or to plant her feet against the ship's framing. The man holding her swore, though laughter rang out from the men working on the lower deck.

"I'm going to drop you down these stairs if you don't stop moving."

That warning didn't deter Fenna even the smallest bit and she began the unrelenting assault of pounding her fists against the man's muscular back. A low growl of annoyance vibrated his torso and, true to his word, he flipped Fenna from his shoulder and she landed with a loud *thud* against the staircase.

Her breath caught in her chest, a shock of pain in her arm, ribcage, hip, and upper thigh from each stair she hit. Laughter broke out again as the man stepped over her in his continued descent to the lower deck, his boot trodding on her fingers as he navigated past her.

Fenna managed to let out a gasping cough that only half filled her lungs as she turned from her side, attempting to curl into her injuries. From the aching soreness that throbbed in each spot, she knew bruises would soon bloom there. The man grabbed her ankle, yanking her down the rest of the steps, where she fell to a crumple in the landing.

There was a crack of knees and a bleary vision of hands between legs as the man bent to a squat next to her. "Next time you'll listen." He stood and Fenna was hauled into the air once more. She groaned when the ball of his shoulder pressed into her sore ribs.

"She's a pretty one, Dukes," a low voice chuckled from behind Fenna, though she heard the connotation in his tone. She wriggled to close the tear in her skirts, one that went north of her knees, and she earned another round of darkened laughter. "You sure the captain wants her below? I'm sure we could find better uses for her."

A hand appeared on her ass, squeezing her cheek hard. She flailed again, whirling around to clobber the hand with a tight fist. More laughs. Her face heated and she felt a zing of shame at it.

"Captain wants her in the brig. That's where she'll go."

The man pushed through the crowd. From her upside down vantage point, she saw swaying hammocks and a crowd of sailors, each eyeing her with a cloying expression that made her stomach twist.

They descended another set of stairs, the creak of the wood beneath her captor's feet ominous and rattling. His footsteps echoed along the narrow walkway, the air steadily growing thicker with the scent of mildew and standing water. With a grunt, the man lifted Fenna off his shoulder and set her on her feet with enough force to buckle her knees. She managed to stay upright, only by flinging out her hands to grasp onto the iron bars of the brig, as he retreated.

"You'll stay here until we reach the capital," he grunted, the metal door clanging shut behind him.

Fenna scanned the cell, taking in the wooden bench bolted to the floor, paired with a grimy, thin blanket torn to near shreds from rat-chewed holes. Three other cells filled out the room and all four were lit by a single, swinging lantern. There was a bucket in the corner, caked in a thick substance that she didn't want to be near. Even from deep within the bowels of the ship, she could make out the muffled shouts of the men working the rigging and sails.

"How long?" Fenna asked, turning to survey her captor, but he had already disappeared into the darkness of the hallway.

She swallowed through the lump lodged in her throat and wiped the moisture from her eyes. No, she wouldn't call them tears. She refused to cry. It was from the smell. She sucked in a deep, calming breath and immediately regretted it. Glancing down at her skirts, she noticed the red stain of blood and couldn't help the tiny smirk that tugged on her lips.

"Fenna?"

She whirled, her incredulous, wide-eyed stare searching the far side of the brig. "Dasos?" Her voice was breathless, disbelief braiding with a giddiness that she couldn't contain. She stepped forward, ignoring the warning throb of pain as she pressed her chest against the iron bars. "Dasos, is that you?"

Dasos appeared before her and Fenna froze, an icy shock sweeping through her body. Long gone was the carefree, bubbly man her brother had grown into. In his place stood a pale-faced stranger with whitened lips and gaunt, sunken eyes. His dark hair was oily and askew, as though he had run his hands through it one too many times without washing it. His clothes hung from his body, loose and unshapely.

Fenna reached a hand through the bars, wrapping it around his shoulder. Where once was muscle now was nothing but flabby flesh and jutting bone. "Dasos? What happened? What—?"

"I've been looking for months now," Dasos said quietly, taking her hand in his. It was thin and clammy. "You just disappeared. I— I didn't know where you went. Imogen and I stood by for weeks hoping that you would come home and—"

"I've been safe," Fenna said, squeezing his fingers tightly. "I traded your debt, Dasos, I wanted to help you."

Dasos blanched, his haunted stare boring into her. "You shouldn't have done that. I didn't ask you to do that—"

"You didn't need to!" She retorted, her voice teetering on shrill. "They were attacking the town, looking for you, might I add." She stopped to take a ragged breath. "People died, Dasos. Innocent people. You weren't in a position to stop it. I only wanted to help."

Sweat dribbled down his temple, a nod to the heat and humidity of the lower decks, and it carved a path to his jawline through the dust coating his skin. "He'll be coming after you, then. If you have a debt, he'll come. *The Specter* always collects what's due to him."

"Don't call him that." Fenna withdrew her hand from his, curling her fingers around the cool, rusted bars of the cell. "He's— he's—"

Dasos lifted a hand to stroke the unshaven column of his throat, scrutinizing her. Fenna shifted from one foot to the other, the tear of her skirts catching on the flaking rust near her knees. Her brother always had the ability to see through her, whether it was happiness, sadness, anxiety, what have you. It hadn't seemed their time apart quashed that talent. Unease flooded her, prickling at her scalp.

He took a step away from her, a sore attempt to gain what little composure he had left, and violently rolled his shoulders. She could sense the storm rising in him. "What was that *thing* to you, sister? What power did he hold over you? What did he do to you?"

Fenna opened and closed her mouth. Her clothes were suddenly too tight, her skin crawling. "N-nothing. He was nothing to me. I thought I owed him a debt, that's all."

"You're lying to me!" There was a ugly twist to Dasos's mouth, one that pulled his hollowed cheekbones into sharp relief. He pointed a finger at her, his stance wide and mocking. "Don't you lie to me. I know how your debt works, I know what you had to do for it. Roll the dice, pledge your soul to him."

"Your debt," Fenna retorted, her own temper rising along with his. "It was *your* debt." She scoffed, shaking her head. "And Devlin was willing to forgive it as long as I was kept on his ship—"

"Devlin?" His brows snapped up and a muscle jumped in his cheek at the tightening of his jaw. "You call him Devlin?" His eyes roamed over her, lip curling into an expression of disgust. "No one calls him by his name, I wasn't sure he ever had one." Recognition dawned on his face. "You're something to *him*, aren't you? After what that beast did to me...after learning who he is...do you love him?"

A range of emotions coursed through Fenna, none of which she was able to identify. Love? Was it love? She cared for him, that was easy to do. She thought back to the jolts when he touched her, the tingling of her fingers when they combed through his hair, how her lungs emptied when he looked at her, the possessive euphoria when he was near.

Fenna had gone her entire life without being loved by someone. At least, not in the sense that she read about in books. She ached at the thought of never seeing him again. The realization slammed into her and her heart stuttered to a stop. It began to beat a moment later, pounding a powerful and vigorous rhythm in her chest. She flicked her gaze to the sludge-covered floor, dipping her chin to her chest.

"I didn't mean for it to happen. I don't know when it did happen," Fenna said slowly, keeping her voice quiet. There was a pain in her that had nothing to do with being dropped on the stairs. She didn't want to lift her eyes, knowing what monstrous glare lay on her brother's face. "Dasos, please—"

Dasos snorted, the sound bitter and punishing. "Are you so starved for attention that you'll take anything you can get? Even an abomination like him?"

"You don't need to be cruel," she retorted, tracking the pacing of his feet with narrowed eyes. "He was kind to me. He protected me. He—"

"Did you like it when he fucked you?" At his stark phrasing, Fenna finally lifted her gaze and pressed her lips into a tight line. When she stayed silent, Dasos went on. "I can tell. You're different." He moved toward the cell, thrusting a hand between the bars and grabbing her upper arm. "What would mother and father say to hear their little girl was being bent over by a—"

Smack

Dasos reeled back, releasing Fenna from his grasp. The palm of her hand stung and her wrist bit in pain, having whacked the bony edge of it on the iron bar when she slapped Dasos across the face. He gripped his cheek, eyes flashing and mouth agape.

The silence was deafening. Dasos's heavy breathing, paired with the rub of his hand against the stubble coating his cheek, echoed through the brig. Fenna watched him with trepidation and, for the first time in her life, was grateful that a locked cell door stood between them.

"It'll all be over soon anyways. It doesn't matter what you feel for him." Dasos swallowed hard. "I was heartbroken over my decision, it tore me up for weeks. But now, I'm relieved. I would rather see you hang from a noose than be with— with him."

"What did you do?" Fenna whispered in horror. "Dasos, what did you do?"

"My sister, the sister I knew, would have never betrayed me like this. Would have never fucked the man who whipped me and beat me and chased me across the continent to get me back."

Anger rolled through Fenna's veins and she tightened her grip on the iron bars, knuckles paling with the pressure. "And my brother would have never allowed dozens of people to die in his stead, people we knew since childhood, so he could hide from his choices like a coward in the root cellar of our cottage. I wonder what mother and father would say about *that*."

Dasos looked as though he wanted to reach into her cell and strangle her. Instead, he merely shook his head and walked away.

Fenna didn't know how long she sat in the brig. It could have been minutes, hours, or days. The lantern never went out and she spent most of her time watching it swing in tune with the dipping of the ship.

Back and forth. Back and forth. Back and forth.

The shadows shifted with it, casting long lines of black onto the slick wooden floor before they shortened to realign with the iron bars.

She had barely grown used to the sour, rotting stench and her stomach clenched each time she inhaled through her nose. She couldn't have been down there too long, she gathered, because no one had brought her even an old scrap of bread to eat.

She was no use to the mercenary captain if she died from starvation.

Dasos hadn't returned, leaving Fenna to ruminate over their argument and what she could have said instead. Thinking about their fight created a strange, swirling mix of disgust and grief that she was struggling to navigate. She had always considered Dasos to be her partner, her best friend, her brother. This divide between them was going to eat her alive.

Clunk, clunk, clunk

Fenna lifted her head from where she had it resting against the framing of the ship, sweeping her gaze along the corners of the brig. There. She pressed her gift forward, tugging on the threads. It felt stronger after her time training with Iris, more in control, and she loved the power it gave her.

She scraped a pleading and soft curl of her mind against the inner wall of the man still obscured in the narrow hallway.

Unlock the doors. Give me the keys. Come find me.

A chuckle skittered across the brig, bristling the hair on the back of her neck, and she was thrown from the man's mind a moment later. Her brain drummed against the side of her skull, and it was just one more piece of her that ached.

"That would have worked on a lesser man, but that man isn't me."

Fenna folded her hands in her lap, adjusting her skirts to cover her knees. "I just haven't found your niche yet, the sweet voice of a lover isn't it. Noted."

The lantern swayed again, lighting up the saccharine smile of the man in the doorway. He was younger than she expected, not much older than Devlin before he had stopped aging. There was an arrogance about him, one that was jilted and depraved. When he stepped into the brig, coming to lean against the iron bars of the cell, Fenna caught sight of a thin, banded scar that ran from his hairline to his chin, bifurcating his face.

"You must be the captain," Fenna said, willing her voice to remain steady despite the bells of alarm ringing in her lower belly. She cocked her head to look at him closer. "I wondered when we would meet."

He smiled again as he studied the cell and Fenna noticed it didn't quite meet his eyes. "I apologize for leaving you alone in the dark. We usually have a man stationed for those I put in the brig." He slid his gaze over to meet hers. "I'm glad I didn't if your first instinct was to use that little gift of yours to free yourself. Good on you." The compliment came out like a purr and Fenna felt a shiver crawl up her spine.

The captain sucked in a deep breath. "When your brother told me what you were, I didn't believe it. Not completely. A woman your age who managed to keep her gift a secret through childhood? Most are killed before then, even those who are merely suspected."

"I had good parents."

"Indeed." He narrowed his eyes. "I overheard your argument with Dasos. Just terrible when siblings are torn apart. And over a man?" He clicked his tongue against his teeth, shifting to place his hand on the pommel of his cutlass. The action wasn't lost on her. "I come with a proposition, one that I think you may agree to."

Fenna tapped her fingers against her knee. "I doubt that very much, but let's hear it anyways, shall we?"

He let out a breathy laugh. "And your brother told me that you're the meek type. How very wrong he was."

"I was the meek type in another life." She made a show of standing, smoothing her ripped skirts, and coming to the iron bars to lean against them in the same fashion that the captain had. "The sea has taught me otherwise."

"She certainly has that ability." He lifted a hand to clasp his chin, rubbing it thoughtfully between his forefinger and thumb. "Your brother was very informative when he landed on the gangplank to my ship. Truth be told, I had no interest in chasing a maiden across the continent. At least...not until I realized who it was you were rumored with. And what the rumor is that you could do."

Fenna turned to glare at the captain. "You're mistaken. My brother would never have told you about my gifts."

The captain smirked. "I believe the words he said were *I was heartbroken over my decision, it tore me up for weeks.* Certainly seems like words from a man who turned you over to a mercenary captain in exchange for tracking you down."

Fenna couldn't help her slackened mouth or her widened eyes. "He wouldn't— he knew— he always protected me, always made sure—"

"Until he thought you were in the hands of *The Specter*, then he was willing to do anything."

His eyes gleamed in amusement, the darks of them dancing in the light from the lantern. "Which brings me to my proposition. You have what I want: an in with *The Specter*, this Devlin. And I have what you want, a way to escape the appointment with the gallows that you'll most certainly have the moment I turn you over to the crown."

Fenna swallowed, her hands trembling. "And here I thought you were going to keep me on your ship. Isn't that what most mercenaries do with people like me?"

"Most? Yes. But I am not most. You'll fetch me and your brother a good chunk of coin— oh yes, don't look too shocked, darling. He'll be paid handsomely, of course. But what good is that when I can have more?"

"What do you want with him?" Unease battered her, swarming every sense and clouding every nerve. She pushed from the iron bars, her teeth sunken into her bottom lip, and she began to pace.

"Want with him? Dear Fenna. I want to *be* him. To hold infinite power over the sea, to collect the souls of those dead and dying, immortal life with unimaginable wealth." The captain became more animated as he talked, his words rushing out in a near babble. "I could buy your protection, you know. We could roam the seas, using your gift as a navigator. I could–"

"How do you plan on killing him?" Fenna let out a loud laugh, shoulders drooping in relief. "He can't die. There is nothing you could do that–"

He whirled on the toes of his boots, hands flying upward to clutch onto the iron bars, his face nearly plastered against the rusted metal. "All that time aboard his ship and he never told you? I cut out his heart, Fenna Terrigan, like he did to the captain before him and what that captain did to the one before him. On and on it goes. I cut out his heart and I bear the burden of his curse."

"I would never allow you to do that," Fenna spat, lip curling as she shook her head. "I thought I wanted to be like my brother. All of those years spent as children, watching him climb the tallest trees and swing from the highest ropes. But I know better now. I will not hide behind you. If I am going to die, it will not be out of cowardice."

The captain's expression had soured and he was silent for a long minute. The ship creaked, waves splashing against the hull above her. Something was dripping in the distance, plopping heavily into a pool of liquid that she hoped was water. Suddenly, as though it had been there all along, his smile returned, wide and bright.

"I understand your position, but you forget one thing." He paused to knock his knuckle against the iron bars and the ring of it echoed into the narrowed hallway. "You're stuck in here and *The Specter* knows where we are headed." His smile grew. "I wonder how close we'll get to the capital before he comes to find you."

"He knows better than that," Fenna said, though her pounding heart betrayed her.

The captain looked at her like he could hear it. "I doubt that very much," he said, turning her own words against her. "But let's see how it goes anyways, shall we?"

Chapter Twenty-Seven

Devlin

"Fucking Nottley," Booker murmured, kicking the desiccated corpse of the dead man with the toe of his boot, "what a waste."

Devlin sighed, hoisting another dead body over his shoulder. Blood dripped onto his back, the feeling of it unnaturally cool against the heat of his skin. He lifted the body over the gunnel and tossed it unceremoniously into the sea, where awaiting sea animals of all sorts had been circling for the last two days.

The Phantom Night was stuck on the outskirts of the cove while repairs were underway. Untangling the mercenary's fallen mast from his own, repairing the hull and the sails, resorting the storage, and inspecting the bulkheads. While the ship stayed afloat, much to everyone's surprise, it was a few days out from sailing.

So, Devlin decided to make himself useful by clearing the bodies, scrubbing the deck, and instructing the crew to place the remainder of the mercenary's men into the brig. He hadn't gone to visit them yet, knowing that he would run each and every one of them through if he did, but time was of the essence and he was running out of it.

"Hull is underway, captain," Loma said, wiping the sweat from her brow. "We've ripped apart the damaged sail to patch it with tar. It'll hold for now, at least until we're in better waters for a true repair."

"Good." Devlin nodded, turning his head to scan the sea. The bright rays of the sun reflected off the waves, adding shiny glimmers to the rippling surface. "Ready the rigging, I want to be off by nightfall."

Booker blanched, his chin flicking up at Devlin's words. "Captain, she isn't nearly ready to sail. Not for that long—"

"We are losing time. Every second we stay anchored here, we are another second closer to Fenna at the gallows." He began his march across the deck, ordering the sails to be placed on the mast and for the anchors to raise.

"She's halfway to the capital already, captain," Booker continued, walking so closely that his toes nipped at the heels of Devlin's boots. "If we decide to go after her, we forfeit whatever time we have left to–"

"That doesn't matter," Devlin shot back as he climbed the stairs to the helm. "She matters, Booker, and I refuse to leave her to the insanities of that monster the capital calls a king."

Booker swallowed hard. "If you do this, if you decide to go after her, then you sentence us to a life of constant pain and suffering. Are you willing to do that to us...to me?"

Devlin whirled around, closing the space that remained between them. "I would do anything to ensure her safety," he seethed, the words low and harsh. "I would take on the entirety of your debt if that was my choice—"

"Is that your choice then, Devlin Cato?"

Devlin stilled, roving Booker's pale and wide-eyed face. With jerky movements that felt akin to a pig being led to slaughter, he glanced over his shoulder to see Liddros leaning against the wheel of *The Phantom Night*.

"There are many things I expected from you, but this certainly wasn't one of them." Liddros let his hand drift across the grainy wood of the wheel. From Booker's eyes, Devlin assumed the motion looked nonchalant. But he had been working with the god long enough to know that it bordered menacing aggression. "Truth be told, I half expected you to leave her to die."

Devlin's responding chuckle was shallow, the sound whistling from his nose. "And what made you think that I would do that?"

Liddros lifted his gaze, a dark brow cocking in amusement. "I remember the very first thing you did the moment your seven years were up and you were allotted access to land. Sailing to the port Verda lived at and slitting her throat in her sleep...that was quite the sight to behold." He offered a bemused smile. "Your brother was certainly surprised. He seemed to believe you were long since dead."

Devlin bristled as Booker darted his gaze between the captain and the god standing before them. "You have..." Liddros bobbed his head back and forth as though contemplating a heavy task. "Approximately two hundred souls on board this ship. Would you be willing to take on the debts of two hundred people to find her? Would you endure thousands of years without her for the chance to save her from the gallows?"

Devlin did not hesitate. "I would take on the debt of every soul on the sea if it meant the chance to save Fenna."

Liddros narrowed his eyes and leaned his shoulder against the spokes of the wheel. "I do have other captains at my employ, their jobs would be quite useless if you did that." He looked past Devlin to rove his gaze over the deck, to where Devlin knew his crew were busy as a hornet's nest to prepare the ship from sailing. "Your crew will do."

"Captain—" Booker warned.

"Done," Devlin said. He crossed his arms over his chest, widening his stance. His gaze was riveted on Liddros. He had told Fenna only days ago that he was willing to kill every man, woman, and child to get to her. That he would burn every town, every forest, and every mountainside to find her. And now, faced with the impossible task of doing so, he knew the extent of how far he was willing to go. He would tear himself apart, would sacrifice every piece of his soul, and would do it without regret and without hesitation.

Even if it meant that she lived a long and happy life apart from him.

Liddros smirked as he turned to set his stare on the quartermaster. "Consider your debt paid in full, Booker Alby." He waved a hand, the muscles in his forearm rippling, and Booker dropped to the deck, unconscious.

Thud. Thud. Thud. Thud. Thud.

Devlin's crew began to collapse all around him, rigging lines and boxes and ropes falling out of their arms as they went. The men reeling in the anchors let go of the chains, sending them crashing into the sea with two splashes that rocked the ship. Devlin's forearms began to burn, the exposed swirling tattoos shifting and changing.

"I've always thought highly of you, Devlin Cato," Liddros said. He went quiet for a long moment, his stare turned to the horizon. "I admired your incomprehensible need to give your crew a choice, even when you owed it to no one. Even when you knew it would mean your downfall. And even when I didn't understand it myself."

Devlin feigned disinterest as the searing heat of his forearms grew to alarming levels; with the debts of the crew members being transferred to him. "You'll get to see thousands of years of it," he finally said as the sensation began to cool and the muscles of his arms relaxed enough that he didn't need to bite the inside of his cheek to keep from screaming out.

A faraway look passed over Liddro's features. "Thousands of years is a long time to retain your humanity. I'll be more interested to see if you're able to do that." He pushed off the wheel, hauling himself onto the gunnel of the ship. "Tick tock, Devlin. She's only three days away from the capital now. It's going to take a miracle to catch up." He stepped from the ship, falling into the oblivion of the sea.

Devlin hurried over to look over the side, searching for any sign of the god's disappearance. The surface was crystalline and peaceful, no ringed ripples cascading outward to alert where Liddros would have gone.

"Captain?" Booker's voice was hoarse and he coughed as he sat up, rubbing the back of his head. "Captain, I'm—" His gaze darted up, eyes clearing, as though he had just remembered that he was late for a very important appointment. "Captain, I'm—I'm—" He felt down his chest, placing his hand over the heart that Devlin knew was beating frantically and free.

"Yes, your debt has been paid," Devlin confirmed, ignoring the sinking feeling of despair in his own chest. There was no getting out of this bargain now. There was no finding a Cognizant to see what future lies before him. Because when he looked now, it was only one of unending gloom and loneliness that he saw.

But, at least Fenna would live. He just had to get there first.

The wind picked up, strong gales whooshing over the deck. A few other members of the crew stirred, their tricorn hats threatening to blow away in the sudden bluster.

"You stupid idiot!" A shrill voice stated, footsteps laying heavy against the wooden stairs. "You absolutely useless pile of bird brains."

Iris appeared at the helm, hand on the kerchief that held her curls in place and her tawny face turned up to glare at him. "Why would you do that? What could have possibly—" She lifted a fist to beat him in the arm.

Devlin winced, his new markings still tender. "The option was leave Fenna to the gallows or—"

"Or take on the debt of every person on this ship?" Iris finished, her tone jumping an octave that Devlin still heard over the drowning whistle of the wind.

"It was out of *love*," Booker said, shaking his head as though he also thought Devlin was a worthless pile of bird brains.

"And did you think about what this would do to me?" Iris shouted, poking her finger so deep into Devlin's sternum that his flesh dimpled against her finger. "To us?" She gestured wildly over her shoulder towards the crew who were each slack-jawed and feeling their own chests. Some took off their hats just to feel the sun against their skin, long since depraved of the sensation.

"You're free, Iris," Devlin said, his lips pinching with annoyance. "You can go, you can do anything you want now—"

"And leave you to find Fenna all on your own? I don't think so." Iris withdrew her finger from between Devlin's pectoral muscles and crossed her arms tightly over her chest. "When do we sail?" The question, though asked nicely enough, had a definite undercurrent of contempt.

"What do you mean when do we sail?" Devlin asked, his head flinching back. "I'm going to drop you lot off at the nearest port and then I'm going to find Fenna myself." The wind blew again, whipping the linen of his tunic into a frenzy.

Iris snorted and turned her beady-eyed stare to Booker. "He thinks he's going to drop us off at a port."

"Stark raving mad."

"An absolute lunatic, I tell you."

Devlin rubbed his forehead, a tension headache building with every moment the ship was anchored. "I've been navigating these seas for one hundred and fifty fucking years. I'm going to do it for two thousand more. I think I can handle the—"

"We didn't give our allegiance to Liddros, Captain Clueless," Iris interrupted him, her head shaking in disgust. "We gave it to you."

Devlin paused to stare at Iris for a beat. For the first time since Liddros had disappeared, he swept his gaze over the quarterdeck. Most of the crew had emerged from the berth, their faces glowing with reverence and turned up to stare at him. The news of his sacrifice spread quickly, as news did on a pirate ship. His throat tightened and he looked down to intensely scrutinize his boots.

"Give us one more sailing, captain," Iris went on, her voice softening as she placed a hand on his shoulder. "Let us help you get her back. We owe it to you for what you did for us."

Devlin looked up again as another gust of wind flapped the half-drawn sails. Booker was nodding, his lips pressed together. Esta was tucked into Loma's side, clutching her arm with her hand. Waller had discarded the new bottle of *fion* he had taken to carrying around, his eyes brighter than they had been in days. Each and every member of his crew was looking at him with expectant, sun-bronzed faces.

Something swelled in his chest, so inflating that he thought his lungs would burst. "Ready the rigging!" he shouted. Whoops and hollers answered, each person darting to their station on the quarterdeck. "Hoist the sails! Weigh anchor!"

Devlin placed an authoritative hand on the spokes of the helm as the sails unfurled, billowing with the wind. His eyes caught on the flag, black with a crescent moon crossed with a cutlass, waving in the sudden gales. Waving the wrong direction from where it should have been.

Liddros was directing them straight to the capitol.

Chapter Twenty-Eight

Fenna

No one would come near the brig, thanks to the captain's orders, but Fenna only bided her time. She knew one of the men would wander down sooner or later, unable to resist the temptation of a woman on board. Even one that they had been warned to stay far away from.

And she was right.

She heard the clunking of footsteps echoing off the narrowed hallway before she saw him. He appeared like a demon in the shadows, the ever-swinging lantern lighting the whites of his eyes. He was pock-marked and dirty, his face covered in layers of dust that made her eternally grateful for the cleanliness Devlin demanded of his own crew. She smelled him, too, before he slipped from the shadows and the sour stench of him made what little food was in her stomach curl.

Nevertheless, Fenna stood from her reclined seat on the wooden bench, splinters pinching against her palms as she pushed herself forward. His gaze dropped to her exposed upper thigh and she swallowed the mounting desire to cover herself up. Instead, she bent her knee and hooked her boot on the horizontal iron bar at the bottom of her cell door.

Fenna smiled at him. She could only imagine how she looked, with her disheveled auburn hair and the slit so high against her leg that she felt the humid, stale air ghost against her sex.

But the man returned the smile, nervously tugging open the laces of his tunic. And Fenna stole her opportunity.

Forcing her mind threads forward, visualizing the furls of smoky mist curling in the air between them, she punched into his mind so hard that his gaze unfocused and his mouth slackened. *Open the door.* She didn't bother with being soft or delicate. There was no time for that.

Grappling with the inside of his doublet, he pulled a single key to match the door of the cell. Realization dawned in his thoughts and he fought against her, pounding and thrashing and writhing in her grasp. *No, no, no, captain, no!* But she held steady, power streaming as she clenched harder and harder. He grunted as he fell forward, slamming his head against the iron bars and crumpling to the floor. The key clattered noisily against the wood.

But Fenna didn't stop. She couldn't afford to have him wake and those tendrils of his still fought against her, threatening to rouse him at any moment. She followed them to their source, where the glowing energy of, what appeared to be, his soul was contained within the center of the tendrils. She had never beheld something so beautiful and she already regretted what she was about to do. She wondered what would happen if she...

Fenna clamped down where his tendrils connected to that ball of energy, imagining her fist choked around the neck of them, until his subconscious weakened, his fight futile. She yanked his mind threads back, dislodging them from his soul like weeds in a garden. Those tendrils slackened and the ball of energy flickered to black. Dead.

Fenna didn't pause to consider what she had done as she withdrew from his mind, didn't pause to reflect on the spectrum of her gift or her sudden realization of why the crown would find her dangerous. She didn't want to contemplate the life she had taken or the fact that a certain pirate captain didn't show up to offer him extra time on the sea. She just bent down, pinching her nose between her forefinger and thumb, and reached her hand under his warm, dirty body. The key was somewhere. It had fallen beneath him.

Cool metal brushed the tips of her fingers and she let out a sigh of relief at the breath she had been holding. Whether that was from his smell or her nerves, it was difficult to say. She stood, reaching her hand through the bars once more to feel for the lock embedded in the door. It clicked open with the turn of the key and the man's body shifted when the door swung open.

Fenna stepped over him, ignoring the emptiness of his upturned eyes and the drool sliding from the corner of his mouth, and crept toward the hallway. She was alone, at least on this deck, and it seemed that the crew had moved their storage far enough away from the brig that temptation was limited. Footsteps thudded above her and murmured voices wafted down from the berth. The air was still stale in the hallway, deep enough in the ship that the fresh salt breeze from the sea was stifled. She backed into the brig, glancing down her front.

If she emerged on the deck above in her skirts and stays, she would be caught before she reached the hammocks. Her stomach bottomed out as she glanced back to the body behind her. He was lithe and short, certainly small enough that his clothes might hide her curves. But, gods, the *smell*.

Fenna steeled her resolve. She stripped the body, the stench so sour that it coated her tongue when she tried to breathe through her mouth. But this would be her only attempt at escape...the captain would certainly not allow it to happen again. She slipped on the breeches and tunic, depositing her skirts and stays on the now-naked body of her would-be attacker, and plopped the tricorn hat onto her head.

Rushing from the brig before someone came down to investigate, every one of her footsteps sounded like a shot from a pistol in the resounding silence of the hallway. She clambered up the stairs, staying on the toes of her boots, and slinked into the shadows of the berth. Some of the crew were napping, their hats resting over their faces to protect their eyes from the light streaming down from the hatch. Others were tucked in the corner, playing cards splayed before them.

"Oi, what are you— oh, it's just Ewald. Gods, he still smells. I thought someone was going to ambush him like we did last time."

"I don't think anyone is willing to get close enough..."

A bolt of appreciation for Ewald's lack of hygiene rocked through Fenna and she sent regards to the dead body in the brig. Precautionary, probing threads zipped from her as she made her way to the stairs, the same stairs that left a network of rounded bruises on the right side of her body. She was listening for any information— when they were porting or how long until they arrived or for a warning that they had caught sight of who she was. Most of the men flitted between thoughts of women or other men on the ship.

Fenna used the stench of her clothes as a shield, skirting to the stairs that led to the quarterdeck. She peered over the edge of the hatch, hands wrapped around the wooden hedges, before hoisting herself through the opening. Night had begun to fall, the golden orange of the sun melting into the dark navy of the night sky.

Stars speckled above her, glinting and glowing. The coast was rocky and littered with high cliffs that lorded over the sea. It could have been home, was close enough that it tugged at an opening in her heart that she had been battling to close. The briny water, mixed with the fresh scent of sun-soaked rocks, barely blew away the smell of her new clothes.

"What are you—"

Fenna whipped around, casting a devastating net of mind threads into the man who had snuck up on her. She punched through the first layer of his thoughts, penetrating deep enough that she found where they connected to his soul. Just as before, she braided those threads with her own and yanked them free. He crumpled to the deck, a hollow thunk sounding into the berth. The murmuring below her ceased and she imagined their eyes dragging up to the hatch door.

"What was that?"

Brain pounding a devastating beat against the side of her skull, Fenna ducked behind the stack of crates tucked against the wall that built the officer's quarters. She lifted a hand to press the heel of her palm against her temple as a series of footsteps bounded up the stairs and stopped just at the hatch entrance. She knew what he was looking at and his shout shot across the quarterdeck.

"It's Byram!" the male voice shouted. Fenna peered through a gap in the crates to see him bending down, shaking Byram as though he were sleeping. "Aye, Byram's down!"

His voice had yet to draw any attention toward him or the now-dead Byram, save for two men that popped their heads up from the berth.

"What happened to—" one of them started, but he paused when his sweeping gaze locked on Fenna's eye in the space between the crates. He opened his mouth to shout, his finger raising toward her, his chest swelling...and then he stopped.

"Milford? What's the matter with you, man?"

Milford had gone suddenly still, gaze unfocused. Fenna was trembling, her eyes narrowed in concentration as she held Milford at bay. His blank stare softened, eyes rolling back in his head, before he fell back and collapsed next to Byram.

The third man didn't quite know what to do, his gawking stare darting back and forth between the two men. Fenna pounced before he could sound an additional alarm, ripping his mind apart with relative ease. She froze as the man doubled backwards and, with a flourish of hands in the air as he attempted to pull away from an unseen death, tumbled down the stairs into the berth.

Where she thought should be grief or regret for what she had done lay only power. It terrified her, the sudden influx of it, and she hated the feeling that rose up inside of her. This wasn't her; what had she done? She balked as she regarded the two dead men in front of her. What had she done? What had she done?

They deserved it. The voice in the back of Fenna's mind was quiet, gentle even. The voice of her mother rarely came to her these days. In fact, she sometimes wondered if she could recall it at all. For a moment, she allowed herself to imagine her mother brushing out her auburn hair by candlelight in the room they shared. She imagined being held as she cried, her mother whispering in her ear.

You did nothing wrong. They deserved it. Your life is in danger. Fenna said the words like a mantra, trying to convince herself of it. She would reckon with her decisions if she lived through the end of the night. For now, she needed to move.

"Fenna? Where did you—" She stood at the sound of her name, her wild gaze connecting with the wide-eyed stare of her brother.

"How did you—?" He trailed off again as he scanned the two bodies around him and the third slumped against the stairs, garnering the attention of those who had been on the lower deck when he fell. "You—"

Dasos made to step forward, but Fenna thrust into his mind just as she had with the other four. She didn't know what her plan was, just that she needed Dasos to let her go. Her head hammered, sweat sheening her brow, as she was met with his resistance and he let out a choked gurgle. He sucked in a loud breath before pushing her out entirely.

"I've had years...*decades*...of your power," he managed to breathe out between pants. "You forget our childhood, how much you *pushed and pushed and pushed* until father found what you were doing. You're lucky you didn't kill anyone before now!"

Fenna took a step back, her boot catching on a spare iron rigging that lay abandoned against the deck. Dasos had turned around, readying to notify the captain of her escape, but she had already bent to pick up the rigging by the rope, the heavy iron bouncing off her ankles. He glanced over his shoulder, alerted to the sudden noise of metal against wood, and devastation blanketed his features for less than a second before Fenna swung the rigging upward.

It smashed against the side of Dasos's head, connecting with a loud *thud*. Blood trickled down his temple as he stumbled back, tripping against one of the dead bodies.

"That'll be enough of that."

Fenna lifted her gaze to find the captain leaning against the railing of the helm, forearms perched against the edge. His brow was cocked, stretching the scar that split his face.

"Killing three of my men–"

"Four," Fenna amended, tightening her grasp on the rigging as Dasos prodded at his injury, reeling back at the blood on his fingertips. "I killed four."

The captain's responding smile was small and devoid of humor. The breeze blew once more, ruffling the ends of his hair. "Four then. Now you understand my position...or that of the king's, if you were to allow me to speak plainly. I can't have you on my ship if I can't control you." He began his slow descent down the steps of the stern deck, his hand running along the railing. "Clairs are dangerous, even the Audients."

Fenna felt a tug of offense at that. It was ironically misplaced considering the position she found herself in.

"Now, you could probably kill most of the men on my ship before you tired yourself out, but you won't be able to get through me or your brother—"

The captain was interrupted by a boom on the horizon that caught the attention of the men on the other side of the ship.

"Sails!" A voice called from the crow's nest, a spyglass pressed tightly against his eye. "Sails, captain!"

"Ready the guns," the captain shouted back, though his tone was bored and unimpressed. He let out a single breathy laugh through his nose. "And you. You'll go back to the brig...and down with the ship if that's her fate. I'll only get a reward out of you, not turn you back over to your master."

"He's certainly not my master," Fenna spat. In the captain's time staring into the distance, she had walked backwards until her lower back nudged the gunnel of the ship. "And I won't be going back into the brig."

In the next breath, Fenna threw herself over the side of the ship, her stomach flipping as she fell.

Chapter Twenty-Nine

Devlin

"Hold your fire!" Loma shouted, her spyglass pressed tightly to her eye.

Devlin braced against the helm as the ship rocked again, a second blast from the cannons sending a deafening shock over the sea. "We're nearly within range! Not much further now—"

"Fenna is hanging from the side of the ship, captain," Loma interjected, twisting to gesture frantically over her shoulder.

Devlin froze, his gaze tracking to meet hers. "Pardon me?" The words were glacial, enough that Loma stilled under the iciness of them.

"See for yourself," she relented, closing the gap between them in a series of steps. "She's on the rope ladder near the keel. Any hit from the cannons could knock her into the sea. She's close enough as it is."

Booker took over at the helm as Devlin squinted into the spyglass, the rim digging painfully into his eye socket. He didn't care. Not when something was gripping his heart like a vice. His heart that had just again begun to beat.

It was Fenna hooked to the side of the ship, to be sure; though she no longer wore her stays and skirts. Her signature auburn braid flapped in the wind and a tricorn hat dipped in the waves beneath her. Three men were leaned over the side of the ship, each tugging on the rope ladder in an attempt to haul her back aboard.

She shimmied further toward the sea with each pull of the ladder. The mist from the crashing waves below licked at the heels of her boots, coating them in brine. She was running out of space and Devlin knew there were but two choices for her to make.

Allow the crew to pull her up, or dive into the churning waters and risk being pulled under by the current created by the rudder. From the hard set furrow of her brow and the near constant glances she was casting toward the sea, Devlin knew what her decision would be.

And, despite the tightness in his chest that made it difficult to pull a breath, a feral grin split his lips. Fenna certainly wasn't going to be hoisted to the deck without a fight. A fourth figure appeared within the frame of the spyglass and Devlin recognized the man in an instant.

Dasos. The unimaginable prick.

Blood trickled from the side of Dasos's face, where a purple welt and a gaping wound had taken up residence near his hairline. He looked over the side of the ship, shooting glaring daggers at his sister. If looks could kill...

Pride bloomed hard and fast in Devlin's gut. "Waller!" he yelled over the helm as the wind caught the sails again, thrusting them through the wake of the mercenary ship. "Where's Waller?"

"Here, captain," The Drunk shouted from his place at the main mast. His hands, surprisingly steady for the first time in nearly ten years, gripped a cannonball that had been passed from the hatch at his feet.

"Can you aim a cannon at the foremast?"

Waller swept a studying gaze over the deck, his thinning hair rippling in the gusts of wind still supplied by Liddros. "Aye. Shouldn't be too hard."

"Ready the chase gun for a single fire."

Loma's brows shot high on her forehead as Devlin caught her in the chest with the spyglass. She grappled with it before she was able to wrap her thick fingers around the base. "Captain, if our aim isn't true—"

Devlin turned to look at Waller, who had already bent over the hatch nearest the mast to shout for the correctly sized cannonball. "Is your aim going to be true, Waller?"

Waller peered up at him, an incredulous expression darkening his face. "And why wouldn't it be?"

That was good enough for Devlin. He sent a trusting nod to the ammunition's expert, one that was filled with words unsaid. Don't hurt her. Don't knock her into the sea. Don't sink the ship.

"Prepare arms. Ready to shorten sails," Devlin snapped over Waller's head. A shiver that had nothing to do with the breeze coiled through the crew. Eyes widened, a breathless adrenaline coursed across the deck, and a rushing eagerness followed. "We board together. A final strike from *The Phantom Night*."

The crew shouted their elation, color high on their cheeks and heads tipping back to yell at the sky. They had been sailing for two days and now...this was it. This is what they had come for.

The following five minutes could have taken three years for all Devlin knew. He watched, seemingly in slow motion, as the cannon was positioned just right against the tracks that held it in place. As the mercenary ship began the slow turn toward the capital, the view of the palace and the sour stink of the city not far beyond the beginning curves of the bay entrance. And as Fenna was being lashed by the waves when she reached the bottom of the ladder, soaking through her breeches and tunic, and plastering her loose locks of hair to her neck.

Devlin sucked in a breath, commanding the release of the cannon, and he put every fiber of faith he had left into Waller's expertise. A boom ricocheted over the water, the acrid smell of used gunpowder filling his nostrils. The boards of the deck trembled beneath his feet.

The split of wood and the resounding shouts from the mercenary ship were unmistakable, as was the warning groan from the mast. The ropes pulled taut as the mast swayed. The ropes finally snapped entirely, whipping dangerously through the air. The mast began to fall backward, tightly locking with the mainmast.

The men in the crow's nest floundered for a brief moment before haphazardly tossing themselves from it in an effort to escape the loose sails, but it was no use. Linen, rope, and metal rigging tangled in a mass that wrapped around the trunk of the mainmast, trapping them in place. Red bloomed large within the bundled sails, where a man had been inevitably quashed against the broken mast.

In their surprise of the chaos around them, the men hoisting Fenna to the deck dropped the rope ladder from their hands, sending her careening into the sea with a scream that felt like a dagger to Devlin's chest.

Devlin watched, waiting with bated breath for her to reappear. The first second felt like an eternity. He was sure the two thousand years of his debt had passed in the following one. He had his hand on the gunnel, readying to throw himself into the sea in the third.

But Fenna broke the surface, sea water in her eyes and auburn hair plastered to her temples. She sputtered as she hooked an elbow around a rung of the rope ladder, taking in heaving breaths so deep that Devlin could see her chest rising and falling from his ship. While her body still jarred from the force of the waves, she had been able to haul herself above the keel.

"Board from the bow!" Devlin shouted, squaring his shoulders to face the mercenary ship. It had slowed in the wreckage, but the full sails at the mizzenmast managed to keep it carving forward enough that Fenna was in danger of slipping under any moment. "Kill all you cross."

At that moment, Iris emerged from the crowd on the quarterdeck, her cutlass in hand and tricorn hat covering her thick curls. "Captain?"

Devlin turned to spear her with a look of unwavering certainty, the muscles of his back stiffening under the tension for every heartbeat he was still on his ship. "Secrets are buried with the men who keep them," he said firmly. "And Fenna's is worth every soul on that vessel."

He grabbed a rope and swung forward, disappearing into the wind above the sea and landing with a dull thud on the stern deck of the mercenary ship. Not a single breath passed before he ran the bo'sun through with his cutlass. The man let out a choked gurgle, blood dribbling from the corners of his mouth, before he fell to the deck. Devlin yanked the blade from his back, red trailing from the tip as he descended the stairs.

"Specter!"

"It's the Specter!"

"Captain, the—"

One by one, Devlin sent the men to Samael, God of the Dead. Liddros would not be enough to contain his fury, his need for revenge. And he thought he could feel the whisper of wings against his back as the god swooped through, claiming man after man after man.

Blood rushed in his ears, replacing the anarchy around him with the sounds of crashing waves and roaring winds. His heart quickened as he scanned the deck for the mercenary captain, the pulsating beat so pronounced that he could feel it in the tips of his fingers.

But the squelching of bodies against his blade wasn't enough. Neither were the screams that cut into babbling cries as they begged for his forgiveness. He was vengeance and there was only one thing on his mind.

Fenna.

Devlin kept her warmth at the forefront of his thoughts. He fixed on her spicy, fresh scent, one that reminded him of ink bottles and old parchment. He thought of her arm touching his when they sat close to one another and how strangely intimate the simplicity of it was.

Then he cut down another man and trod his boot through the puddle of blood.

Booker was there. And so was Loma and Waller. Iris had clutched a man by the balls, squeezing tightly as she held a dagger to his throat. Dozens of his crew raided the mercenary ship, spilling over the gunnel as they swung on ropes and crossed on wooden planks that spanned the gap between the two ships. They fought as though they had nothing left to lose, though Devlin knew they had everything to lose now.

And his chest swelled with the thought of it.

There was smoke and pistol shots and the metallic tang of blood in the air, but Devlin could only think of Fenna.

Relief coursed through him when he spotted her auburn hair shining in the rays of the sun despite the battle around her. Water sluiced from her clothing, thinning the rivers of red that gathered in the seams of the wooden boards. She peered around, wide eyes sweeping across the deck as recognition ignited her features with every familiar face she landed on.

Devlin shoved through the crowd, cutlass abandoned at his side. She was here. She was safe. She made it aboard. He said the words in his head, repeating them again and again as he reached out to wrap his hand around her arm, tugging her into his side. His lips crashed onto hers, tasting the salt spray from the sea.

"You're here...you're..." Fenna trailed off as she pulled away, her gaze wild. "You can't be here, you have to go. It's a trap—"

Devlin lifted his fingers to his mouth and let out a sharp whistle. "Did you believe we would leave you to your fate?" Her answering smile was devastating and, damn, if the sun didn't shine brighter at the sight of her. "What's that smell? Is that you?"

"The clothes. But how did you—" Fenna's gaze darted up to meet his, hazel against seafoam green. Devlin's forearm flexed beneath her fingers and her gaze dropped to the new set of swirling tattoos that marred his skin. She stared for a short moment, her swallow bobbing the column of her throat. "What happened?"

Devlin began to pull her toward the side of the mercenary ship, where a wobbling plank spanned the gap. "I had some help." Despite his desperation to get Fenna off the ship, she dug her heels in as she leaned forward to inspect the new markings...markings that ingested the sunlight like a poison. "I made a new deal."

Her lips parted as she glanced up to him, her eyes clouding over as her brows furrowed into a pained expression. "What kind of deal?"

"Fenna, we have to move. We don't have much time—"

"Why didn't you come when I killed that man in the brig—"

"You did what now?"

"I was hoping you would come and you never did. What happened?"

Devlin heard the crack in her voice, saw the shuffling steps as she struggled to stay still. Her tunic billowed in the wind thanks to the looseness of her sagging shoulders. "Liddros. We were three days behind you. I took on the debt of the crew."

"What does that mean? What happens now?"

Devlin successfully tugged her to the edge of the deck, grasping her under the arms and hoisting her onto the gunnel. She squirmed under his touch, trying, and failing, to plant her feet back on the ship. "Fenna, we can talk about this later. You have to—"

Fenna stumbled as a second hand shot up to clamp around her forearm, yanking her forward. She gripped the rigging to regain her balance.

Dasos. Devlin was never going to be rid of him. Anger flashed, rising like a rushing tide and boiling any semblance of sympathy from him. He lifted his cutlass, the sharp edge of the blade sliding along the brother's throat. The cut was thin, blood barely bubbling through the skin, but the warning was there nonetheless.

Fenna screamed, a hand clutching at her stained tunic. Devlin's chest was heaving in his effort to stomp back every instinct to flay Dasos open and pitch him overboard, leaving his corpse to rot at the bottom of the sea.

"You will not take her," Dasos seethed through gritted teeth. His dulled fingernails, broken and jagged from months of working the mercenary ship, scraped the back of Devlin's hands. "She is not yours to take."

Devlin paused, narrowing his eyes on Dasos's feverish, over-bright face. "She is not yours to sell," he countered.

"I would rather her die than—"

"Do you truly believe the king would kill her?" Devlin retorted, his voice rising above the cries and blows of the battle around them. "She would be forced to be a weapon...one that could take down armies and— don't look at me like that, you know that I'm right." He shook Dasos's shoulder with the hand free of his cutlass, fingers curling into a fist.

"I would rather her be a tool of the crown than be indebted to you."

Devlin let out a breath that whistled through his nose. "You're a fool then, Dasos Terrigan. A fool if you truly believe that I would allow her to stay on my ship another moment through a debt."

Blades clashed around them, striking harder and faster with every rock of the ship and boom of the close-ranged cannons. The burning scent of the battle grew stronger, wind-whipped sails and the groaning creak of broken floorboards replacing the muffled shouts of the injured as they succumbed to Samael.

Dasos was trembling beneath the blade and Devlin could feel Fenna's gaze boring into the spot between his shoulder blades. "We are one, her and I, pieces once spread through the universe that are finally joined in this lifetime. And, despite being given to each other through a binding of the gods, I love her," Devlin finally said, searching Dasos's features for a hint of a crack beneath the mask of malice he wore. "And that love is strong enough to know that it means I cannot have her."

The noise from the back of Fenna's throat, barely a whisper over the battle, was gutted and heartbroken, and Devlin felt it pierce him in the heart.

"Where is my choice?"

Devlin lifted his gaze to the bowl of blue sky above them, curving against the horizon and hazy from the smoke. The deck trembled as Fenna jumped from the gunnel, her boots landing heavily against the wood. She stood between the two men, placing her palm on the flat side of Devlin's blade.

"I get to decide where I want to go. I promise you, brother, going to the capital is not at the top of that list."

Dasos's nostrils flared. "You don't understand, Fenna. He isn't capable of love—"

Devlin growled, shoving the blade further into the column of Dasos's throat, as Fenna took another step forward. The breeze fluttered her hair, tugging it from the braid and kissing her exposed, pebbled skin. "I'm going with Devlin and the crew of *The Phantom Night*. It's my choice."

Dasos's head vigorously shook back and forth, his throat gliding against the blade. He slanted his shoulders away from Devlin, reaching out to grab Fenna's hand. "You no longer have that choice. These men know of your existence, of what you can do. You'll be hunted."

Fenna's eyes brimmed with tears. Her lip curled with enough disgust that Devlin nearly let out a relieving *whoosh* of breath. "You spent the entirety of our lives with nothing, except my welfare in mind. Why would you do this?"

"Because I would destroy anything to protect you, even if that meant destroying you to protect you from yourself," Dasos spat, a vein in the forefront of his brow pulsing in tune with every clench of his jaw. "Because you aren't skilled enough to live in a world that doesn't have me in it."

Devlin curled forward, readying to punch Dasos square in the jaw for his remarks, when Dasos's gaze slid to the side. Devlin was caught off guard when a wild grin split Dasos's lips.

"Well, at least I can protect her from you," Dasos said, his gaze flicking back to meet Devlin's.

Fenna glanced to her right, eyes growing wide with realization and surprise. Devlin didn't have time to react. His boots were slick against the red-stained water that coated the deck, his hand still wrapped tightly in the front of Dasos's tunic.

But Fenna spotted it, the commotion that built behind him. And Devlin watched over a shoulder, in a horror that culminated with a pressure so tightly against his lungs that he momentarily forgot how to breathe. She lunged to shove him out of harm's way.

Dasos's triumphant grin twisted into a wide-eyed scream as he lurched for Fenna, but was caught by a tangle of limbs and the cutlass still at his throat. A blade slashed through the air, silver glinting in the sunlight, and it came down on Fenna with a force that halted her body in place.

Bone and metal ground together as the dagger punched through her flesh and Fenna was forced to her knees. Time slowed to a near stop as Devlin's eyes flashed upward, landing on the captain of the mercenary ship.

The captain's hair was sticky and matted with blood. He shook his head and a gob of flesh dislodged from a knotted lock. He let out a low snort of derision. "What a waste." His arm recoiled, pulling the blade with it. Fenna jolted forward, landing on her hands with a splash of bloody water.

Devlin swung around, his cutlass carving through the air. The blade met its mark, severing the captain's head from his body. It fell with a *thunk* against the deck, the body following a breath later, but he knew he was already too late.

Fenna, face pale and breathing labored, was dying.

Chapter Thirty

Fenna

F enna was cold, despite the warmth of the sun brushing her skin. And she felt light, even though her clothes were still soaked through with sea water. She couldn't feel her fingers. She was rocking, cradled like a baby in a bassinet. Someone above her was crying.

No, they were screaming.

No, no, no...Fenna, no!

Yes, that was her name. But she didn't understand why they were screaming. She was relaxed, her vision blackened behind closed lids, and she lacked any strain or tension that would explain the anguished pleads.

She was sinking beneath the surface of a river, floating into nothingness. She was the wind barreling against the sea and the mist that battered the rocky shoreline. She was made of everything and nothing, bits of the universe strung together, but she felt only peace.

Fenna opened her eyes— did she have eyes?— and peered into the blackness that surrounded her. For a brief moment, she thought she had imagined opening them at all. Her vision shifted, pinpoint darkness yawning open to reveal a flickering light; like one at the end of a long, narrow tunnel.

She moved, not realizing until that moment she was already standing, and began to walk toward it. The golden, glowing warmth seeped into the very essence that was left of her. She thought that light mirrored a sunrise, one that shimmered against the dewy morning beads that sat upon the long blades of grass at the top of the cove.

"Are you sure you want to go there?"

Fenna gasped, her steps faltering as she glanced over her shoulder. There was a man, one that she would have surely passed if he were standing there moments before. She reeled back as she studied him, worry furrowing her brow.

He was handsome, she couldn't deny that, but he looked...she couldn't put her finger on it. Jawline too sharply defined, eyes the color of agate stones, muscles that corded and seemed to ripple under his tanned skin, and pristine fighting leathers that covered the rest of him.

Fenna dropped her stare from his face pausing to take in the dark markings that swirled along his forearms. Markings that looked eerily similar to Devlin's.

"Are you Liddros?" Fenna was unsure of whether she should bow or curtsey. Did one need to do either to a god?

The man quirked a dark brow, a hint of amusement passing over his lips. "Yes, I'm Liddros."

Fenna waited for him to elaborate, but when he didn't, she continued on with, "Why are you here?"

He stayed silent for a beat, the muscle in his jaw ticking in a patterned rhythm that suggested he was deep in thought rather than irritated. He huffed a breathy laugh. "If I'm to be honest, it's because I'm intrigued."

Fenna tried to temper her curiosity and failed. "Intrigued?"

"Your captain's been busy." Liddros sucked in a breath through his teeth and the fighting leathers creaked as he crossed his arms over his chest. Three sapphire gemstones glittered at the hilt of the sword strapped to his back, the stones the same deep blue of the sea. "He's left an impressive trail of bodies."

Even though he was talking, Fenna couldn't help but watch the golden light. It beckoned to her, a mere whisper on the phantom wind, ebbing and growing like it was living and breathing.

Fenna. Please. I love you, I love you.

"You didn't answer my question," Fenna said. The pleading words echoing through the dark chamber from above snapped her from her thoughts.

Liddros waited. Irritation heavily flared with her, and she took in a deep breath to steady herself.

"You stole Devlin's life from him. You ruined so many others." She looked around again. This time, she focused her stare on the darkness beyond, where the glowing light faded into never-ending inky black. A sharp chill ran through her. "How can you live with yourself?"

I love you, I love you, I love you. Wake up.

"Easily. I am not human, therefore I do not have regard for humanity." He tilted his head and Fenna squirmed under his scrutinizing stare. "Though, I am surprised to hear you think I stole his life. Considering how he met you, isn't it possible that I merely gave him opportunity?"

The question lingered between them.

"Devlin. He's— he's okay, then? I got there in time?"

"Time." Liddros assessed her again, his brows knitting and then releasing. His slow, piercing gaze roved over her face. "Time is a funny thing, isn't it? You can't hold it, and you can't see it. But it marches on, content to pillage and pilfer until there is nothing left of you."

Fenna idly twisted a lock of hair around her finger, narrowing her focus on the man as she thought. "I didn't expect to get into a philosophical debate with the God of the Sea. Especially while—" She paused to peer over into the darkness that surrounded her, and she was suddenly unsure of what was up and what was down.

His smile was feline and in sharp contrast to the jarring angles of his face. "While you're in-between life and death?" He didn't wait for Fenna to answer. "Water and time certainly have their similarities, don't they? Ever-changing, ever-shifting, and utterly unending. You can lose yourself in the depths, if you're brave enough to withstand it, or you can stay in the shallows and wade through. Cautious and safe."

"I don't see the point you're trying to make—"

"You didn't stay in the shallows, Fenna Terrigan. You strayed into the depths and got caught in them. And yet...you survived. Thrived even, one would argue."

Fenna swallowed, skirting her gaze back to Liddros. "I didn't survive. I'm here."

"But you aren't there." Liddros pointed toward the glowing light. It had dimmed in the span they have been talking, the kaleidoscope of colors barely distinguishable from one another. "Your tether to life is holding you in place."

"Devlin?"

"Devlin," Liddros said. "More specifically, the curse that you broke."

Somewhere above her, surf was crashing against craggy rocks and the hiss of retreating waves echoed in the darkness. A sudden scent of saltwater and wet stone filled her nose.

"The curse...the curse is broken?" Fenna covered her mouth with her hand, relief pounding a drumbeat into her fingertips. "H–how?"

"Sacrifice." Liddros's response was airy, as though the answer was simple. "Executing every prisoner on his ship wouldn't have mattered. It needed to be done willingly and by the person he is bound to. Out of love, if you will."

The roaring rush of water grew louder, as though Fenna were approaching a powerful set of falls. The air was saturated, the choking humidity thick in her chest, and she could have sworn droplets misted against her cheeks. She lifted a hand to wipe them away, only to find her skin dry.

"Interesting that a sea god would go so far as to create a loophole in his own debt," Fenna said, though her body still trembled. *Whooshing* sped past through her ears, roaring and pounding and rushing. The volume of it pierced into her head, and her eyes watered as she struggled to keep from folding at the waist and clamping her palms over her ears.

That designation was given to me by mortals. It took Fenna a moment to realize the words were spoken in her mind. *Do you truly think a mere god of the sea would be able to manipulate the constraints of time like me? There was Time and there was Death, Fenna Terrigan. And, in the beginning, they were together as one.*

Fenna roared to life, chest heaving and breath sawing at her throat. Her eyes were gummy as she blinked them open and she squinted against the brightness of the sky, sunlight arcing through the smoky haze that turned blue into gray. Was she...where was she?

There was a blade; that much she could remember. It was white hot when it pierced her, lighting a fire in her belly that was only quelled by...everything had gone dark. And then she was awake again.

"F-Fenna? Gods, Fenna?"

She reached forward, blindly grasping onto a hand that was pressed tightly to her abdomen. She blinked again and the fog finally cleared from her eyes.

Devlin was there, tears streaking through the flecks of blood and layers of dust that had settled on his skin. It was in his lap she was perched, her head settled on the crux of his knee.

"Fenna? Is she—is she—?"

She recognized the second voice as Dasos. She had become accustomed to the wavering tremble of his tone the last few days, something that had not existed in their childhood and beyond.

"I'm here. I'm okay," Fenna finally said, slowly sitting up. Devlin's hand was at her back. She was tender with herself, half-expecting to feel a pull of muscles or a sharp flare of pain. She looked down at her tunic, where a large stain of fresh blood had settled into the fabric. "I'm—"

She paused to lift her tunic, exposing her waist to the sun. Dasos averted his eyes from her, but Devlin's hand reached down to brush at the smeared blood on her skin. Fenna had distinctly remembered being stabbed, could feel the blade of the dagger piercing her.

"How is this possible?" Devlin whispered, his awed gaze roving where the injury should have been. "How is this—"

But Fenna wasn't looking at her stomach any longer. In fact, the thought of the injury had left her mind completely. Her stare caught on something that locked her focus into place. "Devlin—" She began, her eyes tracking the movements of his forearm.

"This shouldn't be possible." He hadn't taken notice yet, his attention still riveted on her.

"Captain, what—" Iris started, her boots coming to a sliding halt on the slick deck. She, too, paused and Fenna watched as her enraptured gawk fixed on Devlin's forearms. "Captain."

Devlin finally looked up, decidedly saying nothing to Dasos falling to his knees beside Fenna. "What?"

"I'm sorry, I'm sorry, I'm so sorry," Dasos was saying over and over, grappling for her hand. "I shouldn't have— I didn't— oh, gods."

But no one was paying him any mind either.

The swirling, black tattoos on Devlin's arms were outlined in a brilliant light, licking and consuming the darkness as though the sun was finally given a means to escape. He let out a hiss of pain as the luminous framing tracked inward, burning away the markings.

Devlin's hiss of pain morphed into a shout as the markings burned away faster and faster. He clapped his hands against the tattoos, swiping at them as though he could put out the fire himself. Fenna winched against the deluge of light and shielded her eyes as the bright outline connected in a flash.

The resulting explosion was blinding.

Panic swamped the deck, fearful grunts and cries sounding from the crew who had slowly surrounded them. Devlin was caught within the radiant flash and the blazing heat was so intense that Fenna was sure she would find his charcoaled remains when it finally receded.

The deck of the ship began to vibrate, the pools of water and blood quickening until droplets seemed to float above the rippling rings. Devlin was screaming out and that was the only indication to Fenna that he was still alive.

She was helpless to it, the heat making it impossible to reach out and grab him. Energy crackled along the edges of that light and she sucked in a breath of steamed air that burned from the back of her throat to her lungs.

The burst winked out just as quickly as it began and Fenna squinted her eyes open, spotting darkened dots along her vision. It hurt to swallow. Devlin was on his knees, his kerchief askew, and his breath came out in short gasps.

"It's done," he said quietly, his wide eyes drinking in the sight of his bare forearms. He turned toward Fenna, jaw slackening. "It's done." His mouth split in a wide grin. "It's done."

He repeated the words as though he couldn't quite believe it himself. A prickle of familiarity danced in the back of her mind, something that had happened when she had almost died that she couldn't quite pull to the surface.

"Liddros," was all she was able to rasp out, but Devlin was already leaning toward her.

"It's fucking over! The curse is gone!" Devlin shouted as Fenna wrapped her arms around his neck, pulling him close. "You did it and you're mine!" His hands curled around her waist and he descended on her, planting a passionate kiss on her lips that made her forget she was on a mercenary ship or that she had come close to death or that her brother was still sobbing next to them.

They would figure out the rest later.

Fenna leaned out of his grasp, threading her fingers with his and lifting his arm to inspect the smooth, tattoo-free skin that now lay there. "You had thousands of years to live," she whispered to him as shouts of excitement rang through the crew. "Thousands more memories. And I took that from you."

Devlin's smile was devastating. "No, my love. You gave it all back to me. You gave me back my time. I love you. I love you."

Fenna returned his grin as she kissed him again. "Time is a funny thing. You can't hold it, and you can't see it. But it marches on, content to give until you're so full that you're close to bursting."

She had no idea where the thought had come from, but Devlin seemed to like it nonetheless.

Chapter Thirty-One

Devlin

The cove was the second most beautiful thing Devlin had ever seen and he knew the moment he laid eyes on it why Fenna's mother had named her after it. The rocky cliffside surrounding the small beach let in just enough sunlight that it reflected off the rippling tide whispering against the pebbled sand. There were nooks in the rocks that were perfect for settling, and the cove was private enough that one could sit for hours without being disturbed.

Which, if he was to be completely honest, he was rather enjoying.

"*Gods*, Fenna," Devlin rasped, digging his fingers into the crease of her thighs. "Yes. *Yes.*"

Fenna said nothing, but her responding smile was devastating. She slowed the rocking of her hips over his cock, garnering another moan out of him, and her inner muscles clenched at the new angle when he thrust up inside of her.

Warmth flashed, hot and heady, in her gaze as she planted her hands on his bare chest. "Are you—" She let out a small moan that interrupted her question when he reached up to thread his fingers into the loose locks of her hair, tugging her down to him.

Devlin dragged his thumb over her lower lip and she nipped the pad of it, letting out a small sigh that he swallowed with an open-mouthed kiss. His tongue danced with hers as he pinned her in place, firmly gripping her hips and pistoning, hard and wild.

"*More*," Fenna managed to gasp through the kisses. She planted her hands on his chest one final time to push herself upward, widening her straddle to take him deeper. The sun created a ring against her auburn hair and Devlin was sure, in that moment, she had become a goddess.

His eyes caught with hers, hazel against green, and she was done; clenching and rolling and thrusting as she took her pleasure.

A wave crashed against the rocky shoreline and the mist coming off the sea dusted them, sticking to the sweat sheening their skin. Devlin sucked in a breath as a bolt of arousal zinged up his spine. The scent of her and of him and of them together had him twisting until Fenna was on her back. He thrust into her with deep and long strokes until she tilted her head back and grasped handfuls of sand with tight fists.

They tumbled over the edge together, Devlin's bellow echoing off the cliff sides. He could never have imagined it would be like this with someone...not for a second. He was grateful for it and, after watching the sacrifice she made for him, he knew he would spend the rest of his life worshiping her. Loving her.

Devlin collapsed against her, taking in her panting breaths that ghosted the shell of his ear. If he could live on her alone, he knew it would be enough.

"What are you thinking about?" Fenna asked as he rolled off of her, kneeling in the pebbled sand to tie the laces of breeches back into place. She smoothed her skirts down, a job in itself considering the wind tunneling through the cove.

"You," he answered earnestly, flicking his gaze up to meet hers. "Us."

She smiled again, softly this time, and turned to watch the rising tide enter the narrow bay. He couldn't help, but study her— the furrow of her brow, the graceful curve of her neck, how her hair ruffled in the breeze. He could imagine Fenna scaling the stony cliff walls and coming to sit on the plateau that overlooked the sea, where he knew *The Phantom Night* sat in the distance.

His ship. Their ship.

They had made the weeks-long journey back to Fenna's town. Ordering the crew to port for the second time in months was certainly something Devlin could get used to, though it was going to take some time. The noise of the town, as small as it was, overwhelmed him and the scent of the dirty, shit-covered streets was enough to turn his lead-lined stomach.

Despite having spent decades on *The Phantom Night* with little to no reprieve, he was itching to return to the fresh air of the sea. To feel the sun on the back of his neck as he worked the sails. To hear the waves slap against the hull.

But Devlin promised to bring Dasos home, against his better judgment, and that was what he was going to do. Dasos didn't deserve the kindness that Fenna bestowed upon him, not after what he had done. Devlin wanted nothing more than to strap him to a rope and haul him behind the ship until he was nothing more than fodder for the fish that Fenna liked to talk about so much.

But, Fenna was all things gentleness and goodness wrapped into one, and she was the one who requested it. And, as he had known for quite some time now, he would follow her to the ends of the continent if she asked it of him.

The first night at the cottage Fenna grew up in was the worst. Imogen doted on Dasos enough that Fenna seemed to prickle with discomfort, and Devlin wondered if she were remembering his words.

He would rather you take on his debt, so he can stay in his shitty town and have his bed warmed by the most average cunt he can find.

The second day wasn't much better. Fenna had returned a changed woman and it was under her newly sharpened gaze that the townspeople crossed the road when they walked by. That night, it was Imogen who seemed to prickle with discomfort the longer she was in Fenna's presence. Devlin knew that Imogen and Dasos didn't know what to do with her. They certainly didn't know how to handle a confident, sure-footed Fenna.

By the third day, Fenna had shown Devlin the cove and they spent the afternoon watching sea creatures in the pockets of tide pools that were hidden amongst the rocks. At least, when he wasn't cradled between her thighs.

"What are you thinking about?" he finally asked, allowing for the few minutes that Fenna seemed lost in the memories of her mind.

She glanced over to him, her lips pressing into a slight grimace before she spoke. "I thought I wanted to come back here. But...coming home hasn't been–" She trailed off, taking a deep breath that whistled through her nose.

Devlin leaned against the nearest rock, hooking one ankle over the other. "We don't have an obligation to remain here. We could go somewhere...anywhere."

Fenna scoffed, shaking her head. "And Dasos—"

"Is a man who is capable of making his own way through life. He's gotten this far, anyways."

She went quiet again, turning back toward the bay. He tracked her gaze over the horizon, recognizing the yearning, far-off look that only the sea could bring. Her throat bobbed with her swallow. "There was a time where I thought I was to remain here, destined to work in the bookshop." She paused to glance over at him, squinting against the sun that slipped from behind a thick cloud. "And Dasos would be the one exploring the continent."

Devlin chuckled. "It's fair to say we've determined your brother isn't the one destined for sea-faring adventures."

Fenna sighed, a mixture of hope and sadness braided in the sound. "Where would we go, Captain Cato?"

Devlin pushed off the rock, sauntering forward until he stood in front of Fenna. Something that felt like delight simmered in the spot behind his navel at the way she looked at him. Heated. Wanting. Knowing. He reached a hand down and she grasped it before hauling herself up to a stand.

"I do believe that I promised to show you a jungle," Devlin said, snaking his arms behind her lower back and pulling her into his chest. "And it's Devlin now."

Fenna's eyes brightened as she sucked in a breath that seemed to expand her very essence. "We would need a crew...and some coin." She added the last part as an afterthought.

He tucked his head down to capture her lips in a slow, unhurried way that gripped his heart like a vice. "Coin is easy to come by, pirates we still are after all. And we have a crew, or have you already forgotten? Booker." He punctuated each name with a kiss. "Iris." His lips brushed her temple. "Loma." Then the corner of her jaw. "Oswin." Then the crook of her neck.

Fenna laughed, pulling her head back to look at him properly. "Are you going to name every former member of your ship?"

Devlin smirked. "Only if you keep looking at me like that. And who said former? Most of the crew don't have a family to return to. We've made our own."

"We have, haven't we?" Fenna's lips quirked upward as she pushed away from him, breaking through his embrace. "If I recall, I also remember wanting to see a fire mountain." She began the walk backward toward the lapping waves, her footsteps imprinting in the wet sand.

Fenna lifted a hand to the laces of her stays, unknotting the ties with a quick tug of her wrist. The bodice fell open, revealing tightened nipples under the thin layer of her shift. The skirts came next and she kicked them to the side, where they came to rest atop their pile of previously discarded boots.

The sea was against her calves, then her hips, and her waist. She kept her darkened gaze fixed on him, daring Devlin to follow with a mere tilt of her head. He watched the water splash against her naked form and he was suddenly jealous of the waves caressing the underside of her breasts. He reached upward to tug his tunic over his head, not caring that the air nipped terribly at his shoulders or that the pebbled sand pinched the soles of his feet or that the water would be punishing against his cock.

It would be warmed soon enough, he was sure.

Fenna was magnificent and she was utterly *his*. He was completely *hers*. As he followed her into the depths of the bay, finally settling into that feeling of peace and belonging, he knew, for certain, that he would follow her anywhere.

And, not for the first time, he opened his mind and allowed her to hear every thought.

ACKNOWLEDGEMENTS

I want to first start my thanking my husband, Joe, for the never-ending support and love he has given me. Thank you for letting me cry on your shoulder, for listening to me read passages out loud, and for helping to manage my anxiety when I questioned why I was doing this every other day. You are my life partner, my dream, and my heart. I love you forever!

Thank you to my close-knit family! My parents, who cultivated a creativity in me that still burns brightly to this day. You let me spread my wings and chase my dreams to the tallest mountains. There isn't enough gratitude in the world for me to express. To my sisters, who inspire me and challenge me. Thank you for being my first readers, for your *honest* edits and feedback, and for loving me through every stage of life. I'm so immensely proud to be your big sister!

Finally, you can't read, because you're a doggo. But soulmates come in all forms and one of mine is in you. You, my Sadie-girl are an old lady now, but you have been my road trip partner, my running buddy, my college roommate, my rock during cancer treatments, and much more. You've sat at my feet every single day while I write these stories. One day you'll be gone and I'll endure a lifetime of missing you for the privilege of loving you. I stole your name, so everyone can know a piece of you forever.

About the Author

Sadie Hewitt is the author of stunning, fantastical mysteries that keep readers on their toes. She is an avid fantasy and thriller reader. Sadie is especially passionate about diverse representation and mental health recovery in fiction, allowing her to create wonderfully vivid and relatable characters who jump off the page.

When she's not writing or working as a full-time respiratory therapist, she travels the world, spends time with her two dogs and husband, and scarfs pizza like it's going out of style.

To be the first to know about Sadie's latest releases and upcoming projects, visit www.SadieHewitt.com

Be sure to check out As the Fallen Rise, an urban/paranormal fantasy!

It started with iridescent wings... now one woman must face danger and mystery beyond her wildest imagination.

Created by Primordials, daemons were made in the likeness of humans following a devastating betrayal. And for nearly six hundred years, Agnes was the Mage who protected them, kept them alive, and gave them power. Since her death, the seven factions of daemons have been on the brink of war, inching closer and closer to burning the world to the ground.

Anthropologist Greer Myers believes mythical creatures belong in fairy tales. But when she is unexpectedly thrust into the world she thought only existed in the folklore she studied, the source of her unusual magic is whispered amongst the daemons. The plot for her rise, or her fall, begins in the shadow of a secret society established to hunt her ancestral line.

When a strange man appears with a grimoire and claims that he can help her find her birth mother, Greer- smart and independent- decides to take on the mystery by herself. Weaving lies about her identity and going undercover as a journalist, the mission for information seems safe enough at first, but soon Greer learns the hard way just how sinister and otherworldly her mother's death really is.

www.ingramcontent.com/pod-product-compliance
Lightning Source LLC
Chambersburg PA
CBHW021234310726
48971CB00006B/1812